Clueless in Cleveland

NELLE LEWIS

© 2017 by Nelle Lewis. All Rights Reserved.
First Publication Date 02/01/2017
Hooky Life Publishing Company/ Hookyforlife@gmail.com
Cover design by Estella Vukovic/ estella.vukovic@gmail.com
Printed by CreateSpace, An Amazon.com Company
Available from Amazon.com, CreateSpace.com. and other retail outlets
ISBN (Print): 978-0-9983589-0-1
ISBN (eBook): 978-0-9983589-3-2

Not all those who wander are lost. —J.R.R. Tolkien

For Annette Schneider

Chapter One

The first time I broke my brother's rib, I was six years old. Paul was eleven, deep into his James Bond phase, and hell bent on mastering his 007 Judo chop. I was raging on Fraggle Rock reruns, and while I didn't know Judo from Jordache, I knew how to fend off a radish-stealing Gorg. When Paul came at me with his hand slicing through the air, I jammed the heel of my own hand straight out and met Paul's rib cage with all the force my six-year-old body could muster.

Twenty-five years later, the telltale pop sounded heartier to my ears than it did on his prepubescent rib, but I felt the same awe-inspiring mix of regret and pride that I had when I was six.

"You gotta be kidding me," Paul grunted, dropping to one knee before lowering himself all the way to the floor.

"Gee-zuss." I sank down next to him. "Did I break it?"

"Don't sound so damn happy about it," he said.

"Dude, this was your idea."

"The idea was for you to learn self-defense, not puncture my lung."

"Then what are you griping about? You did your job." I slapped him on his knee and left him on the floor, chasing his breath, while I headed for the kitchen. I fetched ice pack, hand towel, and a bottle of aspirin before making my way back to the dining room.

The house was a two-story bungalow built when my Nana was still in knickers. Paul oversaw its reincarnation into a storefront, following in the tradition of many of his neighbors. The entire block was packed with bungalows, Queen Anne's, and Lakewood Doubles, all empty of kids and bikes, and filled instead with chiropractors, dentists, and the occasional doggie day care. Paul used his as ground zero for his private investigation agency.

We'd turned the dining room cum conference room into our makeshift defense classroom. It was there, braced against the repositioned dining table, that I found Paul when I returned.

"You want help getting to a chair or you want to do this down here?" I asked, wrapping the hand towel around the ice pack.

Paul played mute and reached for the pack. I plopped down on the floor across from him, shook out three aspirin, and fed the meds into his outstretched fingers. I watched as he swallowed each one dry.

"Do you want to hit urgent care?" I asked.

"Nah, nothing they can do. Just gotta wait it out."

"I did good, though, right?"

"Fair," Paul said. "But we still need to teach you more maneuvers for when you get attacked from behind."

"Can we at least say 'if' I get attacked and not 'when'?" I asked. "I'd like to live in a cozy land of denial where this is all just a precautionary measure."

"If you want to spend your days in the office, chasing down electronic rabbit holes, we can go that route, too."

"Nuh-uh. I'm two background checks away from punching

myself in the face, and it's only been two weeks."

"Then you have to prepare," Paul said. He lifted the ice pack from his rib cage and tested his injury with a few pokes. He winced, but kept prodding. Paul's lickin' to tickin' ratio was high. This would slow him down, but not by much.

"How soon can I get out of here and do some real work?" I asked.

"As soon as I'm confident you won't end up dead because you made a stupid decision."

"Or because you didn't show me something that could have saved me?"

"Exactly," he said.

"Control much?"

"Since when have you let anyone control you?"

The front door opened, and I clamped down on the retort that pushed against my lips. A yardstick of a man passed through the doorway. Bland faced and likely approaching forty, though his back was stiff with the posture of an octogenarian. He paused on the threshold. The bungalow was sans foyer. Visitors stepped straight into the living room, which spanned the width of the house, and which Paul had set up as a client visiting area on one side with our desks on the other. Behind that sat the dining room, where Paul and I were lounging on the floor, stowed halfway under the dining room table. It was Sunday morning, and while we didn't advertise open office hours on the weekend, neither did we lock the door. The presence of a stranger surprised us both.

The man remained on the threshold, taking us in with a confused frown. I scrambled to my feet.

"Hi there," I said. "Welcome to Carter Consultants. I'm Samantha."

"I'm looking for Paul Carter," he said to a spot beyond me, then pointed his prematurely receding hairline at Paul's sprawled form under the table. "Is this a bad time?"

"Not at all," Paul said, shifting his weight and cautiously

getting to his feet.

"We were just working on some things and I, uh, accidentally hit him," I said, inadequately filling the silence as Paul made his way to the door.

The man studied me like I was a cat with two different colored eyes. Curious about what he saw, but not sure he liked it. Paul reached the threshold and offered his hand.

"Sorry about that," Paul said. "I'm Paul Carter. How can I help you, Mr…?"

"Pentley. Jerome Pentley."

Jerome met Paul's hand with a one-pump shake. "I'm looking for some assistance to solve a problem for my wife."

"Be happy to," Paul said with a smile meant to reassure. Jerome Pentley did not look reassured. "Why don't we all grab a seat, and you can walk us through what you need."

Paul motioned us toward a small table and chairs tucked into one corner of the room. Jerome hesitated, tossing a look at me before turning back to Paul.

"Sam's a consultant here and maintains the same confidentiality with clients that I do," Paul said. He picked up legal pads and pens for both of us, and joined me at the table without a backward glance at Jerome.

Looking short of mollified, Jerome approached the table and took a seat. He levered one long leg over the other, pinching the pleat of his pant leg with two fingers as he went. He reclined all of three inches and crossed his wrists on his lap before resting pensive eyes on Paul. Every move came off deliberate and controlled, but Jerome seemed to vibrate in his chair. I peeked at Paul. He was listing heavily to his injured side, but had his game face on.

"Mr. Pentley, why don't you tell us a bit about your wife's problem?" Paul asked.

"Tracy is stepping outside of our marriage," Jerome said.

"You think she's having an affair?" Paul asked.

"I don't think. I know."

"What's brought you to believe that?" Paul asked. Jerome narrowed his eyes at Paul's use of the word 'believe'.

"Many things. Some small, some not so." Jerome said. Paul and I sat, pens in hand and eardrums perked, waiting.

Jerome shifted his weight away from me and faced Paul head on. I angled my head casually down toward my armpit. I was showered and twice deodorized, but the distaste coming my way was ripe as week-old pierogi.

"Why don't we go through them all? Small and otherwise?" Paul asked.

"Very well. I have, on many more than one occasion, come home to find certain oddities."

"What kind of oddities?" Paul asked.

"Hair in the shower pan that is neither mine nor my wife's. Cologne on the sheets. Once, a cufflink on the floor next to our bed. On my side."

"And I take it you're more of a button man?" I asked.

Jerome raised both wrists in front of his face, revealing the sleeves of his well-worn broadcloth button-down shirt, devoid of both cufflinks and taste. He executed this maneuver without ever so much as glancing my way. Paul smothered a smile and sent me a look letting me know I was very close to earning a time-out.

"Mr. Pentley," Paul said. "Did you ask your wife about the cufflink or any of the other, ah, oddities?"

"Yes, the cufflink was the fire starter. Tracy told me that she had been melancholy over missing her father, who abandoned her when she was a teen. She was sorting through a box of his personal effects in what she described as a fit of sentimentality and says she must have dropped the cufflink on the floor."

"And did she seem believable?" Paul asked.

"Would I be here otherwise?" Jerome asked. Paul smiled and let it pass.

"Even in situations of deception, not every incident is related,"

Paul said. "Part of what I do is to help sort through what is and is not pertinent."

"In that case, I believe you may find it pertinent that I have also been informed by one of my neighbors that a dark blue Mercedes has been gracing my driveway repeatedly over the last few weeks. Always on Mondays. And before you ask, I do not know anyone who drives a Mercedes."

"How about Tracy? Does she have any friends who may own a Mercedes?" Paul asked.

"None, to my knowledge."

"What type of work does she do?"

"She sells residential real estate," Jerome said.

"Any chance the Mercedes owner could be a client coming to see your wife?"

Jerome snapped his head back and forth, once to each side, his headshakes as succinct as the rest of his movements. "Tracy sells low to mid-end houses. The list price on a decent, used Mercedes would rival the mortgage amount on some of those homes. Besides, she never brings clients home. I wouldn't allow it."

"Mind me asking why?" Paul asked.

Jerome looked like he minded it very much, but answered anyway, seeming to choose his words carefully. "Her work is her work, as mine is mine. Home is about us, not anyone else."

Paul nodded in neutral assent. "How about this neighbor of yours? Any reason he might be giving you bad information?"

"Why would he?" Jerome asked.

"For fun. To stir the pot. I've seen neighborhood squabbles over the height of one's grass turn into assault. Have you had any issues with this gentleman in the past?" Paul asked.

"Not a one," Jerome said. "There's no pot-stirring here. In fact, he came to me to congratulate me. He thought the car was mine, that I had just purchased it."

"But he said he's only seen it there on Mondays?" I asked.

"Yes," Jerome said. He looked at me as he answered, so I

pressed on. Give me an inch and all.

"Always at the same time?" I asked.

"Near so, at least always in the afternoon. My neighbor said he works an early shift on Mondays and usually gets home just before four o'clock."

"And where are you on Monday afternoons?" I asked.

"At work. But I participate in a softball league and we have a game every Monday evening."

"Do you go straight there from work?"

Another military-precision nod. "We play right at six and I'm home by eight thirty."

Paul flipped to a new page on his pad. "Mr. Pentley, what would be an ideal outcome here?"

Jerome studied Paul for a beat. "I would think it obvious. I want you to confirm she is having an affair."

"And if she is, what do you plan to do with the information?" Paul asked.

Jerome looked caught off guard for the first time. "What is the relevance?"

"I like to have a general feel for what my clients' end goals might be."

"Because you're worried a husband might seek retribution?"

"Partly," Paul acknowledged.

"Mr. Carter, I'm not out to hurt my wife. Nor even to divorce her if she has, in fact, taken up with another man. If she has, it will be my immediate job to woo her back."

I'd bet a dozen sprinkled donuts this man couldn't woo a dead bird into a cigar box.

"Mr. Pentley," I said. "When you came in this morning, you said you needed help solving a problem for your wife. Seems more like it's a problem *with* your wife, not for. What did you mean?"

Surprise colored Jerome's features. "If Tracy is doing something to disrupt our home, then that is as much a problem for her as it is for me. Whether she knows it yet or not."

Chapter Two

Paul and I succumbed to another mind-jostling hour with Jerome before sending him on his way with a copy of a contract, our assurance that we wouldn't exceed his exceedingly modest retainer, and a promise that we'd would be on the case come Monday morning. We pried from Jerome details about his and Tracy's relationship, family, and work. He was about as forthcoming as one would be if we were asking about newly discovered offshore accounts. Gleaning information about Tracy's habits, schedule, likes, and dislikes came a bit easier. From the pile of minutiae, we ruled out the relevance of Tracy's disdain for eggplant and ruled in the possibility that tomorrow afternoon would be an ideal time to check out the comings and goings of the Pentleys' driveway.

We sketched out a plan of attack for the next day, and I took off to pick up my childhood friend Angie, who'd invited me to her yoga class. I figured the kicking and screaming I'd done in response to the invite was a workout on its own, but I'd just moved back to Cleveland after a decade away, and I had some making up to do.

We had time to kill before class, so we made a pit stop to see my little brother, Vinnie. Angie and I coasted into the parking lot of Dazio's, my family's pizza shop. My dad opened Dazio's nearly thirty years ago, and my brothers and I were playing there before our heads cleared the dough prep counters. I'd stolen pepperoni slices faster than my Nonni could count rosary beads and even after a decade away, the smell of warm yeast and oil brought me back to being five years old and running from the threat of my brothers wielding the pizza paddle behind me.

All the spots were full in front of the pizza shop, but I managed to cram my Jetta into a slot in front of the laundromat three doors down, next to an ancient Monte Carlo with a Dazio's delivery roof sign attached. In addition to the laundromat, the strip also housed a Polish bakery, a tanning salon, a convenience store, and a cramped bar largely frequented by the third shift guys from the automotive plant down the street. It was an exact copy of one out of every five west-side Cleveland strip malls.

As Angie and I hit the front door of the shop, a muscle-bound young man named Danny pushed through carrying a stack of pizzas. Danny was one of Dazio's delivery drivers and had had a crush on me from the time I babysat him a dozen years earlier. It'd be endearing if he didn't perpetually take it one step too far.

"Hey Danny, how's it going?" I asked, as Angie held the door to let him out. Danny leaned against it instead, putting his back to her.

"Wow, Samantha. I'm liking the yoga pants." I could smell the testosterone rolling off him. It smelled like motor oil and hops.

"Thanks, Danny," I said. He remained lodged in the doorway.

"No, I mean it, Sam. I like them a lot. Like I like football. And beer."

I waited.

"And my mom." And there it was. Angie cringed at me over Danny's shoulder and pantomimed throwing up in her cupped hand.

"Alrighty then," I said. "Why don't you get on the road before those orders get cold?"

I squeezed past Danny and slipped into the shop.

"Hey Sam, why don't you and me—," Danny started. I turned back and pushed him out the door, then snatched Angie's arm and dragged her in. I forced the door closed and waggled my fingers at Danny through the glass. He raised his fist to his ear, pinkie and forefinger extended, and mouthed "call me" as he turned and headed for the Monte Carlo.

Angie stood next to me, peering out the glass door as Danny climbed into the Monte Carlo. "You do know that boy is going to be on Dateline NBC at some point real soon here, right?" she asked.

"Obviously. I just pray I'm not on the same episode." I turned and headed behind the counter, which was manned by a cute, blonde high school girl.

"Hey, Cece, is Vin here?" I asked.

"Office." Lots of cute, not lots of articulate.

I bee-lined for the office in the back of the shop, passing the ancient brick oven on the left, dough machine and prep counters on the right.

Angie detoured to beg some mozzarella off the kid tending the oven. Given she looked like a 5'2" version of Jessica Rabbit, the begging wasn't necessary.

I made my way to the rear of the restaurant and popped my head into the office. My brother's head of curls was buried in a laptop on a tiny desk, spreadsheets and calculator at his elbows.

"Knock, knock," I said, pulling a lock of hair on the back of his head. Without turning around, Vinnie's hand rocketed back and smacked mine before I could steal it away.

"Too bad, so sad." Vinnie's ultimate verbal comeback our entire childhood. Thumb wrestling, slap jack, you name it. If it required reflex, you couldn't beat him. Growing up, Vinnie could catch a fly by one wing. The fact that he spent so many hours trying to do so didn't help the rep he had with the neighborhood kids of not being the sharpest knife in the drawer. Vinnie never let on that the teasing bothered him, but I didn't think it was coincidence that he spent his teen years religiously covering himself in muscles and tattoos.

"What's shakin', bacon?" he asked as he swung his chair around to face me.

"Not much. Dinner's at six. Can you bring some garlic bread? Mom's making chicken casserole."

"Man, I hate that casserole. I was hoping to hit the Y for a pick-up game at seven." Vinnie said, throwing his head back on the chair rest and pantomiming a three-pointer.

I leaned in and smacked him on the side of his head. "Can you humor her a little? This is the first time she's shown some interest in something since Dad died. You can eat and still hit the Y with plenty of time to spare."

Angie appeared in the doorway with a handful of mozzarella. "Plenty of time for what?" she asked.

"Aaange," Vinnie popped his chairback upright. Vinnie has been in love with Angie since high school. Unfortunately for him, Angie married her junior high sweetheart, popped out three kids, and her husband Tony was still chasing her like a greyhound after the mechanical bunny.

"Hoops," Vinnie said in answer to Angie's question. "Sam's trying to rope me into going to Mom's for dinner."

"You have to go! She's probably lonely," Angie said.

"She's making her chicken casserole."

"On the other hand, you don't want to coddle her."

I pinched Angie's arm. "Whose side are you on?"

"Sam." Angie cut her eyes at me. "I love your momma, but sweetie, that woman can overcook a salad."

It was true. In a neighborhood overrun with Italian and Polish women pumping out hundred-year-old family recipes like paintballs from a gun, Mom was the unwritten disgrace of the block. She could barely cut a cantaloupe, let alone bake cannelloni. Dad had been the cook of the family and since his passing, Mom had stocked her fridge with little more than cottage cheese, Hagen Daz, and Diet 7-Up.

Until last week, that is, when she made the grand announcement that we should start having Sunday Dinner at her house. Which as a result of my unplanned return home, was also my house. Vinnie rented a cozy studio apartment, Paul had a fiancé and a house, and I had Mom's guest bedroom with unlimited sharing privileges of the hall bathroom. Forcing Vinnie's attendance at that night's dinner might have had a smidge more to do with sharing my pain than humoring our mom.

"Here's the deal," I said, sensing Vinnie gearing up to ditch me. "I'll cover you for a shift this week." Vinnie ran the restaurant and was short an assistant manager, leaving him to shut down the restaurant most nights. He'd had to let the last manager go after Vinnie had found him in the storeroom getting intimate with a fresh bowl of pizza dough and a bottle of imported olive oil.

"Three shifts," Vinnie countered.

"One."

"Two."

"One."

"Deal!" He threw a fist-pump into the air and turned back to his laptop. "Just lemme finish these supply orders and I'll be at the house by six."

"Sweet," I said, and escaped for the front door while Angie said her good-byes. She met up with me at the car and looked at me steadily over the roof while I dug out my keys.

"Don't say it, Ange."

"He thinks he negotiated with you."

"I'm aware."

"And won."

"Get in the car, Ange."

Chapter Three

I dropped Angie off at home to relieve Tony from diaper duty, then drove the last few miles to Mom's house. Mom lived in Parma, a small town on the west side of Cleveland made up of a mix of retirees, blue-collar workers, and young families. Mom's pocket of the neighborhood was devoted to the holy trinity: football, bingo, and pierogi.

Mom still lived in the same bungalow that my brothers and I grew up in. Two bedrooms on the ground floor that my brothers and I shared, one bedroom in the second half-story where she and my Dad hid from us kids, and a full basement that was appropriated by my brothers' friends from elementary through high school.

The house was a marriage of faded red brick and white siding, with a long front porch and a stoop on which I spent many an hour growing up, waiting for the boredom to end before it chafed me raw.

As soon as I opened the front door, I smelled it. A cross between burning metal and dry rot. Mom's chicken casserole.

"Mom?" I called out.

"Hi, baby," Mom said as I hit the kitchen doorway. Long dark hair with the barest of gray strands knotted messily above her head, she hacked randomly at a pile of vegetables on the counter, dumping them helter-skelter into a nearby salad bowl. The smoking casserole was resting on the stove top, charred to a chalkboard black.

"Can I help?" I asked, studiously avoiding the chopping, waiting for the inevitable bloodshed.

Before she could answer, I heard the front door open and close. A moment later Paul paused behind me where I was still in the doorway, cowering from the smell.

"Jesus," he whispered.

"Stay strong," I whispered back.

"You do know I'm standing right here, yes?" Mom stopped chopping and turned, gesturing at us with her knife arm.

"Whoa." Me.

"Shit." Paul.

We both turned in the narrow doorway, trying to back out, and tripping each other in the process. Vinnie came through the front door at the same time, caught sight of Paul and me making a run for it, and turned back toward the door.

I untangled myself from Paul and crossed the room in three running steps, snagging Vinnie's shoulders and propelling him toward the kitchen.

"Mom, Vinnie's here," I sing-songed.

Vinnie shot me a dirty look and mouthed the words "one hour". I delivered him a beatific smile while Paul hauled the still-smoking casserole to the table, and we sat down to eat.

Paul dished plates while Mom passed around the garlic bread, hot and nearly spongy with butter. Vinnie busied himself by pouting and drowning his salad in a pool of dressing.

"How's the job so far?" Mom asked in my direction.

When Paul had called to tell me that he thought Mom was struggling to get over our dad's death six months earlier, I agreed to come home right away and temporarily work for Paul while we figured out how to help her.

"She's pretty good," Paul answered for me. Paul had thus far tasked me with simple jobs like credit and criminal checks, running skip traces, and interviewing accident witnesses. It wasn't terribly exciting work, but would keep me flush while helping get mom back on her emotional feet. And by emotional feet, I mean get her back to playing bingo.

"I got a call from Uncle Gino today," Mom said, after forking through the casserole and failing to come up with a char-free bite. Paul, Vinnie, and I all stopped picking and stared at her.

Every family has that one relative. That one whose DNA you think you can't possibly share, despite the dead-ringer looks they have of some great, great grandfather. That one who hasn't done anything textbook pornographic–or at least gotten caught at it–but you know it's only a matter of time. That one who you make sure at family parties you don't get caught with alone in the kitchen. That's my Uncle Gino.

I glanced between Paul and Vinnie, whose eyes all told me I had just drawn the mental short straw. I blew out a sigh and put down my fork.

"What's up with Uncle Gino?" I asked.

"He heard you're back in town and wanted to know what your plans are," Mom said.

"My plans for what?" I asked.

"For your future. He was disappointed that you haven't called him. His little house down on Lincoln Avenue is just standing empty since he moved out to River."

"And?" I asked.

"He says you could move in there."

"Mom, I can't live in Uncle Gino's house."

"Why not?"

"Do I have to say it?"

"Samantha, he's your father's brother. He's hurting, too, and maybe this would be a way for him to feel closer to kin. Don't you think you could show a little respect to them both by at least discussing it with him?"

"Mom, it's not about respect. It's about cooties." I didn't dare tell my mom my main worry was what a black light might bring up on Uncle Gino's furniture.

"Don't be ridiculous, Samantha. Besides, he said you can live there rent-free. Wait, where are you going?" Mom asked.

I was halfway out of my chair. "To buy a Swiffer and some bleach." I said, grappling with my purse and throwing a wave at my brothers.

"Hey!" Paul and Vinnie yelled in unison.

"Every man for himself. Thanks for dinner, Mom."

"TWO SHIFTS!" Vinnie screamed at my retreating back.

Chapter Four

Monday morning, I landed at Paul's office, my trunk jammed full with every cleaning agent, mop, and scrub I could find. As soon as I finished work, I was meeting Uncle Gino to get the keys to the Lincoln Ave house and to scour the yellow pages for an exterminator, fumigator, and exorcist.

I locked the Jetta and ran up the steps to the office. Paul was already there, talking to what sounded like a prospective client on the phone. He was scribbling fiercely, face intent.

I dropped my bag at my desk, which sat opposite Paul's. The desks were both oversized teacher's models, monster relics from an old schoolhouse on the east side that got renovated into some type of massage school years before.

After filling a mug of coffee and securing a handful of Red Vines from the giant tub on my desk, I settled back in my chair and watched Paul. The brush of gray at his temples was new since I saw him at the funeral and it made me wonder just how hard the last six months had been with Dad gone.

Paul finished the call and nabbed my untouched coffee.

"Dude" I said, mouth full of Red Vine. "Can't you get your own?"

"The bigger question, *dude*, is how can you eat candy for

breakfast?"

"It's not just candy, it's Red Vines. Show some respect. And not all of us can have a fiancé who fills our larder with fresh-pressed kale juice," I said, earning a frown from Paul. "So what's the deal with that call? You were full-on Ned the Note Taker."

"We have a new client."

"Nice!" I threw my licorice up in a victory V. "What's the skinny?"

"Guy named Jerry Stanislowski. He suspects his business partner might be in cahoots with one of their competitors. He's worried the partner is trying to sabotage their business so the competitor can swoop in and buy them out, then the partner will go to work for the bigger guy."

"Who's the competitor?" I asked.

"Polaski's."

I freed the licorice from my lips.

"Polaski's?" I asked. "Like the donut place?"

"One and the same."

"Wait," I said. "What's Jerry's business?"

"He owns Lakewood Bakery."

"But there are donut shops all over the city. What's the big deal? If this Polaski guy buys out Jerry, there are still like a thousand other places to compete with."

"It's not just donuts. We're talking bread, kolaczki, cakes, pies. If it's got sugar and flour, they sell it. Birthday parties, bowl games, catering, weddings, funerals. It's evidently big business. I guess there's a lotta dough—." He stopped at the sight of my upheld hand.

"Don't say it."

"In donuts."

"Cheap, even for you," I said. "Let's cut to the bottom line here. I've got three backgrounds to run down this morning. Do you want me to start researching the donut mafia while you do the surveillance on Tracy this afternoon?"

"Nope, change of plans for the Pentley case," Paul said.

"You're not going to watch the house?" I asked.

"Nope. You are."

"Really?" I clapped my hands and am ashamed to say I may have squealed a little.

"Yes, really. You have to learn surveillance sometime. May as well start on this one."

"Do I have to follow her? Do I get to jump in a cab and yell 'Follow that car!'? Buy an overcoat and hide behind a newspaper in a hotel lobby?" Chain-yanking Paul fell in my top five favorite hobbies.

"Calm down, Sparky. You're not following anyone anywhere. You're just gonna park down the street from the Pentleys' house and watch. We'll set you up with binoculars and a camera. All you need to do is get some good pics of the Mercedes owner, get his license plate number, and not get noticed. Basic stuff here."

"What if I don't see them actually touching each other?" I asked.

"Doesn't matter. Get pictures anyway. Let's establish who he is, then we can work on figuring out if he's selling Tupperware or playing Mr. Woodpecker Drills a Hole." Nice. And yet he somehow conned a woman into saying yes to marriage.

"What if I have to pee while I'm waiting?" My number one life concern, given I have a bladder the size of an acorn.

"Don't drink anything before you head out," Paul answered with a shrug.

"What if I get bored?" I hedged.

"Bring a book."

"What if I get a leg cramp?"

Paul lifted his eyes to the ceiling and appeared to be counting. "Sam. You've sat longer on I-480 trying to get through crosstown traffic than you will trying to get a shot of this guy, and that's even if he shows. I don't think we need to worry about your electrolyte levels just yet."

"What if I fall asleep?"

"What if I smack the shit out of you?" Paul asked.

"You mean like now, or as a remedy in case I fall asleep?"

"God help me. Come on, let's go up to the equipment room and get you outfitted."

***

Four hours and three mind-numbing background traces later, I cruised into the Pentleys' neighborhood with a high-resolution camera, a copy of *50 Shades of Gray* to which I was only 10 Shades in, two packs of Red Vines, and an empty bladder.

The Pentleys' neighborhood was ripe with towering trees and large homes, a clash of new money and old that was rare for the west side of town. Most neighborhoods were distinctly one or the other and those lines were preserved like pickles in a jar.

The Pentleys either had family money, or new money and old taste. Their Tudor home was smaller than most of the other estates, but bore the same age and feel. Two stories with a gabled roof on the left, wide three-paned windows spanning the second floor and a massive bay window on the first. The intricately paved driveway ran up one side of the house and disappeared. A double stone archway created a four-foot long entryway shrouding the front door in the fading daylight, the lengthening shadows cut only by one lone sconce embedded in the stone.

The neighbor's house to the left sat a dozen feet away, and an empty patch of land sat to the right. Past the rooflines, I could see massive trees rising in the backyards.

I drove past the house, turned at the next corner and made a quasi-legal three-point turn back onto the Pentleys' street. I angled my car into the curb four spaces back from the Pentleys', semi-hiding my car behind a Lincoln sedan that allowed me a good view of the house. The Pentleys' long driveway was empty, and it was impossible to tell whether a garage stood in back. The autumn light was fading fast, despite being late afternoon, but it wasn't dark enough for me to feel like risking a walk around back to check it out. The Pentleys' neighbor had allegedly seen the Mercedes out front anyway, so I decided to park my hiney where it was for the moment.

I set up the camera, adjusted the lens the way Paul had shown me, then settled back and waited for the Mercedes to appear.

A half hour later, I had devoured half a pack of Red Vines and five more *Shades*, feeling equal parts sugar-sick and frisky. Several cars had come down the street, but only one slowed anywhere near me, a neighbor who turned into the driveway directly opposite the Pentleys'. I wondered idly if that was our observant neighbor who'd tipped Jerome to the Mercedes, but the car rolled straight into an adjacent garage and I couldn't see who was behind the wheel. I had dressed warmly, jeans and sweater layered over a long-sleeved thermal tee and tennies, my Ohio State knit sock hat tugged down low over my brow, covering half of my long curls. Even so, I was starting to feel the chill.

I waited another quarter hour, seat-dancing to Whitney and karaoking to Meatloaf. I tacked on another three excruciating minutes trying to understand the attraction to Coldplay before deeming myself officially bored.

Still no Mercedes. The flow of cars coming in and out had slowed, despite the proximity to the post-work hour. Paul had told me to stay in the car under all circumstances, but I desperately needed to stretch, and dark had fallen enough for me to entertain a quick walk up the drive. I was itching to see if there was a garage or parking pad in back. Jerome's neighbor said he'd always seen the Mercedes parked in view from the street, but how would he know otherwise?

Jerome Pentley said his ballgames typically lasted until 8:00pm, so if Mrs. Pentley's alleged lover hadn't shown up yet, it was unlikely they'd have enough time to do the deed without chancing getting caught. I liked my chances.

I slipped out of the car and hopped up onto the sidewalk, doing my best impression of someone out for a casual stroll. A dog would have been a primo prop. Note to self.

I cut up through the empty plot of land next door, thinking if the Mercedes happened to come right at that moment, I could pass myself off as a potential home buyer. Never mind that there wasn't a For Sale sign on the plot, I figured it would work in a pinch. My undercover skills may have been just the tiniest bit lacking.

Sticking close to the tree line bordering the back of the empty plot, I stopped twice under the guise of surveying the property, while surreptitiously scanning for neighbors. No one was outside, nor did I see any faces in the windows that were starting to light up along the street. Most had drapes drawn against the chill. I quickly crossed the last twenty feet and slipped behind the Pentleys' house. Once in their backyard, I could see there was an oversized two-car garage connected to the driveway, and a crushed gravel walkway linking the garage to the house. Odd choice for northern Ohio, and I wondered how they managed to shovel the snow off it. Next to the walkway were two trash cans and several wooden crates, the type offered up in lieu of bags at discount liquor stores.

Reassured by the silence, and seeing curtains drawn across all the back windows of the house, I took a look-see through the garage windows. The window built into the main roll-up door had been frosted over with a dark material, blocking my ability to see anything more than shapes inside. High up on the side of the structure, sat a small window. Even a boost from Lebron James would have left me a mile short. I ran back around the garage and retrieved three of the liquor crates, stacked them under the window, and gingerly tested my weight with one foot. At 5'7" and a fistful of licorice over my ideal fighting weight, I worried I was pressing my luck, but the crates held without so much as a squeak of complaint when I boosted my other foot up.

Inside the garage sat a dark green Audi, the space next to it empty, but roomy enough to accommodate a second car. An oversized nightlight set into the back wall cast a glow that allowed me to make out four tall wire racks on the far side of the garage, all choked with boxes and plastic tubs. The back wall held bike hooks staggered three high and next to those, a work bench well-stocked with an assortment of tools.

I leaned shakily to the side and had just craned my neck to see the remaining wall when I was yanked airborne, one strong arm creating a vice grip around my waist and another clamping tightly around my mouth.

Unable to scream or open my mouth wide enough to bite down on it, I tried to pry the hand away with one arm, while the other was pinned to my side by the arm encircling my waist. I gained momentary purchase on the ground and attempted to wrap my leg around my attacker's ankle, but only succeeded in drawing his hard chest and stomach closer to my back. It wouldn't have mattered if Paul had taught me another fifty moves, I couldn't even remember the first one. Sweat popped out on my forehead and panic set in as I felt my attacker's weight shift and he started dragging me backward toward the edge of the property.

When we hit the tree line, I felt warm soft lips on my ear and heard a whispered "It's okay. I'm not going to hurt you. Look at me, shhh, it's okay."

I felt the tight grasp on my waist loosen slightly. I took a steadying breath, twisted my head to the left and looked up.

Gee-zuss.

Chapter Five

"Johnny?" I whispered hoarsely, an unleashed scream still coating my throat.

"Long time, kiddo," he whispered back.

Too stunned to be scared, I turned fully around, Johnny's arm still secure around my waist and his chest pressed to mine. With his free arm, he inched my knit cap up my forehead and smiled down at me.

"Miss me?" he asked.

The fear that had turned to shock now turned to full blown anger. Not the hey-you-just-cut-me-off-in-the-fast-lane kind of anger, but more like I-will-cut-you-down-and-take-away-everything-you-hold-dear kind of rage. I raised both hands to push him away and opened my mouth to tell him exactly how much I didn't miss him, when his eyes shifted past me at a beam of light that began to arc our way.

"Company's here," he sang softly. He circled his arms tighter around me and walked me backward, farther into the trees. He stopped and turned me back around in his arms, crouched low, and pulled me down to nestle between his legs. I mutely complied.

A set of headlights continued to crawl up the Pentleys' driveway, easing to a stop a good forty feet short of the tree line. It was a late model Mercedes, midnight blue.

The driver cut the headlights, but Johnny and I maintained our spooned crouch, not moving a muscle. Curiosity, and maybe a tinge of worry that Paul would find out I'd broken the don't-leave-the-car rule, kept me rooted to my spot. I belatedly realized that I left the camera in the car while I took my exploratory jaunt to the backyard, and now I had no way to capture Lover Boy exiting the Mercedes.

The car door opened and out stepped a tall blonde woman. Even in the encroaching dark I could see she was dressed to the nines. Blood red skirt and matching silk blouse peeked out from under a camel leather trench coat. Matching suede heels highlighted large, toned calves. Behind me, Johnny tensed slightly. I couldn't tell if it was from surprise, recognition, or a cramp.

The blonde cut across the grass to the front door, stumbling a bit in her heels before she disappeared from view. I sprung up from our hiding spot, Johnny rising with me but not letting go of my waist.

"Sir Grabs a Lot, heel," I said, smacking his hands away. I took off along the tree line, walking quickly, squelching the desire to bolt for the car and my camera. Johnny stuck right alongside me, matching my pace stride for stride. Which meant I was trotting and he was strolling. Johnny was tall enough to climb.

"What are you doing here?" I asked.

"What are you?" he asked back.

I came to a stunned and sudden stop. "You want me to give *you* answers?" I asked. Johnny's mouth dropped open, and I bolted across the grass.

Johnny Rosato barreled into my life my sophomore year of high school and left like a robber in the night three years later, leaving me behind with a burgeoning crush and zero good-bye. He'd been both spontaneous playmate and sincerest sympathizer to my grandiose dreams, but what hurt the most was that he ran out on my brother Paul. His best friend.

Paul never talked about it, and a decade had passed, but I couldn't imagine Paul would be stoked to see Johnny.

I felt exposed when we neared the sidewalk and jammed my thumb down on my car's remote. I hustled in and slammed the door lock, but not before Johnny jumped in the passenger side.

"Get out." I dug around for my camera, adjusted the lighting control, and aimed it at the house. Tracy may not have been dallying around with another man, but we could at least document things to reassure Jerome.

"Sam," Johnny turned sideways toward me in his seat. I continued to maneuver the camera, refusing to look at him. "Samantha," he whispered.

I raised my head to him. Hazel eyes that blazed green when he was happy and gray when he was serious, were now the flat gray of a battleship's hull. My stomach flipped for the briefest of moments.

"No," I said, shaking my head and turning my attention back to the house. "You don't get to waltz back into my life and expect to pick right up."

"Baby doll, I didn't exactly waltz into your life. You came tiptoeing into my investigation and I plucked you off a beer crate to stop you from ruining it."

"Your investigation?" I shrieked. "You walked into mine. Wait," I said, turning fully toward him in my seat. "You're investigating Tracy Pentley?"

"No. Jerome Pentley."

"Why?" I asked.

"He's supposedly been holding auditions for How Much Wood Would a Woodchuck Chuck, and forgot to ask Mrs. Pentley to try out." Paul would have been delighted. I was not amused.

"I think you might have gotten some bad information," I said. "Jerome Pentley hired Paul to look into his *wife*. He thinks she's the one who's looking for a new baguette to bake in her oven." Johnny squinted one eye at me. I should probably leave that game to him and Paul.

"My point is," I said. "Why would Jerome Pentley tell Paul to watch his wife on a Monday if Tracy Pentley is telling you to watch her husband on the same day?"

"She didn't."

"You just picked Monday randomly?" I asked, looking back at the Pentleys' house for any sign of movement.

"I didn't pick a day at all. I was just here for the cake."

I swiveled my head toward him. "For the what?"

"Cake. My Aunt Jeanette lives four blocks over, remember? It's Little Tony's birthday, and she made cassata cake."

"Her version or the real version?"

"Hers."

I sucked in a breath. Cassata cake is an Italian sponge cake that's typically soaked in liqueur, glued together with ricotta and covered in marzipan. Colozza's Bakery made it with layers of strawberries and custard, and a whipped cream top. Colozza's version was a west-side favorite, but Aunt Jeanette's rendition could make a grown woman cry.

I wiped a tear from the corner of my eye and simultaneously caught a flash of blonde. Tracy's visitor emerged from the house. I raised my camera as she crossed the Pentleys' lawn back to the Mercedes. She had her head down and hands buried in her pockets. I snapped pictures continuously as she climbed into the car, but she never raised her head enough for me to get a clear view of her face. I got three good shots of the car and the plate number before the car began to back down the drive.

"Okay, show's over. Out," I said.

"You're not going to follow her?"

"Paul told me not to get noticed."

"Do you listen to Paul any better now than you did when we were kids?" he asked.

"Good point," I said, starting the car and whipping out from the curb. The Mercedes was already two blocks ahead and I gunned the car forward, attempting to pick up ground.

"Yo, Speed Racer," Johnny said, planting his palm on my thigh. "Just keep sight of her. You don't need to ride her ass."

I slowed slightly.

"Hey, Johnny?"

"Yeah?"

"Did you want to take your hand off my thigh?"

"Just trying to help."

I took his hand and placed it on his thigh. "Help yourself."

The Mercedes approached a yellow light and her brake lights flashed. I tapped my own brakes in response. The light still yellow, the blonde must have had a change of heart. The Mercedes surged forward and sailed through the red, leaving me caught at the light.

"Crap," I said. The light was a short one, but by the time I crossed the intersection, the Mercedes' taillights were long out of view. We cruised around for a few minutes, but the car was gone.

I wound my way back to the Pentleys' street and slowed as I passed their house. The driveway was still empty and the Lincoln that I'd used for cover had disappeared as well.

"Where's your car?" I asked.

"There."

"Which one?" I scanned the street.

"Behind the Jag," Johnny said, pointing at a very familiar motorcycle.

"Oh, my."

Johnny grinned, popping a dimple in his cheek. "You remember."

I felt a little whisper downstairs. My whole body remembered.

"It's probably one of the last times I'll have her out before winter comes. Wanna go for a ride?" he asked.

Yes, yes, yes. "No," I said, focused on my lap, willing my chichi to calm down.

Johnny reached out and gently wrapped one of my curls around his forefinger, stroking my cheek with his thumb as he went.

"Okay, well thanks a bunch. This has been fun. Good to see you," I said.

What the hell was I saying? I eased my head away from his hand and shifted the gear back into drive.

Johnny laughed as he opened his door and stepped out. "God, I've missed you."

Gee-zuss.

Chapter Six

"Oh, dear God," I whispered, and blinked rapidly in the dark, trying to suck up a full breath. "Please get me out of this. I'll take Nonni to bingo for a month of Sundays."

I loosened the drawstrings and slipped the hood of my sweatshirt back off my face. So much for the power of prayer. I took in the avocado fridge, peeling linoleum kitchen floor, and chipped tile countertops. I turned back toward the living room and spied the two-toned carpet, patterned paisley with stains. Orange, brown, and green flowered wallpaper ran through both rooms. Its abstract flowers looked like they were modeled after a seventh-grade sex-ed diagram.

"I, um," I faltered. "Uncle Gino, this is really nice of you to offer, but wouldn't you rather rent this out to someone? Make some money off it? I'm honestly good staying with mom for a while."

"You kidding? Family takes care of family. You'll stay here as long as you want." Gino dropped an arm around my shoulders and waved a hand across the living room with the other. "Really, Sam, where you gonna find a better deal? You don't even need furniture. Just move right in."

Sure, I thought. As soon as the bleach dried.

My gaze followed his arm to the sofa, sloped jarringly to the left from years of untold abuse, and I whimpered. But that might have been due to Gino's arm, which had begun to slither its way from my shoulder down to my rib cage.

My cell phone vibrated in my pocket, and I detangled myself from Gino as I answered.

"Hey," Paul said. "You still at Gino's?"

"Involuntarily."

"Can you get back over to the Pentleys' house?"

"Yeah, what's up?" I asked.

"It's Tracy Pentley. I'll explain when you get here."

"I'll be there in ten," I said, glancing at Uncle Gino, who had taken a seat in an armchair and was busy cleaning his teeth with what looked like a folded receipt. "And, Paul? You're taking Nonni to bingo next week."

***

I left Uncle Gino with a half-hearted promise to call him later, substituting his departing hug with an awkward high five, and headed back to the Pentleys'. When I turned onto their block, I could see two cop cars at the curb and an ambulance idling across the street. The back doors to the ambulance stood open. An empty stretcher rested inside. Two EMTs stood nearby chatting, looking anything but hurried.

I parked several houses down and saw Paul trotting in my direction as I climbed out of the car.

"Hey," I said. "What's going on?"

"Jerome came home from his game and found the kitchen trashed. Glass on the floor, chairs knocked over, couple drawers flipped out onto the floor. He called 911."

My eyes flicked to the EMTs. "Is Tracy okay?"

"No idea. She's not in the house. The police are checking out the woods at the back of the lot, but I don't know much beyond that. Jerome called me right before I called you."

"Is…" I hesitated. "Is there blood?"

"Not that I've heard so far."

"Is her car still here?" I asked.

Paul cut me a look. Ooops. During my drive over to Uncle Gino's, I'd called to debrief Paul on the Mercedes sighting. He wasn't exactly stoked about me leaving the car to scope out the backyard.

"Yes, and the police want to talk to you. I told them what you told me, but they'll want to hear it from you," Paul said.

I nodded, staring at the Pentleys' Tudor. "It had to have happened after the blonde left. She wasn't in there very long, and she definitely came out of the house alone."

"But you were in the backyard for a while, right? If she did try to attack her, Tracy could have gotten out the front door without you seeing," Paul said.

"I mean, it's possible. But don't you think she'd have tried to get help somewhere by now? That she'd have called her husband or the police?"

"Yes, unless she's afraid."

"Of what?" I asked.

Paul shrugged his shoulders. "This woman. Who knows what she may be involved in? It's entirely possible Tracy got wrapped up into something bad, and going to the cops or Jerome would force her to reveal it."

"Mmm-hmm," I said. "Or…"

"Or, what?" Paul asked.

I chewed my lip. What I hadn't told Paul during our earlier debriefing was that Johnny had shown up at the Pentleys'. Or that Tracy had hired him to check out Jerome. I was torn. On the one hand, it might help the police to know that Johnny was checking out Jerome Pentley, but on the other, I wasn't sure if Johnny's reappearance would upset Paul. Assuming even a slim possibility that the info would help find Tracy, I took a deep breath and plunged in.

"So, listen," I said. "Don't get upset, but I need to tell you something."

Paul looked at me warily. "Let me guess, while you were traipsing through the Pentleys' backyard, you took the opportunity to pop in the back door, too?"

"No, of course not. But while I was scoping out the garage, I ran into—"

Over Paul's shoulder, I saw a familiar figure walking toward us. Familiar because it had hijacked me from a crate not three hours before.

"Paul—" I said, but Paul had already turned at the sound of the footsteps behind him.

"Long time, no see," Johnny smiled at me, but his eyes held a mixture caution and curiosity.

Paul slapped an abbreviated handshake into Johnny's palm.

"What's up, man?" Paul said. "You get anything from Roman?"

"Not yet," said Johnny. "I think he's waiting to see what they've got before he decides what I get to know."

I looked first at Paul, then at Johnny. My lips parted, then closed, my brain fighting to find words. They each glanced briefly at me, then at each other. Paul shuffled back and forth a couple steps, while Johnny jammed his hands in his front pockets and threw a glance back over his shoulder at the Pentleys'.

"Sam…" Paul began.

"Paul," I said

"Sam."

"Now that we've got that down, why don't you tell me what's going on?" I pointed at Johnny. "This one disappears for ten years and you're suddenly sharing secret handshakes?"

"Not exactly," Paul said. "Johnny came back to town a few months ago, to work for a PI agency down in Akron. We kind of crossed paths on a case he was working."

"And you guys just patched things up?" I asked. "Your best friend jets on you without a word and it's suddenly all okay?"

I glanced over at Johnny, who was looking at me like I was about to walk into a tree and didn't know it.

"What?" I said to Johnny, then looked back at Paul. "What aren't you telling me?"

Paul took my arm and walked me backward several feet. Over his shoulder, I saw Johnny turn and stride back toward the Pentleys'.

"Sam, Johnny didn't bail on me. His uncle offered him a job down in North Carolina. I knew he was leaving."

"What? Why didn't you tell me? Why didn't *he* tell me? Do you know how long I was pissed over that, thinking *you* were pissed?"

"Look, I knew you had a crush on him. He was going to say good-bye to you, but I asked him to let me tell you instead."

"Why?" I asked.

"I figured if it looked like he just took off, you'd be mad for a little while and get over it instead of pining away over him."

I gawked at Paul.

"I know, it sounds stupid now," Paul said. "But I didn't think you'd get so bent about how I'd feel."

I willed my jaw to close, but couldn't quite crank it all the way.

"Gimme a break, Sam. We were kids. I'm sorry."

"So, Johnny knows all this?" I asked. "That's why he's looking at me like I'm the fat kid who just dropped her cupcake?"

"He does now. He called me after you guys left the Pentleys'."

Good god. I was living with my mother, taking orders from my brother, and had just blown a tizzy because my girlhood crush had blindsided me. Again. I was a thirty-one-year-old woman living the life of a third-grader. I could only hope there'd be a pudding cup in it for me somewhere.

Paul silently watched me work through my internal seizure.

"You gonna be okay with this?"

"Do I have a choice?" I asked.

Paul grinned. "Tell you what. Johnny's got a cop buddy here named Roman who doesn't mind sharing sometimes. You want to go see what we can find out?"

I stood rooted to the ground. Paul reached out and patted my head twice. "Oh, just come on. I'll help you hold your cupcake, fatty."

Chapter Seven

I ran my hands over Johnny's chest and made my way to his mouth, his breath hot on my neck. I turned my face to his and arched against him. His hand slipped into my waistband, before both his progress and my dream were cut off by the sound of mom's coffee grinder slicing through the air.

I rolled over in my childhood twin bed, knocking my knee into the wall. Paul, Johnny, and I had spent another three hours at the Pentleys' last night, answering questions for the police. I answered the same five questions a dozen times, described every scratch I could see on the Mercedes and how many buttons were on the blonde woman's red silk shirt. By the time I turned onto my mom's block, it was close to four in the morning. Between three hours of sleep and Mom's appliance acoustics, I was one cranky kitty by the time I landed at the office.

Paul was already at his desk, coffee in hand. Johnny sat across from him, propped on the edge of my desk, a length of Red Vine jutting between his lips.

"Hey, kids," I said, slipping between them. I snagged my purse strap on the arm of my chair, ricocheted back, then half fell, half slumped into my chair.

"Smooth," Paul said.

I lowered my burning face and busied myself with turning on my computer and fussing with my phone. I worked at ignoring the butt on my desk that I had so thoroughly inspected an hour earlier in my dreams.

"Good timing," Johnny said. "We were just talking about Tracy Pentley."

"Any update?" I asked. I'd missed out on meeting Roman the previous night. My statement was taken in the cramped butler's pantry by an officer who'd apparently enjoyed a recent salami hoagie.

"There's not much," Johnny answered. "Police never found Tracy's purse and her car is still missing. Outside of the mess in the kitchen, they didn't find anything disturbed in the rest of the house. No blood, no defensive weapons of any obvious kind. No signs of forced entry."

"Do they think it could have been a burglary?" I asked.

"If it was, they were looking for something specific. Electronics are still there, including Tracy's laptop. Jerome checked her jewelry and couldn't tell if anything was missing, but there was a diamond necklace and bracelet sitting in a tray right out on her dresser."

"Who's to say she didn't leave on her own accord and toss some stuff on the floor to tick Jerome off?" I asked. "If she thought Jerome was cheating, maybe she decided to cut bait."

"Then why bring me in?" Johnny asked. "She only called me two days ago. If she planned ahead well enough to stage a scene like that, hiring me would be pointless."

"But what if she found real evidence of an affair after talking to you, and just didn't bother to call you off?" I countered.

"Possible, but I don't see it," Johnny said.

"Did Roman say how the police are approaching this?" I asked.

"They're talking to the family on both sides," Johnny said. "They're also trying to figure out who owns the Mercedes, which

I'd imagine they know by now. I'll check with Roman later."

"I'm curious about that myself," I said. "That blonde was fairly tall, but she didn't seem all that steady on her feet when she went in the house. I don't see how she could handle Tracy if she put up a fight."

"Not unless she had a weapon," Paul said.

"But then where's Tracy? We saw the blonde leave by herself."

Johnny's cell rang and he walked back to the kitchen to answer it. Paul and I considered each other, both silently working through the scenarios.

"I have to take off," Johnny said, walking back into the room. He freed another Red Vine from the nest in the tub and headed toward the door. Angie walked in the front door just as Johnny reached the threshold, and stopped in her tracks. She looked at me, then up at Johnny, over at Paul, then back at me. She tilted her head back toward Johnny while keeping her eyes on me.

"Am I protective-angry-bitch-face, or am I unaffected-don't-even-see-you-there-casual?" she asked me.

"We've moved on to so-what-it-was-a-long-time-ago-fake-smile," I said.

Angie shrugged and beamed at Johnny. "Hey buddy, good to see you." She slapped his shoulder as she moved past him. Judging from Johnny's face, there might have been a little more punch than slap involved. For Angie, high school grudges lasted longer than a Nancy Grace diatribe.

"Good to see you, too, Ange," Johnny said. "You're looking good."

Angie cut a look at him. "I'm aware. And be advised, I just got used to the fake smile phase. We're going to have to work up to the bullshit chitchat phase."

Johnny tipped her an imaginary hat, winked at me, and was out the door.

Angie plopped down on the corner of the desk that Johnny had vacated. She was sporting blue workout tights and a cherry red tank top that peeked out from under a zip-front jacket. Her hair was braided up into some kind of bun that I couldn't achieve if I had two days and a diagram. "There's a rock climbing class tonight at that new gym down on Lorain. Come check it out with me."

"Can't," I replied. "Uncle Gino's offering the Lincoln Ave house to me and I need to get over there tonight to de-Gino it."

Angie snorted. "Two fortnights, a crane, and a bomb couldn't get Gino's funk out of that house. What are you thinking?"

"He's not charging me rent and I desperately need my own space."

"So what, you save on rent and spend all that money on the herpes meds you're gonna need from sleeping in his bed?"

"Hey, ladies?" Paul interjected. "There's nothing more I'd like to do on this beautiful, sunny morning than to explore the enticing topic of my uncle's theoretical genital warts, but can we get to work?"

Angie hopped off the desk and gave Paul a salute. Her eyes dropped to his desk as she slung her purse over her shoulder.

"Hey, is that Tracy?" She reached out and picked up the picture of Tracy Pentley that Jerome had left with us. "You working for her?"

Paul and I gaped at Angie.

"You know Tracy Pentley?" Paul asked.

"Of course I know her. So do you," Angie said, tossing a look at me. "She used to be Tracy Simmons, from Parma Park Middle."

"Get out," I said, scooting my chair around to Paul's desk. I'd seen the pictures when we first met with Jerome, but except for her eyes, this woman looked nothing like the Tracy Simmons I remembered as a girl.

"Are you sure?" I asked Angie.

"Completely," Angie said.

I studied at the picture some more. Tracy and I had been best friends for all of two years, somewhat by default. Her parents were divorced, and her dad had moved to LA to chase a movie career pipedream. Tracy's mom doted on her to excess and there was never even a question that Tracy would stay with her. Tracy had been a loner at school and her only sister, older than us by four years, spent her waking hours hopping between loser boyfriends and fighting with their mom.

Tracy and I shared an affinity for books and a mutual dislike for the girls who spent all their time on hair, make-up, and all things boy. By the time we hit high school, Tracy's mom got a new job and they had moved two towns over. Our relationship didn't survive. It was a measly twelve-mile divide, but insurmountable in the days of one house phone and no wheels.

"I never would have recognized her," I said.

"Rumor has it she's had a little work done. It's definitely her, though. She was in my cycle class last Fall. I ran into her at an open house I went to when my sister was buying her first place."

"That would be her," Paul said. "According to the bio I've been putting together this morning, she's been an agent for the last few years."

I looked up from the picture, surprised. "Why are you doing a bio? Does Jerome seriously want you to keep trying to figure out if Tracy was cheating?"

"Not exactly. He called me this morning and asked to me to investigate her disappearance. That's what I wanted to talk to you about before you two started climbing the family herpe tree."

"I'm out." Angie headed for the door.

Chapter Eight

"Please tell me those are rosary beads. Like, really big rosary beads. On a really short chain," I said.

Vinnie stood holding the plastic baggie he had unearthed from under Uncle Gino's bed, a shit-eating grin riding his face. "Well, all right. Go, Uncle G," he said.

"Good gravy," I said and held my palm up flat in front of me, in an attempt to ward off the baggie-encased cooties. Vinnie laughed and shook the bag, taunting me from across the bed.

"Yeah, keep swinging that thing. Let it break," I said. "You think Gino washes those things any better than anything else around here?" Vinnie dropped the smirk and the bag.

Paul and I spent the morning digging up what we could on the Pentleys', then I'd wrangled Vinnie into helping me with the decontamination project at the Lincoln Ave house. For the price of one twelve-pack of Blue Moon, he was my labor for the afternoon.

Two hours in and we'd already hit the gigolo jackpot. In addition to the, uh, rosary beads, we'd found the ripped top sheet from a satin bed set, three half-empty packs of incense, and a jar of fingernail clippings that I fervently hoped were all Uncle Gino's and not souvenirs. At the back of the attic closet, we also found a stack of abandoned VHS tapes. Uncle Gino seemed to have a respect for the classics. *Assablanca, On Golden Blonde, The Way We Came.*

The two other small bedrooms were blessedly empty and we'd already thoroughly scrubbed down the kitchen and living room. Once we sterilized the master bedroom, I'd theoretically be able to move in, but my willie factor was still off the charts.

"Anything new and exciting in the high-stakes world of credit checks?" Vinnie asked, opening and closing bureau drawers, a plastic grocery bag wrapped around his hand for a glove.

"Actually, yeah. We were hired by a guy who thinks his wife's cheating on him, and she turned up missing the day we started watching her," I said. I started spraying down one of the nightstands. "Hey, you probably remember Tracy Simmons from middle school?"

"Nope, don't think so," Vinnie said, then stopped wiping. "Wait, maybe. She the one with the big shnoz and the kinky hair? You guys hung out constantly?"

"That would be her."

"Yeah, I remember her. She carried that Molly Ringwald lunch box around all the time, like a purse, right? Weird chick."

"This coming from the kid who carried those little green army men around in his pocket," I countered.

"So?"

"You were fifteen."

Vinnie took a renewed interest in wiping down the bureau.

"So, what's the deal? Did she run away?" he asked.

"Not sure. It looks like she may have been taken unwillingly, but a lot of things don't add up. That's what Paul and I are trying to figure out."

"Why aren't the police doing that?" Vinnie asked.

"They're investigating, but Tracy's husband is paying Paul to look into it. He thinks the police will figure that Tracy's just run off."

"What are you and Paul gonna do to find her?" he asked.

"Learn more about her marriage, talk to friends and family, find out if she had any spats, money issues, that type of thing," I said.

Paul and I had learned some general info that morning, courtesy of the internet and public records. The Pentleys' had been married just shy of four years, living the entire time in their current house, which they bought two months before the wedding. Tracy had gone to college but didn't graduate, and held a series of odd jobs for a handful of years before eventually getting her real estate license a few years prior. The realty agency website revealed she'd sold a respectable number of listings, so she must have found her niche.

Jerome Pentley was born in Connecticut and grew up along the East Coast, moving to Cleveland for college. He'd moved north again for a job in Michigan, where he'd also been married for a short time, before landing back in Cleveland working as a mid-level research analyst at a local university. We didn't know yet how Jerome and Tracy had met or how long they'd been together before marrying, but Paul was working on tracking down Tracy's sister and mom.

Strains of the Brady Bunch theme song started jangling in Vinnie's pocket. I moved to the windows at the front of the room and showered them with glass cleaner. Behind me, I heard Vinnie apologizing to his caller.

"Sorry, can't tonight. I'm closing the shop," he said. "But, Sam can."

I whipped around.

"Sam can what?" I mouthed.

Vinnie smiled at me and walked backward toward the hallway. "Yeah, I'm sure of it. I'm with her now, and she's totally free tonight."

Oh, what the fresh hell. "Vin! Who is that?"

"Cool, call ya' later, Ma."

It hit me like a five-year-old with a piñata stick. It was

Tuesday. Mom could only want one thing. I dropped my head in defeat.

"Say it," I mumbled.

"Ma thinks she's coming down with a cold. You gotta take Nonni to Bingo."

Chapter Nine

It's not that I don't love my Nonni. Even the bingo isn't so bad, though I never made it out of there without my hands and wrists covered in purple bingo marker and a healthy dose of guilt. Nonni only went to Bingo at the Sisters. More formally known as the Sisters of the Charity church. Or what I liked to call, the Big Time Church.

While both my parents were raised Catholic, and Nonni raised my dad with twice-weekly mass, they didn't go to church regularly while we were growing up. They raised us at home in the Be Nice religion. Be nice to other kids, be nice to your teachers, be nice to your elders. They overlooked a lot of our scrapes, swearing, and general hell-raising. In exchange, they fully expected that we wouldn't go to jail, turn into coke-heads, or get knocked up. Or, in my brothers' case, do the knocking. Sitting in a church, for any reason, always left me feeling like a five-year-old dipping into the proverbial cookie jar.

I finished up at Uncle Gino's and stopped off for a plate of chicken Paprikash at the Club House. I'd called Angie on the way and convinced her to skip the rock wall in favor of a night with Nonni and the Sisters.

Nonnie loved Angie. Angie is the granddaughter I would

never be. Church-going, married to a sweet and dependable man, devoted to her kids, and could stuff the hell out of a manicotti shell. Little did Nonni know that Angie's favorite "F" word wasn't "Father" nor that her sweet, dependable husband tried to stuff Angie's shell in every backseat, movie hall, and restaurant bathroom this side of the Valley View Bridge.

I swung onto Angie's street as she came trotting down her driveway and she hopped in as soon as I rolled to a stop. I waved to Tony, who was standing at the front door with a two-year-old hanging on his leg, and took off.

"Thank God you called," Angie said. "If that man touches me again any time soon, I'm gonna start to chafe."

"On the good news front, at least it's your tail he's trying to chafe."

"Tell that to my hoo-hah. She's starting to look like a California Raisin."

Angie lived less than a mile from the church. When we hooked into the lot, it was already three-quarters full. Bingo at the Sisters was a hot draw. Where most of the town shut down by eight, the Sisters rocked bingo until almost eleven. Mom had arranged for Nonni's neighbor Eunice to drop her off at the church, so Angie and I made our way to the lobby to look for her.

We found Nonni on a bench along the far wall, sitting with an impatient look on her face. She sported a coral colored polyester pants set, which would have been somewhat pretty if she didn't have a head full of peach hair to match. Nonni'd had beautiful auburn curls when she was young and thought the peach rinse kept her connected to her youth. No one had the heart to tell her it looked like she'd raided an Oompa Loompa's spray tan collection.

Nonni had her stack of bingo cards resting in her lap, her monster purse by her side. She could have packed for a three-day trip to Chicago in that thing. When we were kids, whatever you needed, Nonni had it. Umbrella, tissues, toy train, cough drops, lipstick, sweater, gloves, books, crackers, puzzles, eyeglasses, once a full loaf of sausage bread. The purse weighed more than she did.

Nonni saw us and gestured frantically. "Get your cards. Agnes Cravatelli already has her seat and the tables are filling up fast around her."

I hooked a hand under Angie's elbow and hustled her over to the table that was set up by the Sisters to hock bingo cards, markers, and scratch-offs. I cobbled together two sets of everything, passed the Sister a twenty, and we shuffled back toward Nonni.

"Who's Agnes Cravatelli?" Angie whispered.

"She's Nonni's arch nemesis," I said. "Nonni takes the 'keep your enemies closer' adage to a whole new level. She can't stand for Agnes to be out of her sight at these things."

"How does an eighty-five-year-old woman have an arch nemesis? More importantly, *why*? At that age, I'm thinking my greatest focus in life will be not shitting my pants."

Nonni stood up as we approached. I heaved her purse onto her shoulder and we took off for the main hall, her barely five-foot tall frame disappearing in the crowd of old ladies pushing into the room. I scanned through the jumble of beauty parlor-ed heads, trying to find the spot of peach in a sea of blue.

By the time we found Nonni, she'd already set up base camp. She'd thrown sweaters over two chairs, no doubt rescued from the depths of her purse, to save for me and Angie. In front of her, she'd laid out eight bingo cards, four markers in various colors, and two troll dolls. One doll wore a sombrero and poncho, while the other bore an eerily close resemblance to Michael Jackson. To her left, she had set out two baggies of Fig Newtons and an inch-high brass elephant, with a slot cut into its back for her "lucky penny".

Angie and I spread out our loot, which looked like Ikea milk crates next to Nonni's Ethan Allan suite. Angie dug into her bag and came up with a wadded roll of Lifesavers, a wet-nap, and a pacifier. She spread these out above our cards, then we joined the long line at the snack bar to get Nonni some decaf to go with her cookies.

Angie surveyed the room while we waited. "I think we've got four of the last eight working ovaries in this room," she said.

"Maybe three. I feel like my left one isn't really pulling its weight," I said.

"Maybe it's just afraid of commitment, like her mommy."

"Funny."

"Hey, check it out. Two more for the Ovarian Club," Angie said, surreptitiously pointing with her elbow to the back corner of the room. "We're up to twelve." She cut a look at my belly. "Well, eleven."

"No really, you should take that act on the road," I said.

I looked at the table Angie had gestured toward. Sitting alongside the full cast of the Golden Girls was a brunette who looked a shade younger than me and next to her, a woman I assumed to be her mother. The younger woman was a knockout. Cindy Crawford hair, Grace Kelly face, and Dolly Parton bringing up the rack.

Neither of the women were interacting with any of the Girls and they had only two playing cards apiece, the international symbol for bingo newbie. Maybe they were on Nonnie duty, too.

I scanned the rest of the room as we inched closer to the front of the snack line. I saw several familiar faces from my youth, friends of my Nonni's and nonnis of my friends. Only one other person our age, a wispy red-head, leaned over a much older woman to her left, and dabbed at her playing cards. Probably filling all her Free Spaces before the games started. Bingo Prep was not to be taken lightly. I'd seen amateur women try to start with eight cards and by the fourth game you could find them curled in the corner, tears streaming down their faces, mindlessly dabbing at the air with their markers, whimpering "B6, B6, O64, wait, wait, go back..."

We picked up our drinks and headed back to our table just as one of the Sisters started the opening announcements.

"Okay, everyone," Sister said. "We've got twelve rounds of regular play, three lightning rounds with one winner only, and Ruth will be coming around with two supplements at the first break. She's also got instant tickets, folks. Six games tonight, two with a $1299 payout," Sister pushed out, all in one breath. She pointed to a middle-aged woman wearing brown corduroy pants and a Day-Glo orange apron pilfered from the local Home Depot. Ruth's apron pockets were bulging with the aforementioned instant tickets, which were the real draw. Bingo entry was only five bucks, but these ladies would collectively spend thousands in instants during the night. Husbands all across town thought their wives were tee-totaling bingo cards, when in fact they were throwing down like they were at an illegal Monte Carlo night in an underground speakeasy.

"Our number caller tonight is Marion Hedgley–thank you, Marian," Sister continued. "And please make sure you support the Sisters with a visit to the snack bar. All proceeds go directly to the church. A big thank you to Jerome Pentley, our gracious benefactor who has so generously donated all of the snacks and drinks for this evening."

A smattering of applause spread through the room as Sister pointed to a man stacking boxes near the doorway to a storage room. Jerome Pentley turned around at Sister's introduction and gave a tight smile to the room.

"Here we go, ladies and gentleman," Marian Hedgley boomed. "First ball is in the monitor."

Two and a half hours later, Nonnie had won a lightning round, Angie had won a hundred dollars on instants, and I had green marker on both elbows and a cheek.

At Sister's intro of Jerome Pentley, Angie and I had both craned for a better look, but he had disappeared into the storage room and never came out. We were halfway through the last game of the night, and a quarter of the room had emptied of players sighing in disgust when one wrong number after another had come up. Half of the Golden Girls quartet had given up, as well as the mother-daughter pair we'd seen earlier.

Angie had crumpled up her last playing card and was scrolling through Google images of Richard Gere on her smartphone. Like Uncle Gino, she appreciated the classics. I knew Nonni would fight it out until the bitter end, if for no other reason than to prove her stamina to Agnes.

At last, "BINGO!" came on a feeble shout from an octogenarian at Agnes' table, and there was a collective scraping of chairs and securing of lucky charms as folks made a dash for the parking lot. We'd followed the herd and just gotten Nonni settled in the front seat, her behemoth purse at her feet, when she started patting her pockets in a frenzy.

"Nonni, what's up?" I asked.

"My Ponchi. I can't find him."

Angie shot me a look from the back seat and started slowly twirling her finger by her left ear. I reached back and twisted her finger until she let out a little yelp.

"Nonni, who's Ponchi?" I asked tentatively.

"He's my lucky doll. I had him on the table, I know it." Nonni levered her purse halfway up her leg before getting stuck.

"Was he the troll with the sombrero?" I asked, lifting the purse the rest of the way into her lap.

"Yes. I bet that whore Agnes took him when I went to the Ladies'."

My mouth dropped open and I heard a whispered "Holy Christ" from the backseat.

"Ange," I said. "See if that thing's in Nonni's purse. I'll run back in and check our table."

***

I jogged through the lobby and pushed on the doors to the bingo room, but they were locked. I circled back around to the lobby and trotted down the hall toward the church offices and day school. I knew from previous visits that the bingo room was connected to the offices through a second shorter hallway shooting off the side of the room.

Both the main hallway and the connecting one were dark, but a weak light spilled out from a partially open door on the right, where I heard faint voices. I continued down the hallway to the door at the end that led to the main room. The door was unlocked and I wound my way through the tables to where Nonni, Angie, and I had been sitting. The table was empty, as was the floor around it. I snatched out a folding chair to duck my head under the table and there was Ponchi, sitting patiently on the chair. I snatched him up, shoved him in my pocket, and headed back to the side door. The light I had seen earlier had been turned off, but I still heard voices, now farther away.

I turned the corner into the main hallway and came up short. Fifty feet away, tucked into a decorative alcove supporting a statue of a cherub, was the young brunette Angie and I had seen earlier.

Only it wasn't her mother's mouth she had her tongue halfway down. It was Jerome Pentley's.

Chapter Ten

I dodged behind a statue of a saint, wedging myself between it and the wall. The saint had his hand on his hip, allowing me to peek underneath his armpit to see Jerome and the brunette still playing grab-ass in the nook. I scanned the main hall, judging the distance back to the bingo room. It wasn't far, but it had been sheer luck that the pair hadn't seen me when I came around the corner. If I waited them out, and they came back my way instead of toward the main doors, they would see my butt hanging out from behind the statue.

I tip-toed sideways along the wall, careful to step straight up and down so my sneakers wouldn't squeak on the polished floors. Feeling along with my left hand, I kept my eyes trained on the couple. Jerome had both hands down the back of the brunette's jeans, a small marvel given the jeans were tighter to her skin than plastic to a fruit roll-up.

A loud rattling followed by insistent banging started up in the lobby. Jerome released the brunette, they both looked toward the main doors, and I jack-rabbited across the hallway and back into the hall leading to the bingo room. I heard footsteps running somewhere behind me in the main hallway, but didn't take the time to look back. I pushed through the side door to the bingo room, ran around the stage where the number caller sat, and scuttled underneath the cloth apron that hid the framework of the stage.

I heard the door open and close, but no more footsteps. A moment later, I heard the sound of a door slamming behind the snack bar. Two more minutes passed in silence, and I was about to crawl out when I heard the door open again. I froze.

"Hello?" said a male voice.

"Sam?" Angie said. "Sam? Did you find Ponchi?"

I lifted the stage skirt and half rolled, half crawled out. Jerome Pentley and Angie were standing near the door. Jerome narrowed his eyes at me while Angie worked to get the smile off her face.

"What are you doing under there?" Jerome asked.

Digging the doll from my pocket, I held out my hand, revealing Ponchi in my palm. "My Nonni's lucky charm. She left it behind."

"Under the stage?" Jerome asked, looking at me like his bullshit meter was about to hit red.

I shrugged and opened my eyes wide. "Must have fallen and gotten kicked under there when everyone was leaving." I picked a little lint off Ponchi's sombrero, patted his head, and smiled at Jerome. He didn't return the favor.

"So, you donated all the snacks tonight, right?" I asked. "That's really great."

If Jerome knew how to take a compliment, he didn't show it.

"Tracy volunteered us to do it," Jerome said.

"Who's Tracy?" Angie asked, blinking innocent eyes at Jerome.

"My wife," Jerome said, glancing at me, then toward the door.

"Oh, is she here tonight?"

Jerome quickly scanned Angie's face. "No. And it's time for you two to go."

***

"Why didn't you just stay under the stage?" Paul asked.

As soon as we parted ways with Jerome Pentley, I hustled Angie, Nonni, and Ponchi safely home, then hightailed it over to Paul's house.

"What was I supposed to do, leave Angie out there alone with him? She told him she came in to look for her friend. I don't think he would have just said 'oh, okay' if she said never-mind."

"Angie could get herself out of a Swahili prison with a smile and a piece of gum," Paul said. I shrugged. It was true. In high school, Angie had gotten caught coming out of a stall after smoking a clove cigarette in the girls' room. She got out of it by telling Mrs. Clinedale that there must have been a sewer back up and she had poured some of her perfume down the floor drain to help with the smell. She followed up by suggesting Mrs. Clinedale have the principal call her cousin Lonnie, a local plumber, who could come out in a jiff to look into it for a great price. A confused Mrs. Clinedale headed to the principal's office with Lonnie's number and Angie went back to geometry class.

"Are you absolutely positive he didn't see you out in the hallway?" Paul asked.

"Pretty sure. I was around that corner within a second and I heard footsteps behind me, but they had to have been the woman's. I think Jerome sent her to sneak through the snack room to the rear exit door, while he went to let in Angie."

"And you didn't recognize the woman?" Paul asked.

"No. Neither did Angie and we saw her during bingo, in good light."

"Okay, my turn," Paul said, turning around and retrieving a beer from the fridge. "Johnny called a couple hours ago. Roman told him they found a car abandoned out near Sandusky. Tracy's cell phone was on the floor in the backseat and there was a little bit of blood on the case."

My stomach did a slow roll. "How much is a little?"

"Not enough to say anyone was hurt badly, but there's no way to tell if it came from an injury that happened in the car or before the person got in. But the fact that the car was left the way it was is enough for the police to think Tracy may have been taken against her will."

"Whose car is it?" I asked.

"So far, they traced it to a guy who says he sold it for cash a couple days earlier."

"Can we get the record of the sale, or the title?" I asked.

"That's the catch. The guy didn't give the woman who bought the car a receipt, or even discuss title. The car was a junker and he just needed the cash, but he was more than willing to admit to the shady sale after he heard the car was involved in a missing person's case. Roman said the guy was ready to cop to every petty crime he'd committed in the last ten years. Which would have been a waste anyway, seeing as how the guy got into a fistfight in a bar later and a dozen witnesses could alibi him for the day Tracy went missing."

"Anything on the Mercedes yet?" I asked.

"That's another odd thing. The plate number belongs to a 1999 Ford Focus."

"No way."

"Way," Paul said, taking a pull from his beer.

"Go back," I said. "The police said nothing was noticeably disturbed outside the kitchen, right?"

Paul nodded.

"And no forced entry? Not a scratch on the doors or the windows?"

"No, neither front nor back showed any signs of being forced. When the blonde went in, she either had a key, the door was unlocked, or Tracy invited her in."

"I'm going with door number three," I said. "Seems most likely Tracy let her in. But then, why would the blonde bother with putting on fake plates?"

Paul rubbed the top of the beer bottle against his lower lip as he considered my question.

"I've got calls out to both her sister and mom. If they don't call back by noon tomorrow, I'll drive out to her mom's place. You wanna come?"

"Definitely," I said, rubbing my eyes. "I'm going to move my stuff into Gino's in the morning. Maybe we can stop off for a tetanus shot on the way to Tracy's mom's?"

"You bet." Paul polished off the second beer and set the bottle on the counter behind him. "Let me ask you something and don't get all defensive."

"Mmm, too late," I said, smiling.

"You and Johnny," Paul said. I lost the smile.

"Yeah?"

"When we were kids, how much of that was..." Paul trailed off with a pained look.

"How much was what?" I asked.

"Look. I know you guys talked about shit that you wouldn't tell me."

My face flushed and Paul held up a hand. "I don't care about that. I just wondered if you guys, uh, if there was anything more to it. I don't need details, just yes or no."

"How about 'kind of'?" I asked.

Paul pumped his head up and down and thought about it.

"Why does it matter?" I asked.

"I'm picking up a lot of work, and Johnny's offered to give me a hand for a while. And, I'd like him to help train you."

"And you want to make sure we're not playing footsies," I said.

"Something like that."

I was disappointed and it must have shown.

"I'm not saying I think you wouldn't focus on the job." Paul's words rushed out. "I just don't want to make it harder than it has to be. For either of you."

"What's that supposed to mean?"

Paul gave me a wary look.

"You think Johnny could be distracted?" I asked, throwing my fingers up in air quotes.

"Shit, Sam, I'm not nineteen anymore. I can see the way he looks at you."

My flush burned deeper.

"And you may have this whole resentment thing still going on with how he left things before, but I know you. You'll get past that. You two have always connected and I need to know it won't be a problem while Johnny's helping out."

"You have my word."

Chapter Eleven

After another long night of playing Sleuth Barbie, I was dead on my feet by the time I got back to my mom's house. I wiggled my toothbrush across my teeth enough to hopefully fake out the tooth fairy, wrestled my jeans off, and toppled into bed.

I woke up four hours later to my mom's face hovering inches from mine, her fingers roughly pushing the hair off my forehead, whisper-shrieking my name. "Sam. Sam. Samantha."

"What? What's wrong?" I asked, pressing my head back into my pillow so I could look her in the eyes.

"You have a visitor," she said.

"Angie?"

"Johnny."

"What does he want?"

"I don't know. But baby," she paused.

"What?"

"Before you go out there, you might want to do a little something with yourself first."

I rubbed my eyes and pulled away fingers smudged black with mascara. "I'll get a comb."

My mom eyed my hair, then my face. "Hmmm."

Mom scampered out while I unwound myself from the sheets,

yanked on yesterday's jeans, and snuck down the hall to the bathroom. I raked my hair up into a ponytail, rinsed my face, and downed a shot of mouthwash with a water chaser. It was obvious my outfit was on its second wearing, so I skipped the make-up. Lipstick on a pig and all.

By the time I hit the living room, Mom had plied Johnny with a Diet 7-Up and a salad plate heaped with Oreos. Never mind it wasn't nine in the morning, my mother wasn't going to be thought of a bad hostess.

"Hi," I said, taking a seat on the far end of the couch and tucking my feet up underneath me. Johnny sat on the adjacent armchair, elbows on his knees, rolling the can of 7-Up between his palms.

Mom retreated to the kitchen and we soon heard the sound of dishes clanking around in the sink.

Johnny combed his eyes over me, a smile tweaking the corner of his mouth. His hair was a shade on the long side, and he was boasting a two-day old shadow. I could smell his cologne and all the old feelings came roaring back. Had I not been painfully aware that I smelled like the underside of a church stage, I would have crawled into his lap to take a closer sniff. Old habits die hard.

"Late night?" Johnny asked, the smile becoming broader.

"Did you come over bright and early just to give me a hard time, or was this the only slot you had in your calendar?"

"Neither. I came to offer my help."

"With what?" I asked.

"Paul said you were moving this morning. He thought you might need help, but he's caught up in that bakery business."

"So he asked you to come in his place?"

"I offered."

"Why?" I asked, twisting the toe seam of my Hello Kitty sock.

"Sam, I thought we were at the it-happened-a-long-time-ago phase."

"We are," I sighed and looked up at him. "I may have had a

momentary set-back."

"Is this going to be a long setback, or something we can knock through by lunch?"

Thirty minutes later, I was washed, dried, and dressed. I chugged a cup of coffee and crammed a granola bar into my mouth while Johnny loaded his truck with my clothes and small collection of boxes, then we took off for Uncle Gino's. We stopped off at a paint and hardware store and picked up four gallons of paint, tarps, and a handful of brushes.

By noon, we had my meager belongings unloaded and the paint stored in Gino's garage for me to douse over the walls later.

***

"Oh, Samantha. Look at you."

Tracy's mom wrapped her arms around me in a tight hug, then drew back and framed my face with her hands. Her eyes sported the red of a recent cry, but were momentarily dry.

"Hi, Mrs. Simmons. How are you holding up?" I asked.

"Oh, you're not twelve anymore. Call me Carol," she said. "I'm as fine as can be expected of me. Come in, come in." Johnny and I followed her into the house, through a massive foyer, and down a step into a sunken living room.

I introduced Johnny, and Carol pointed us toward a couch flanked by matching blue side chairs. Pictures lined the mantel above the fireplace, all in heavy silver frames. I saw a few of the Tracy I remembered from middle school, and several of her that must have been from high school and beyond.

Carol's eyes tracked my own. "How long has it been since you've seen Tracy?" she asked.

"Not since shortly after you guys moved away."

"I always thought it was such a shame you two didn't stay close, though I can understand why," she said. "Tracy talked about you for a long time, you know. She always considered you very dear."

"Me, too," I said, surprised to feel my throat constrict. Angie and I had become best friends the year after Tracy moved away. I adored Angie, but Tracy understood my yearning to get out into the world better than anyone.

"Carol," I said, finding my voice again. "We were hoping to learn more about what things have been like for Tracy the last few years. I know the police are working on this and you've spoken with them, but Jerome has asked Paul to look into things, too."

I didn't know how much Paul had disclosed about why Jerome hired him in the first place, but I thought "things" was a nice euphemism for "possibly shtupping someone else". It had been a lot of years, but I didn't have reason to think Carol had taken Tracy off the pedestal she'd built for her.

Carol leaned back and used two fingers to manipulate a moist-looking tissue from the pocket of her pants. After dabbing both eyes, she looked up and nodded, more to herself than to us.

"What would you like to know?" she asked.

"Are Tracy and Jerome happy, from what you can tell?" I asked.

Carol shrugged her shoulders slightly. "Happy might be a strong word. Complacent is probably a better description."

"What do you mean?" I asked.

"Tracy didn't have a lot of boyfriends in high school, and never was one to have crushes. When she met Jerome, it wasn't fireworks, but that just wasn't ever Tracy's style. She and Jerome seem compatible more than anything else."

"Wasn't she excited to get married?"

"More like she took it in stride. She was ecstatic when they bought the house, though, and I think she really loves selling homes. It took her a long time to find work that she enjoyed. She just bored easily, I think. Been that way since she was a girl."

I remembered that about Tracy. She always seemed a bit caged and uncomfortable in her own skin, which may have been why we got along so well.

"Did you ever see them fight, or did Tracy ever talk to you about problems they had?" I asked.

Carol gazed at the mantel, eyes darting wetly back and forth between the childhood photos.

"Not really." She looked back at us and her eyes were wet again.

"What do you mean?" I asked.

"I never saw them fight, but I never saw them really love either. Jerome is perfunctory. Cold, if you ask me."

"Did Tracy think so?"

"Tracy says he's just a solitary person. She knows he can come across chilly, sometimes condescending. She says it's just that he doesn't have patience for silly things or people."

Carol freed a clean tissue from its box on the coffee table and blew her nose. It was a nostril by nostril affair that Johnny and I silently waited out.

"Did she have a best friend?" Johnny asked when the sodden tissue disappeared into Carol's pocket. "Someone you think she would have talked to about her marriage?"

"I don't really know who her friends are," Carol said.

"Is there anyone she talks about when you two get together?" Johnny pressed. "People from work, maybe? Women she goes out with?"

"I'm sorry, but I simply don't know." Carol sat back and wrapped her arms around her sides.

"I'm sorry," I said. "We don't mean to upset you. We just want to do everything we can to help find Tracy."

"And don't you think I do?" Carol snapped.

"Of course you do," Johnny said, leaning forward. "I can't imagine anything harder than not knowing where your child is. We want to help find her and so does Jerome."

Carol cast a nasty smirk at Johnny. "Jerome wants to help, huh? He hasn't been over here even once since Tracy's gone missing. He's only called once and I'd bet dollars to donuts he only did that to keep up appearances."

"It's hard to know how people will react in situations like this," Johnny said, keeping his face neutral.

"If your wife went missing, wouldn't you be out there searching for her? Talking to people, trying to figure out what happened?" Carol bent forward, jutting her tissue hand out at Johnny.

"I know it looks bad," I said.

"Looks bad? What it looks like is like he did this to her. He's the reason she's gone."

"Carol, Jerome was at a softball game when Tracy went missing. It's not likely that he could have been at the house when this happened."

"Then he had someone else take her," Carol said.

"Does Tracy have any money?" I asked.

"Not anything to speak of, I don't think. She tells me about every house she sells. Not bragging, mind you. She just loves it so much and is so proud."

The corners of Carol's mouth drooped down as she shook her head back and forth, releasing a fresh torrent of tears.

"Maybe we should let you get some rest. I'll check on you later," I said, digging a notebook and pen out of my purse. "Here's my number. If you need anything at all, please don't hesitate to call." I knelt near Carol for a moment, but she didn't look up. I tucked the card under a vase on the coffee table and we left.

Chapter Twelve

Johnny swung past the police station so I could update his cop friend, Roman, on my bingo adventure. Roman wasn't at the station, but Johnny caught him on his cell and we agreed to meet at a sandwich shop down the street. Roman walked in ten minutes after we sat down and gestured to the waitress for a Coke before settling into the booth across from Johnny and me.

"How we doin', kids?" Roman asked as he shucked his coat. He had a linebacker's body, but folded himself into the booth with the grace of a ballerina. He reached for a menu with a hand that could palm both my head and a banana, with room to spare.

"Thanks for meeting us," I said. "I don't know that what I have is going to be all that helpful, though."

"Well, I appreciate anything you've got. We're not exactly holding a fat bag of answers right now." Roman's eyes drifted to Johnny's before settling back on me. "Did Johnny explain our agreement to you?"

"Yep," I said. "Mum's the word on anything you share with us."

Roman's smile spread across his face like hot jam as he looked back at Johnny. "Oh, please tell me you said 'mum'."

"And 'crumpet'. You should have been there," Johnny said.

A waitress appeared and we placed our orders. When she was gone, I gave Roman the rundown on bingo night and the brunette.

"Did you hear any of their conversation when you first came out into the hallway?" Roman asked.

"No, I heard their voices, but not any particular words," I said.

"Were they arguing, laughing, upset, happy?" he asked.

"I really didn't hear any specific conversation, but given they were plastered to each other I'd guess they weren't engaged in a heated debate."

"Did he say her name at any point?"

"He may have, but it would've been hard to hear what with her tongue in the back of his throat," I said.

Roman slid eyes at Johnny.

"Sorry," I said. "Low blood sugar."

Roman searched my face, the shadow of a smile painted on his. "Tell me more about this woman."

Before I could answer, the waitress delivered our plates. She planted a greasy carousel of ketchup, mustard, and relish on the tabletop and hustled off.

"Like what?" I asked.

"Height, weight? Anything memorable about her looks?" Roman asked.

I thought for a moment as I chewed on the cheese sticking out the side of my patty melt. "I'd say she was probably a few inches shorter than me, maybe 5'3". Petite, slim. Other than being very pretty, she wasn't particularly memorable."

"Age?"

"Maybe late twenties?"

Roman jotted a couple notes down in a small spiral notepad, deftly managing to eat his sub at the same time. I was impressed. I would have had more mustard than ink on the page.

Roman looked up at Johnny. "You said when Tracy hired you she thought Jerome was cheating on her. Did she say who with?"

"Nuh-uh," Johnny swallowed and wiped his mouth. "She

didn't know for sure, or if it was even a one-woman thing. She was pretty vague in her suspicions overall, actually. Said he was working more than usual, sometimes really late. He seemed less interested, a little disconnected."

"Couldn't that just be a reaction to working more?" I asked. "Maybe he was just tired or stressed about his job." The Jerome I'd met looked entirely in control, but public appearances could be deceiving.

Johnny shook his head. "I've had other suspected cheating cases with a whole lot less to go on and ultimately uncovered a lot of dirt. Sometimes people's gut instinct is all they need."

Roman chimed in. "I've seen domestic altercations start over nothing more than a pot of burned mac and cheese. You never know what's underlying in a relationship that no one's talking about."

"Paul said Jerome was married once before." I said to Roman. "Are you looking into that at all?"

Roman leaned back, spreading three feet of shoulder across the back of the booth. "We prefer to use guesswork and Magic 8 Balls to solve our crimes."

I nudged my chin at Johnny. "Low blood sugar?"

Johnny smiled into his roast beef.

"Of course we're looking at his past relationships," Roman said. "I don't know if he was running around during his first marriage, but we do know that his wife died."

"Of what?" Johnny asked.

"Death certificate states natural causes."

"But?" I asked.

"Med records show she'd been in and out of the hospital for the better part of a year. Stomach stuff. Rashes, fevers. Muscle weakness. She got the standard run of tests, but nothing popped."

"What'd Jerome have to say about it?" I asked.

"Nothing. He lawyered up before he was even formally questioned."

"Seriously?" I asked. "Doesn't that seem hinky?"

"Sam, let me ask you something. How many episodes of *Law and Order* have you watched in the last decade?"

"Um, like seven kajillion?" I said.

"How about *Dateline*?" Roman asked.

"Most every Friday night for the last three years."

Roman and Johnny exchanged a look, smiles battling a breakout on both their faces.

"Oh, stop," I said. "I record it."

Roman looked down at his plate while Johnny shoved a wad of fries into his mouth.

"I go out!" Silence. "I do!"

"Okay, okay," Roman said finally, holding up a hand. "My point is that the everyday John Q. Public has a general understanding, or at least thinks they do, about how this stuff goes down because they see it on TV all day. It's common knowledge that we look at spouses first when a husband or wife is murdered."

"But nobody thought she was murdered, they just thought she was sick," I interrupted. "That's what makes it so hinky."

"I don't disagree, but it doesn't mean he murdered her. Jerome could've watched a 'kajillion' TV shows too, and was paranoid enough to get a lawyer. Or he could have taken someone else's suggestion. Who knows? At the end of the day, the death was mysterious, but we found no evidence of murder let alone a murderer."

I chewed my bottom lip and breathed my frustration out through my nose.

Roman pointed a potato chip at my face. "Does it make you feel any better to know your brother's got a hot date to go see the detective who handled the case up in Michigan?"

"Infinitely."

Chapter Thirteen

"Come on with this four horse!"

"Good lord," Johnny said, clapping a hand over his ear.

I pushed past him and leaned into the rail separating gamblers from the six tons of thoroughbred beast crushing toward the finish line.

"Nooo!" I hollered, slapping my program against the rail when my horse lost by a nose.

"You really need to learn to express your emotions more," Johnny said. "This wallflower act is a snooze-fest."

"Come on," I said, turning toward the concourse. "There's a long-shot at Santa Anita. I need to find a simulcast TV."

Johnny caught my hand and reeled me back toward him. "At exactly what point in our afternoon of investigating did you plan to actually, you know, investigate?"

"Patty's on until seven. We have plenty of time." Tracy Pentley's sister was working the second shift at a bar inside the Thistledown Racino. With two weeks left in the racing season, I voted for an in-person meet over a phone call.

Johnny called dibs on two stools at the bar while I placed my bets. When I caught up to him, two glasses of what looked like pop sat in front of us and Patty was spooned into the bar, batting game-winning lashes at Johnny. She was only a few years older than Tracy and me, but no one would call me a liar if I claimed her as my aunt. She sported a rust-colored blush, liberally applied under what I can only assume was a night light. The blush matched the spotty dye job on her hair and the only distraction from her inch-long roots was the mountain of boob she had pressed in Johnny's direction.

"You didn't tell me on the phone that he was such a lollipop," Patty said to me. "I would've agreed to meet *after* work." Patty gave Johnny a playful wink, which he returned. I cut my eyes at him, but he purposely ignored me. Or was distracted by Patty's display.

"Patty?" I asked, trying to pull her attention toward me. "How are you doing? It must be hard right now," I said.

"I guess." Patty's body English was laser-focused on Johnny, but she twisted her head in my direction in time to catch my surprise.

"It's not that I'm not worried," Patty said. "Tracy and I just aren't all that close."

"Why's that?" I asked.

"No one special reason."

"Always been that way, or did you two have a fight?"

"We fought some when we were kids, but it's not like we hate each other. We just never had anything in common and I don't think either of us cares enough to put in the energy."

"Do you spend any time with her and Jerome?" I asked.

"Not especially. I see him at holidays, mostly."

"Is he good to Tracy? Has she ever complained about him?" I asked.

Patty shrugged. "Couldn't tell you. I've never seen them fight, but I've never seen them gooey-eyed either. Honestly, they strike me as seriously boring. I picture lots of nights filled with PBS in that house."

"I hear Masterpiece Theatre is the new Cinemax After Dark,"

Johnny said. Patty beamed.

"Do you know any of Tracy's friends?" I asked.

"I met one gal at a baby shower last year, but they may have been more work acquaintances than anything. I can't remember why I got that vibe at the time, but they didn't seem super close."

"That's a pretty specific memory from a year ago," I said.

"Yeah, I guess it stands out because I almost felt like she was trying *not* to be friendly, but wanted to. I'd get it if Jerome were around. I don't know, maybe Tracy was worried it would get back to him."

"You lost me," I said. "Worried that what would get back to him?"

"That Tracy had a friend," Patty said. "Jerome wasn't a fan of her having a lot of friends."

"Did she tell you that?" I asked.

"No, actually," she said, fluffing her hair and quickly scanning the bar. "Ma told me. I guess Tracy was having problems with a co-worker of hers that was her friend for like, a hot minute. Then they became total enemies. Ma was at dinner with Tracy and Jerome one night when Tracy was talking about it. Ma said Jerome seemed happy about the friendship going south."

"Did your mom say what the fight with the co-worker was about?" Johnny asked.

Patty screwed her face up at the memory. "I think it was about business. The friend was also an agent and they had to go after the same clients or one stole a client from the other, or something like that. Ma explained the details to me, but to be honest, I kind of tune her out after a while."

"I feel ya'," I said.

"Any idea why Jerome doesn't want her to have friends?" Johnny asked.

"I really don't know. Maybe he wanted her all to himself, but like I said, all I've ever seen is a plain-Jane relationship," Patty said.

"This maybe-friend from the baby shower...do you know her name?" I asked.

"Mmm, Anna Beth? It was a two-namer. Maybe Beth Anne? Sorry, can't remember." Patty didn't look sorry. She looked hungry. For Johnny. I angled my head back into her line of sight.

"Patty, what about old boyfriends?" I asked. "Any past relationships that didn't end well?"

"I don't think so," Patty said. She looked past Johnny and waggled her forefinger at a customer down the bar who was signaling for their check. She turned to the register and started punching keys. "I only know of one other guy she spent any time with, and I don't think it was all that serious. Kind of hard to tell with Tracy, though."

"How so?" Johnny asked.

Patty appeared thoughtful for the first time. "Tracy has never been the most emotional person. Sometimes growing up it felt like she was saying what people wanted her to. Best I can describe it," she said with another look down the bar as a customer tapped it with the bottom of his glass.

"Look," I said. "Go take care of your customers and we'll get out of your hair. Thanks for the chat. If you think of anything that might help, will you call?" I asked, jotting my number on a bar napkin.

Patty shoved the napkin in her apron pocket and selected a fresh one, on which she sketched out a phone number. I reached my hand out to take it, but she pressed the napkin at Johnny. "In case *you* think of anything that might be helpful."

***

"I need a favor," I said.

"Kind of busy over here," Angie replied.

"I meant after we get off this stupid wall. The only thing I need right now is to get rid of this wedgie," I said, tugging on the repelling rope that was tied around my backside. My foot slipped and I slammed the side of my body into the wall. The bad news was I feared I hairline-fractured my elbow. The good news was the wedgie was gone.

"What is it?"

"The rope, but it's out now."

"No," Angie said. "What's the favor?"

"I want you to check out one of Tracy's co-workers. She's an agent, too. I need you to act like you're in the market for a house and meet up with her to see some places."

"Oh, I'm totally in. I'll take Tony. We can play newlyweds looking for our first nest."

"Oh no, I don't want to get blamed for kid number four," I said, pushing off the wall with the balls of my feet and dropping a yard before losing control and kissing the wall with my hip. "Besides, I'm going with you. You're my decoy."

"Why do you need a decoy?"

"Because I need someone to help loosen things up, but I can't take Johnny on any more interviews with women," I said. I pushed off again, got my ankle caught in the rope and swung right back into the wall.

"Can't stand to watch your man getting some action?" Angie smirked.

I bit back my yelp and refrained from looking down at my shin, picturing layers of skin peeling down into my sock.

"He's not my man and I don't care what kind of action he gets," I said. "It's just hard to hear any answers over all the panting."

"Don't be bitter. You could do with a night or two of quality panting." Angie pushed off the wall like a fairy on meth and sailed past me.

"Not my point, Angela Marie." I called down after her.

Angie's voice floated back up to me. "All I'm saying is, you see an unrealized crush coming back to haunt you whereas I see untapped opportunity."

"For a roll in the hay," I said.

"For starters, yeah. But you never know where it could lead."

"Ange, I don't know." I managed to repel down parallel to her, but averted my eyes.

She reached out and steadied my rope, forcing me to look at her.

"Let me guess. You don't know if you're going to stay. Is that it?"

I looked over at her, but it was her turn to avoid me. "Ange."

"Tell me what I need to ask this agent."

"Ange, come on. It's only been a few weeks."

Angie looked over at me. "Just tell me."

I watched her a moment longer, but her face had shut down.

"My thought is you could kind of test the waters." I said. "Look at a couple houses. Act super interested in one, then hedge a bit."

"How?" Angie asked.

"Tell her you really liked a house you saw last year, but your agent botched the offer, you lost the house, and you don't know if you want to go through all that again. Then slip it in that Tracy was your agent."

"Why can't I just ask her if she knows Tracy?" Angie asked. "I can say I saw her name on the website and that she looks like someone I went to school with. It's closer to the truth and that way I don't have to trash-talk Tracy."

"But I do want you to trash talk her. Tracy supposedly had a falling out with one co-worker over a business deal and she was kind of buddy-buddy with another. I found a woman named Maribeth, who might be the buddy. If she and Tracy are friends, she'd probably know something about the falling out. I'm thinking that if you say something bad about Tracy, maybe it'll be our foot in the door for Maribeth to defend her."

"What if she's the co-worker Tracy was fighting with?"

"Then the trash talk helps us even more."

Chapter Fourteen

The next morning, I dragged myself out of bed and took inventory in the mirror. Two bruises on my right leg and three on the left. Streaks of fire ripped down the backs of my arms in place of triceps. No more rock wall with Angie. No more yoga. And definitely no more trapeze. That little stunt our sophomore year left me looking like a humpback just in time for the Homecoming dance.

I brushed my teeth, scraped my fingers through my hair, and padded out to the kitchen.

"Good morning, Samantha," my mom called out as I came through the doorway.

"Good morn—. Geezuss," I stopped short and tugged at the hemline of my sleep shirt.

"Good morning, Samantha." Johnny was propped against the kitchen counter, holding a half-eaten bagel in one hand and a knife full of shmear in the other.

"What on God's green earth happened to your legs?" Mom asked. She wiped her hands on a dish towel and scuttled over to bend down for a closer look.

"They're fine, Mom," I said, trying fruitlessly to back away from her. "I just tried something new with Angie last night."

"What, boxing?" Mom asked.

"Double solitaire?" Johnny asked. I moved to punch him over my mom's head, but my aching muscles wouldn't let me get my fist that high. I settled for an evil eye. With my day-old mascara, it may have come off more sad-clown.

"Samantha, you need to be more selective in your choices."

I frowned at Johnny. "Preaching to the choir, mom."

Johnny busied himself with shmear.

Mom returned her attention to the stove, where a pan of scrambled eggs sat, willing themselves into a rubber mound.

"Why are you here?" I asked Johnny as I squeezed in next to him at the counter to pour myself coffee.

"Samantha!" Mom scolded behind me. I closed my eyes and counted to five before turning around.

"Johnny, it's so fantastic to see you. What can I do for you this fine morning?"

He bent his head toward me. "You're not going to put on pants?"

"Will it make you tell me why you're here any faster?" I asked.

"No," he said, popping the last of the bagel into his mouth and turning to the sink to rinse his knife. "Paul called me this morning. He was supposed to drive up to Michigan today to talk to that Detective, but he's still wrapped up in the bakery case and he asked me to go."

"Killer. You'll call me when you're done?" I asked.

"I'm thinking you should hear it firsthand," Johnny said.

"Oh, no sir, I don't think so," I said.

"Why not?"

I bit into a bagel and chewed on how to tell him I didn't want to be alone with him. My lingering resentment over how he left things was trickling away and creeping in its wake were memories of good times we'd had. I desperately did not want to get caught up again, but didn't want to admit it. I needed a solid, unemotional, and believable excuse.

"I have a hair appointment." Not a good day for feminism.

Johnny swept my hair back with one hand and gathered it at the nape of my neck. He wound it around his palm, then slid his hand down the length of it.

"Looks good to me." Johnny said.

My vocal chords thrummed and pushed a whimper to my lips. I was saved by the sudden realization that my mom was watching the whole display from the stove. She stirred a pot of plain water, head buried forward, eyes cut sideways at us.

Johnny smiled conspiratorially at my mom as he shifted away from me and picked out another bagel from its box.

"So, you're willing to let down Paul? Over one little road trip?" Johnny asked.

"Oh, Samantha." Mom swallowed the bait. "You have to help your brother. Look how much he's helped you."

"Mom, Johnny's exaggerating. If Paul needed my help, he would have called me."

Mom crossed her arms over her chest. "He shouldn't have to ask. He's your brother."

I hung my head. Maybe I should have learned boxing instead of rock climbing. I could have avoided the last blow.

"And you know how much you love a road trip, sweetie. You always have."

***

Freshly showered and dressed, a bag of soggy sandwiches shoved into my reluctant hands by my mom, I was buckled into Johnny's truck. We flew down the turnpike that connects Cleveland to Toledo, Chicago, and all points westward. The route to Toledo is a flat, farmland-dominated ride, interrupted only by the sleepy town of Sandusky. Sandusky is famous nationally for its unparalleled rollercoasters and locally for its unparalleled smell of week-old sock that floats off the limestone quarry. The sulfur stench peaks in the heat of summer, but the autumnal cool delivered a leftover whiff through the truck's heating vents as we drove.

I'd spent the first part of the ride reading through the file Paul had culled together on the first Mrs. Pentley's life and death. From Paul's notes and the local news articles, I didn't learn much more than what Roman had already shared. By all accounts, Abby Pentley had been ill off and on for an extended period of time and her death was not a huge surprise to the local community.

"What do you think?" Johnny asked as I returned the clippings to their envelope.

"Not much here, but I find it interesting that there are three news articles about her death, all written by the same publication. If no one was surprised and there wasn't anything that stood out as suspicious, why did it get so much coverage?"

"She was young and pretty," Johnny said with a nod to the envelope in my lap. "You know how it can be in small towns."

"Still, I'd like to get Detective Schmidt's take on it," I said. "Speaking of, how do you want to tackle this?"

"Tackle what?" Johnny asked.

"The interview. Do you want to lead it and give me the high sign if you want me to jump in?"

"No, I thought we would do it together. Play it as it comes." Johnny threw a confused glance at me before gliding into the exit lane. "Why?"

"I just don't want to mess it up," I said.

"Mess up what? All we're doing is asking some questions like we did with Tracy's family."

"Yeah, but I kind of know those people. This feels more, I don't know, official." The words felt lame on my tongue and Johnny's face agreed.

"Sam, you were a reporter once upon a time. You must have interviewed a thousand people. How is it any different?"

"That was a lifetime ago and I wasn't exactly covering hard-hitting news. I wrote society articles and interviewed vapid, rich women holding Gucci-wearing lap dogs."

We rolled up to a red light and Johnny looked over at me. I feigned interest in two women jogging behind matching strollers as they crossed the intersection.

"What's going on with you?" Johnny asked.

"I just don't want to disappoint Paul," I said to the windshield.

I wasn't ready to admit to him that my great escape from Cleveland hadn't exactly been the road to Oz and that I was now second-guessing my abilities. I'd spent my childhood dreaming up visions of how I was going to conquer the world by running to big cities and bigger opportunities. Instead, the reporter job that I thought was my ticket out ended up being a ticket to an even smaller town in Colorado. I escaped from a place where everyone knew my name to one where nobody knew it and didn't care to. It went from suffocating to isolating.

An office manager job in Denver followed the reporting gig before infinite boredom sent me following an enterprising boyfriend to Dallas. He was convinced the food truck business would be the next great thing, which it was – years after we opened and closed ours. By the time my dad passed, I was managing a mold infested motel billed as a beach resort in Tampa. When Paul called asking me to come home, I was three layers deep into Google, looking to see if clown colleges were still a thing.

"I really don't think Paul could be disappointed in you," Johnny said.

Johnny had never lied to me and didn't seem to be now, but the worry still gnawed at my belly. Somewhere around the third move and fourth career change, I'd started glossing over a lot of details with Paul about how life was going. I wasn't at all sure he'd be impressed with my path.

I snuck a peek at Johnny's profile. The oblong scar on his cheek from the childhood car accident that took his mom and brother had faded underneath a layer of age. The night he told me how that loss had changed him flooded over me, reminding me of the boy I could once say anything to. I opened my mouth and shut it again. This was also the same boy who thought little enough of our friendship to let his buddy bid me good-bye.

"I guess we'll see," I said.

Chapter Fifteen

Detective Larry Schmidt was just this side of albino. Pale skin, white blond crew cut, milky fingernails blurring the line separating cuticle from knuckle. The ghostly look was shattered by crystalline green eyes that bounced across the desk between Johnny and me.

"Our suspicions of Jerome Pentley never amounted to much more than circumstance and gut feeling, neither of which could get us an arrest warrant, let alone a chance at a conviction," Schmidt said.

"What was the circumstantial evidence?" Johnny asked.

Schmidt's well-worn chair let out a metallic whine as he reclined back and tented his pale digits. "Abby was admitted to the hospital four times for undiagnosed stomach issues. Except for the first time, she hadn't left her home for the better part of a week prior to the illnesses and Jerome was the only contact she'd had."

"That's a long stretch to go without leaving your house," I said.

"That's partly why it stood out to us." Schmidt creaked his chair back up to the desk and tapped the case file that he'd hauled out when we arrived. "Abby, by all accounts, was woven into the town fabric. Involved in her church, volunteered for multiple causes that had her out and about routinely. Friends said when she and Jerome first moved to town, she was shy as a beat dog, but that all changed. She had regular lunch dates with her friends. Movies, museums, shopping. This was not a reclusive person we're talking about."

"Anything useful in the hospital records?" Johnny asked.

"They ruled out more than they ruled in. Abby's first two visits were close together, but not close enough for a flag to go up. Both times, she was given intravenous fluids and eventually sent home. The assumption was she had some type of stomach bug."

"And the other two?" I asked.

"The third and fourth visits were both at different hospitals from the first two incidents. The description of symptoms were similar to the first two, just more severe. The notes from that last visit say Abby also had respiratory issues that they attributed to a bad cold she'd had in the prior couple of days."

"Do we know if the cold was real, or was that a story Jerome was peddling?"

"The receptionist at Abby's church corroborated the cold. Abby had been in to help set up for a fundraising event and the receptionist remembered her having a wicked cough that day."

"Did she die at the hospital or at home?" I asked.

"Hospital. She was admitted during the last trip to the emergency room and died there the following afternoon."

"Paul's notes didn't say anything about the autopsy," I said.

"Because there wasn't one," Schmidt said.

"Why not?"

"Officially, it was a combination of factors. The hospital's policy is to only do an autopsy if the family asks for one. The medical examiner could have ordered it if they suspected something other than natural causes, but they usually only do that if the patient dies less than a day after they were admitted, which was not the case here."

"But what about the other times Abby was sick? Didn't the

last hospital know about those? It's not like Jerome could really hide that," I said.

"He probably wouldn't want to hide it, though," Johnny said. "Kind of helps him in a way."

Schmidt nodded. "The trail of previous illness, all undiagnosed, set up a pattern for what was seen as an ongoing health issue. The fact that he got her care is huge. If he were trying to kill her, he wouldn't get her help, so the multiple visits would have disguised his intent, if anything."

"What's your unofficial opinion?" Johnny asked.

"Poor judgment. The circumstances may not have clearly defined her case as qualifying for an autopsy, but in my mind if you got a young and by all accounts active young woman with an unlabeled illness? You err on the side of caution."

"You think Jerome was making Abby sick?" I asked.

"Yes, and slowly. I think that the first time she got sick, Jerome was testing the waters. That was the only time where Abby had been with other people, multiple people in fact, in the days prior to her going to the hospital. So he could have easily given her any number of tainted things to eat or drink and if the hospital had caught on, it would have been a fairly muddy pool of suspects at that point."

"What's your theory on why he would have done it?" Johnny asked.

"I'd guess money," Schmidt paused. "Abby was covered under a million dollar life insurance policy."

"But I thought I read in the file that her brother was the beneficiary?" I asked.

"He was," Schmidt nodded. "When they bought the policy, Jerome was named beneficiary. Abby had it changed three weeks prior to her death."

"So, it's possible Jerome didn't know," I said.

"One would presume, but when we questioned him, he was adamant that he knew he'd been removed from the policy."

"Which kind of kills your motive," I said.

"We tried every which way to show he couldn't have known. Abby visited her insurance agent's office in person to make the change and the agent swears there was no electronic or phone communication afterward. The office did mail a hard copy of the policy to her, but it was postmarked the day after Abby died. We pursued it with the prosecutor, but we had no way to prove Abby and Jerome didn't talk about the change before it was made."

"Can't you exhume her body to do the autopsy?" I asked.

"Not without family consent and we don't have enough evidence to get a court order."

"Let me guess," I said. "By 'family', you mean it has to be with Jerome's consent?"

"You got it."

"How does that make any sense? Can't Abby's family demand one if they think Jerome was involved?"

Schmidt nodded, patting the case file. "They could, but the only family Abby has is her dad and her brother and neither of them wants to press the issue."

"Press the issue?" I echoed. "Can't they see something is hinky here?"

Schmidt rubbed a palm over the lower half of his face. "I talked to both of them personally. Repeatedly. I doubt Abby's dad has seen one sober day in the last two decades and her brother's got four kids. Including a three-year-old who was real sick. My guess is that's why Abby changed the policy."

"Then she had to have believed she was going to die soon. You think she knew Jerome was going to kill her?"

"Hard to know," Schmidt said. "But when Abby died, the little boy had already gone through three rounds of chemo and doctors told the family it didn't look good. The boy died six months later."

"But why wouldn't she just leave Jerome?" I asked.

Schmidt dropped his eyes to the case file in front of him and rubbed it softly. "I wish I knew."

Chapter Sixteen

My brain had tripped its off-duty light by the time we rolled back into Cleveland and I couldn't face the reality of my first night in Uncle Gino's bed. Johnny dropped me back at my mom's instead, but Mom was nowhere to be found. I had just settled cross-legged into the couch with a bowl of lukewarm soup when I heard a giggle on the porch, followed by a key scratching the lock on the front door. The door swung open to reveal my giggling mother trailed by the hairiest jockey-sized man I'd ever laid eyes on. His tiny arms circled Mom's waist and Mom caught sight of me just as they crept up her rib cage.

I felt a trickle of warm soup hit my chest as the spoon I'd had halfway to my mouth slipped out of my grasp.

"Samantha!"

I felt my brain short-circuit as it tried to process what it was seeing and block it right back out.

"Heyyy." I stood up and shoved a square of napkin under my pajama collar in a vague attempt to sop up the soup.

I could see my mom mentally warring between good manners and her obvious displeasure at my presence. Manners won.

"Wally," Mom said, clutching her purse like a talisman in front of her. "This is my daughter Samantha. Samantha. This is, uh, Wally," she said, waving a hand toward him like he was a European vacation prize on the Wheel of Fortune. Her other hand remained locked on her purse.

Wally turned three shades of a cherry Gobstopper, but managed to eke out a "Good to meet you, Samantha. Your mother has told me a lot about you."

Hunh, wish I could have said the same. I couldn't help but eyeball him from top to bottom. Angie's seven-year-old had a longer inseam than this guy did.

"It's very nice to meet you, too," I ground out, stepping up to shake his sweaty but surprisingly firm hand.

"Sam," Mom said. Syrup-coated tension bubbled in her voice. "I thought you were getting your, ah, nest settled at Uncle Gino's tonight." Her cheeks reddened into frostbitten patches. Standing next to Wally, they looked like a pair of jovial garden gnomes.

"Uh, I was, but I got back from Michigan really late and I haven't unpacked sheets or anything."

Mom's eyes bored into mine. "I have sheets here," she said.

"I know, they're still on my bed," I said.

"That you can take to Uncle Gino's.

"Oh."

"Now."

***

"Stop laughing. This is not funny."

Angie clung to her front door, snorts escaping from her nose, while I fumed on her front step.

"It—. I can't—. Oh, god—." She clutched her belly.

I stood on her stoop, still in my soup-stained unicorn pajamas, having been too stunned to change before I left Mom's house. It didn't keep me from throwing a jacket over the whole mess and parading into the United Dairy Farmers on the way to Angie's. If the sight of my mom pre-shtup with Danny DeVito didn't justify a late-night banana milkshake, nothing did.

"I swear I will cut you. Move, it's freezing out here," I said. I pushed her backward into her hallway and closed the door.

"Oh, come on. This is delicious," Angie exhaled, finally turning and leading the way into her living room. She danced effortlessly through a trail of kids' toys, books, and blankies, while I wove in and out like a drunk with a failing liver.

"Really?" I asked, tripping over an eyeless Mr. Potato Head. "Would it be just as scrumptiously delicious if it was your mother?"

Angie tucked herself into an armchair and clapped her hands like a child. "The woman who can't even say 'immaculate conception' without whispering? That wouldn't be delicious. That would be a divine gift from the baby Jesus himself."

"Oh, hell," I said, sinking into the sofa. "Here's the honesty. Part of me is freaked from the ick factor, but there's another part that's saying 'what the hell, good for her'."

"You're not getting an argument from me. I think we should all be living this ride like the amusement park's about to close. But what about your brothers?"

I unearthed a worn bunny from between the sofa cushions and massaged a clubbed ear. "You know Paul, it takes a lot to faze him. But this might be rough for Vinnie."

"Any chance they already know?" Angie asked.

"I highly doubt it. I don't think Vinnie would be able to hide something like that and I don't see why Paul would try."

"Paul didn't tell you about Johnny."

"True, but he thought he was protecting me. And I just can't see him lying about this," I said.

"What are you going to do?"

"I need to talk to my mom."

"Are you gonna be mad if this has been going on for a while?" Angie asked.

"Don't get me wrong, it is a little weird. I always knew on

some level that Dad would probably die before my mom. But I never actually pictured her being with someone else. Like, the little book of life running in my head didn't even have that chapter. But if it makes her happy? I can't be mad at that."

"Would you leave again?" Angie asked softly.

"I don't know." And I didn't. "The whole point of my coming home was to help Mom."

"Was it?"

I stopped worrying the bunny. "What's that supposed to mean?"

"I'm just wondering if there's more to it."

"Can we do the Dr. Phil thing later? I don't think I can digest two life crises in one night."

"Fine, but cut the drama. I wouldn't call your mother having a boyfriend a crisis," Angie said.

"I haven't had a meaningful relationship in two years. My mother's been single six months and is getting more action than I am. What would you call it?"

Chapter Seventeen

"And here's the master bedroom, including a fully renovated en suite bath. How gorgeous is the marble in that shower?"

Maribeth Collins ushered Angie and me into a spectacular gray-and-white parade of marble and glass that matched both the color and taste of Maribeth's dress. I really needed to look into this realty agent gig, I thought.

The bathroom was indeed exquisite. I thought of Uncle Gino's cramped upstairs bath, with its blue tub and gold fig leaf wallpaper, and rapped my head into the door.

"Ohmigosh, are you okay?" Maribeth asked, reaching out to pat my head.

"Oh, Debbie," Angie said, using what she decided on our way over was my undercover name.

Angie propelled me past Maribeth back into the bedroom. "A touch of the vertigo," Angie stage-whispered to Maribeth. "What's the square footage on this one again?"

Maribeth's eyes lingered on me for another second before she dragged them back to her listing sheet. "Eighteen sixty, not including the basement. That will give you nearly six hundred more to play with."

"Is it finished?" Angie asked.

"No, it's not," Maribeth chirped. "But that gives you such a wide range of possibilities. TV room, craft room, storage." Maribeth paused and looked between us hopefully.

"Hmmm," Angie said. "I'm not sure what I'd use all that for. Maybe I should be looking at something smaller."

I nodded encouragingly. "This does seem like a lot of house."

"But," Maribeth said. "Think about room to grow. You mentioned on the phone that you and your husband were looking to start a family. Why not buy the house that fits your future now? It's a bit like building a field of dreams, no?"

Oh, no. Not Costner. "Ange, you—" I started.

"That's a good point, Maribeth," Angie cut me off and headed toward the kitchen with a dreamy gaze. Maribeth followed with a knowing smile.

"No. No, it's not a good point, Maribeth," I said, chasing after them. "I mean, it is, but not for Angie. Angie's future won't be quite this big."

Maribeth was still smiling, but with noticeable effort. "It sounds to me like Angie thinks it might be," she said.

"I know it sounds that way, but she doesn't really," I said. "Angie's future is about fifteen hundred square feet, with one and a half baths and two cramped bedrooms for three kids. Maybe four if she doesn't lay off the box wine, but even then her future will just have to get bunk beds."

Maribeth and I caught up to Angie, who was at the kitchen island, stroking a gooseneck water faucet that hung above the stove. Maribeth extended a bejeweled wrist from the cuff of her silk shirt and pointed at the faucet.

"You can fill your spaghetti pot right there on the stove," Maribeth cooed.

Angie turned fevered eyes on me. "I can fill my spaghetti pot right here on the stove."

I stepped forward and began to ease the faucet out of Angie's hands. "Sweetie. You don't make spaghetti. You make Easy Mac."

Angie's smile dimmed. "In the microwave." She let go.

"See, Maribeth," I said, popping the faucet back into its base. "This is where Angie could really use your help. She's tried to find the right house before, but she had an agent who was probably more in it for the money than for what was right for Angie."

"I appreciate how that can happen, but that's not how I work," Maribeth said. "I do everything I can to find what my clients want." She tipped her shiny blonde coif in Angie's direction. "Whether that's a faucet or a finished basement."

Angie turned a hungry look back to the sink. I looped my arm around her and squeezed her arms against her sides.

"I'm sure that's the case," I said. "But, well, Angie's last agent was also from your agency, so I just want to make sure she doesn't get off track again."

"Wait, are you still with that other agent?" Maribeth asked. "I really shouldn't be working with you if you're already in an agreement."

"Oh, no," Angie said. "It was a long time ago. I don't even know if she's still working there. Tracy Pentley?"

Maribeth's expression remained neutral as her body stilled. "I know Tracy. When did you work with her?"

"Last year."

"And you're saying she tried to sell you more house than you could afford?" Maribeth asked. Her eyes held Angie's.

"I think she may have been thinking about her commission a little, yes," Angie said, unease straining her voice.

"It's common for an agent to show a client some options that stretch their budget a bit," Maribeth said. "It often helps the client see what's possible. Especially if their wish list and budget are far apart."

"The client's wish list or the agent's?" I asked.

Maribeth stiffened. "I think we're done here."

Chapter Eighteen

I dropped off Angie, pit-stopped for a late takeout lunch from a nearby deli, and headed over to the office. I wanted to spend a couple hours clearing through my rising stack of background cases before heading over to Dazio's. Vinnie had called earlier and cashed in my chip to cover a closing shift.

Paul wasn't at the office or returning my text messages. I wanted to catch up on the Pentley case, but he'd been incommunicado the last couple days. I unwrapped my meatloaf sandwich, opened my laptop and set to work. At the top of the list was a background check on a woman named Wanda Ames who claimed she hurt her back in a work accident. Co-worker gossip countered that the injury wasn't what it seemed. Wanda told the disability rep that she was all but laid up in bed. A co-worker confirms Wanda was laid up, but alleges it was on top of a bar dispensing liquor shots. From her belly. Another reported that Ms. Ames was an avid bowler and since the injury, she had been spotted keeping her injured back loose with a little therapeutic midnight bowling. The insurance company had contracted Paul to do some digging.

I made calls to Wanda's co-workers and confirmed their statements, learning little in the way of additional detail, though one did supply me with Wanda's favored bowling alley. I plugged away at two more uneventful, dirt-free background searches and typed up my reports for Paul to review before I sent them to their respective clients. I had just started researching an auto insurance claim suspected of being part of a bait-and-hit ring when Johnny pushed through the front door.

My belly warmed and I hoped it was the meatloaf. Johnny nudged my case folders to the side and leaned a cheek on the desk.

"What do you have against chairs?" I asked.

"Too much of a commitment. Speaking of, got any plans tonight?"

"Hot date with some pie."

"Has it gotten that bad?"

"Pizza pie," I said. "I'm closing at Dazio's tonight."

"What time will you be done?"

"Why?"

"It's Friday night. Thought we could see if Jerome is having date night with his friend the brunette. See where it takes us."

"Let me ask Paul. I was planning on tracking down some info for another case. I don't want to get behind."

"I just talked to him a little while ago. He's on board," Johnny said.

I sat back.

"When did you talk to him?" I asked.

"About an hour ago. He told me you'd left him a message that you were heading over here and I said I'd stop in to see if you want to go with me."

I tried to hide my irritation.

"Look, I don't know what time I'll be able to wrap up at the shop. You should go on without me." I returned my attention to my laptop.

"I've got no problem waiting," Johnny said.

"It takes a while to shut down," I lied. "Even if Jerome goes out tonight, he could be back home by the time I'm ready to roll."

"I was thinking I could keep tabs on him and then when you get done, you could just come meet me."

"Why are you pushing this?" I asked.

"I'm not pushing anything. Just trying to make it work," Johnny said evenly.

"Why? You don't need me for this."

"Can't I want you, though?"

My belly flushed with heat again and momentarily distracted me from my irritation. I sent a silent prayer to the patron saint of loose girls that I could keep from dragging his face down to mine. I scrutinized my watch until I trusted myself to look up.

"I'll call you when I close up the shop and we'll go from there. Deal?" I asked.

"I'll take it."

Chapter Nineteen

"New perfume?"

"Cute," I said as I climbed into the passenger seat of Johnny's truck.

"No, it's hot. An exotic blend of sausage and yeast. And is that—?" Johnny touched a finger to the tip of his nose and sniffed the air. "Is that a hint of pepperoncini?"

I popped my seat belt back out of the buckle and aimed for the door handle. Johnny reached his arm across me and grasped the belt, dragging me toward him.

"Nuh-uh, not so fast," he said. "We have work to do."

"Um, Johnny?"

"Hmm?"

"Does that work involve you staring at my mouth all night?"

Johnny dragged his eyes back up to mine. "It's not you, it's the sausage."

"Hmm," I said.

Johnny slid his hand down the length of my belt and snapped the buckle back into the lock, grazing my torso as he went. I sucked air in so fast, I hiccupped.

"Doing okay there?" he asked.

"It's the sausage."

"Hmm." Johnny eyes raked over my mouth a final time before starting the truck.

I forced myself to think about baseball, which only made me think of baseball players. Crap. That trick does not work for girls, I thought. I flashed back to my chat with Paul the previous night and sobered up like a girl who just donned a purity ring.

"So, what's our boy up to?" I asked. We were sitting on the far end of a parking lot across from an Italian restaurant on the border of Middleburg Heights and Strongsville.

"Not sure yet," Johnny said. "I followed him here from his office and he went in alone two hours ago."

"Any women go in after him?"

"Not any who were on their own. But for as long as he's been here, he's gotta be with someone."

"Not necessarily. I've been here," I said. "They serve food in the bar and have two huge TVs. Maybe he just doesn't want to stay at home and think about his missing wife."

"You mean the same wife that he probably put away someplace nice and safe?"

"Hey, we don't actually know that he had anything to do with it, right? He could be shtupping this other woman and still love Tracy. Or at least want to stay with her. It happens."

"Shtupping?" Johnny cocked his head.

Before I could respond, the front door of the restaurant opened and Jerome appeared. No brunette, or blonde for that matter, dangled from his arm. He stood on the curb and scanned the cars parked immediately in front of the restaurant, which were few given how close it was to closing time.

"Looks like he's waiting for a ride," Johnny mused.

"Or maybe he got stood up," I said.

Johnny threw an appraising glance my way. "Sherlockian."

Jerome stepped out into the lot, walked down past the restaurant and stood in front of an adjacent sporting goods store. He stayed there for several minutes, tossing an occasional look back toward the restaurant door.

Minutes passed before a trio emerged from the restaurant. Two guys wearing tee shirts with the restaurant's logo, followed by a brunette who was ripping her hair out of its ponytail as she simultaneously unraveled the straps of her apron from around her waist. Jerome stepped away from the store front and strolled slowly back toward the nest of cars in front of the restaurant. His casual gait belied the intent look he had set on the brunette.

"Bingo," Johnny said.

"Literally," I said. Johnny shook his head at me, but a smile was plastered over his face.

The trio scattered and the brunette trailed off to a small, badly rusted white sedan.

"Is that Jerome's car?" I asked.

"Nope. He's the blue Lexus."

As the brunette fussed with the car lock, Jerome called out to her from ten paces away. We were parked too far away to catch anything more than the baritone of his voice. The brunette turned and launched herself at him, attempting to wrap him in a hug. Jerome trapped her wrists in his hands and dragged them down between their bodies, glancing around the parking lot. The other two employees had climbed into one car and were already pulling out. Only two other cars remained, their owners unaccounted for.

Jerome bent low to the brunette's face and they exchanged a few words before she turned her attention back to the lock. She fiddled some more, then the pair retreated to Jerome's car two aisles over. Jerome beeped the locks on his Lexus and held the passenger door open. He again lowered his face to hers and they exchanged a kiss that escalated quickly. From the height of Johnny's cab, we could see Jerome slip his arms down around the woman's buttocks, hiding the move in the V created by the open car door. There was some rubbing and jostling for a moment and the brunette appeared to lean up and whisper in Jerome's ear. Jerome snapped his head back and untangled his hands from her pants. He spoke to her in a rapid fashion, flashes of anger on his face cutting through the shadows. The brunette's face crumpled as Jerome pulled her away from the car and closed the door. He held her by the elbow and hustled her back to her car. She quick stepped next to him as she spoke, pulling at his arm like a petulant child.

Jerome ripped the brunette's purse off her shoulder and jammed a hand into it. She pawed at his shoulder, keeping up a stream of words in his ear. Johnny had motored both of our windows down a couple more inches, but I still couldn't make out what either was saying. We could hear the woman's plaintive tone as Jerome extracted a set of keys from the bag and unlocked her car. He pressed her into it, tossed her purse in after her, and tried to close the door. She stuck a leg out just as he made contact, and she squealed.

"Damnit, Vanessa!" Jerome roared as he wrenched the door wide and shoved her back in by her foot. He slammed the door, turned and took off at a trot toward the Lexus. He didn't look back, wasting no time folding his body into the car and taking off with a little chirp of his wheels.

We heard Vanessa's ignition turn and fail, turn again, and catch. She screeched out of the lot on badly balding tires and managed a decent clip as she took off in the opposite direction.

"Him or her?" Johnny asked, starting the truck.

"Her," I said. "If she's got any dirt on him, this is the perfect time to get it."

"Hell hath no fury like a woman scorned?" Johnny asked.

"Hell hath no fury like a woman left fondled and alone."

"I'll keep that in mind."

We pulled out of the lot and followed Vanessa exactly three blocks before she turned into a convenience store parking lot. We angled into a spot on the side of the adjacent gas station and watched through the plate glass as she pointed at the liquor shelf above the cashier's head. He pulled down a bottle of clear liquid and rang her up. Even from this distance, I could see her mascara-smeared cheeks under the lights as she exited the store.

Vanessa slumped back into her car and we followed her down Bagley Road for several miles before she turned into a residential neighborhood. The streets were nearly empty and riddled with stop signs, making our slow pursuit more challenging.

"Well, this doesn't look obvious or anything," I said.

"That woman's so upset, I doubt she'd know if a parade of leprechauns was behind her."

Vanessa turned into a driveway barely held together by pieces of broken cement. We cruised by and turned left onto the next side street. Johnny made a U-turn in the middle of the road and came to rest at the corner. Vanessa was extricating herself from her car, purse and liquor bag clutched to her chest.

I popped my seatbelt and reached for the door handle. "Hang tight," Johnny said.

I looked back toward Vanessa. A woman had emerged from the house, arms held in front of her as she made her way down the uneven walkway. Vanessa rushed into the woman's hug and they stayed there a moment before turning and retreating into the house.

"Well, that puts a crimp in things," Johnny said. "I was hoping for a one-on-one chat."

"We can still get it. We've got a first name now, and I know that woman. She was with Vanessa at bingo. It has to be her mom."

"I'll swing back past. Write down the house and plate numbers and we'll see what Roman can dig up."

"Done and done," I said, digging a scrap of paper from the console.

"It's late," Johnny said. "You want me to just drop you at Gino's and you can pick up your car tomorrow?"

I twisted slowly in my seat and beamed a smile at him.

"A beautiful woman, smiling at me invitingly, late at night. Why is my first reaction fear?" he asked.

I reached out and fiddled with his collar, then tweaked his

chin. "How do you feel about bowling?"

Chapter Twenty

"What size?"

"Fourteen," Johnny said to the bowling attendant.

I sunk my incisors into my lower lip and turned my head away as the attendant handed a pair of multi-hued shoes over to Johnny.

"Calm down," Johnny said.

"You wish," I said.

The attendant smirked as I snagged my shoes from the counter and turned toward the lanes. We had struck out with Vanessa, but I was determined to accomplish something before the night was over. We arrived with fifteen minutes to spare before midnight Cosmic Bowling started.

I'd done a walk through when we first arrived, and spied a woman resembling pictures of Wanda sitting with two middle-aged women and a much younger man. She was sitting with her legs stretched out across the molded plastic bench, beer in hand and laughter stretched across her face. I'd seen two photos and a grainy cell phone video of her at a workplace training session. Her hair was shorter now and streaked with pink, but when she leaned over the shoulder of the man working the scoring monitor, I got a glimpse of a lower back tattoo and knew for sure it was Wanda. Tattoos may be a dime a dozen, but how many alligators with teddy bears riding them do you see peeking out of a woman's waistband?

A couple playful giggles and some well-placed arm stroking with the desk attendant had earned me the lane of my choice, and Johnny and I settled in three lanes down from Wanda. I perused the ball rack and plucked out the first one I could easily lift. Meanwhile, Johnny rubbed and weighed each one like he was picking melon for a picnic.

"It's not tournament play, sport," I said.

Johnny air-bowled an emerald green ball, deemed it the winner, and placed it next to mine on the return carousel. He came around the scoring monitor where I'd just finished entering our names, and folded himself into the seat the next to me. He draped an arm around my shoulders and leaned in close.

I cut my eyes at him and he grinned.

"Just playing the part," he said.

"And exactly what part do you think you're playing?"

"The part of a man out for a midnight bowl with his girl before he takes her back home for a canoodle."

"Canoodle?"

"Shtupping?"

"For the record, there will be no canoodling. Or shtupping. Or taking a girl back home," I said.

"Any girl, or just you?"

Maybe Paul's concerns hadn't been completely off the mark.

"I feel we've gotten off-topic," I said. "Can we just bowl and keep an eye on Wanda, please?"

Johnny dropped a kiss on my forehead and undraped himself from his seat. "Yes, ma'am."

While Johnny palmed his ball and stepped onto the boards, I took a gander at Wanda's lane. The man in their group was bent over, poised to release his ball. The other two women watched the arc of the ball, but Wanda's eyes were glued to the man's rear. Desire lit her face. Or maybe it was the beer.

"Your turn."

I swung my gaze back to our lane, then to the score board. "A strike?"

"Yup. A girlfriend who cared would have clapped. Done a little cheer, you know?" Johnny threw up jazz hands and shimmied his hips. I resisted a smile and lost.

"Who said I had to be your girlfriend in this little charade? Why can't we be friends who have mutually exclusive relationships with other people?" I lifted my ball and danced my fingers over the tiny fan at the end of the carousel.

Johnny laughed. "Sweetheart, that would never happen in real life."

"Sure it would. I have male friends that I hang out with a lot."

"Straight guys?"

"Yes."

"Who have girlfriends?"

"A few." Uh oh.

"And do you go out with them alone?"

"Sometimes," I said defensively.

"At midnight?"

I hesitated. "Once."

"And how did that turn out?"

It turned out that he'd been trying to get into my pants, but I wasn't going to admit it. Instead, I turned and shot my ball down the alley. And landed flat on my ass.

Do not cry. Do not—. Stop crying. Stop crying.

I raised my sleeve and dashed at my eyes, then turned on all fours and came eye to foot with a boot.

Johnny stood there grinning, hand stretched out to help me up. I slapped it in a high five and crawled past him. When I got to the end of the carousel, I perched on the edge of the deck and rubbed my tailbone. Johnny came over and crouched in front of me.

"Did Wanda see me?" I asked.

"Baby," he said softly. "Everybody saw you."

"Shit."

"You want the upside?"

I raised my face halfway and peered at him through my lashes. "What?"

He pointed to the scoring monitor and I twisted around.

I got a strike.

***

"Better?"

"Mm-hmm," I said, picking up another nacho as I chewed the first.

Johnny shook his head, pushed the napkin container toward me, and leveraged a wad of nachos onto his plate. After my little spill, we'd turned in our shoes and retreated to the snack bar where I could check out Wanda from a distance while I fed my injury.

Half the lanes had cleared out and Wanda had yet to pick up a ball. I was on the verge of calling it a bust, but didn't want to give up. Well, that and there was still half a platter of nachos left. I wolfed down another clump then wiped my hands and was dabbing my mouth when old Wanda stood up and sauntered over to the ball carousel. She stretched side to side, glancing at the lanes on either side of her. She completed a little girl's pirouette, scanning the back of the alley as she spun.

Our table in the snack bar sat directly behind Wanda's lane and I curled into Johnny, nuzzling his neck while I kept sight of Wanda beneath my lashes. Johnny had a nacho halfway to his mouth and in his attempt to backtrack it, got it caught in my hair.

"Aw, man." He tossed the chip on the plate and freed a piece of cheese from my hair. "Woman, what are you doing?"

"Wanda turned this way. I had to do something."

"Sam, she doesn't know you. What do you think she's gonna do?"

"Nothing," I said, watching a jalapeno bit fall from my hair.

"But I may need to scope her out again and it won't help if she recognizes—. Look, look." I pointed a knuckle toward the lanes.

Wanda had finished surveying her audience and stretched over the carousel, where she picked out a shiny pink ball. I activated the camera on my phone and prayed to the picture saints.

The man in the group stood next to Wanda, wrapping an arm around her as if he was showing her how to throw. Wanda gave him a playful push and stepped up to the deck. She took a last peek to each side of her, strode three long steps, and whipped the ball down the lane.

"Strike," Johnny said.

"Strike out," I said with a grin, reviewing the pics I snapped.

Johnny threw me a side-eye. "Really?"

I sat back in my chair, satisfied. As much from what I had just seen as from the nachos. Maybe a smidge more from the nachos.

"Don't give me a hard time," I said. "In the span of six hours, I've tossed four dozen pizza shells, fallen flat on my ass, taken a nacho hair rinse, and put up with your cute remarks. How much can a gal take?"

Johnny tilted his head back and roared with laughter.

"Okay, it's not that funny," I said.

"Oh, yeah it is," Johnny said, catching his breath. "Now you get to go sleep at Gino's."

Chapter Twenty-One

When the pillow hit my face, I fought it hard enough to launch myself off the futon and onto the hardwood floor.

"What the hell?" I rolled onto my back and looked up to see Paul towering over me, attack pillow in hand and a question on his face.

Could I ever just wake up to an alarm clock?

"What are you doing here?" Paul asked.

I hiked myself up into a sitting position and casually slung one arm back over the futon cushion.

"I borrowed the office couch for the night," I said.

"Yeah, that part I got. Why?"

"It was super late when I got done last night and it was easier to come here to crash." I fought to keep my voice airy.

"Where were you?" Paul asked.

"Parma," I said, rolling the name slowly off my tongue, wanting with every bit of me to roll it back in.

Paul crossed his arms and rocked a bit on his feet.

"Sam."

"Mmm?"

"How long did it take you to get here?"

"Fifteen minutes."

"Un huh," Paul said. "And how long would it have taken you to get to Gino's?"

"Fine," I said, dragging myself off the floor. "It would have taken the same time either way." I sidled past him and hit the stairs.

"Sam," Paul called after me.

"I haven't even got sheets on the bed at Gino's yet and I was exhausted. I don't know the lay of the land. I coulda taken a header down the stairs trying to get to the bathroom in the middle of the night," I babbled.

I retreated to the kitchen and discovered that Paul had started a pot of coffee brewing before he came hunting for me.

"I knew I'd be safer here at the office and you have the extra space upstairs any way. No harm, no foul. In fact," I said, twisting around to face him. "Maybe I should just move in here. I could pay you rent and kind of keep an eye on the office at the same time." I selected a coffee mug and ignored Paul's shaking head.

"The commute would be good and you'd always know where to find me. There's really no down side." I filled my mug, splashed in a lug of cream, and handed it to Paul where he had lingered in the doorway during my rant.

"You can't stay here," Paul said, taking the mug and a seat at the table. I joined him.

"Is it because of the licorice?" I asked.

"No." Paul laughed.

"Is it because you don't want to risk getting tired of my face?" I asked with a toothy grin.

"Definitely not."

"Is it because I didn't come home right away after Dad died?"

Paul lifted his head away from his mug mid-sip and focused a startled look at me.

"Why would you say that?" he asked.

I rubbed at the inlay on the wooden table, my fingers swirling circles around the delicate grooves.

"Sam, come on."

"I just wondered."

"Sam, I'm not mad at you and never was," he said.

"Okay," I said. I scooted my chair back and fetched a mug for myself.

Paul turned in his chair to watch me. "Did you really think I was mad?"

I sat back down. "Maybe. I don't know," I said, rubbing my face.

"What?" Paul asked. "Just spit it out."

"It's just been hard to get a hold of you lately. It feels like you talk to Johnny more than me, which is cool. I get that you're friends, it's just weird when I call you and he gives me a message from you instead of you calling me back."

"I told you, it's been getting busy," Paul said. "I'm working on some ideas to expand the business and I trust Johnny to fill in for me."

I nodded, fingertips back to fussing the grooves. Paul leaned forward, resting his forearms on the table.

"You thought anymore about staying for a while?" he asked.

I raised my eyes to his. "I've thought about it." That was the truth.

Paul nodded, his head bobbing like one of those dashboard Chihuahua dolls.

"Do you think you'll at least stay the year?" he asked.

When we first talked about my coming home, we thought it might take a year or more to help get Mom back on her feet. Given what I walked in on the other night, or rather what walked in on me, it didn't look like getting on her feet was even Mom's goal. Oy.

"Maybe," I answered, and decided to test the waters. "How do you think Mom's doing?"

"I don't know. She seems okay when I see her, for the most part. But she cried the other night."

"About Dad?" I asked.

"Sort of. I was telling her that I was thinking about signing me and Erica up for a couple's cooking class and it reminded her of Dad's meatloaf recipe."

"She's obviously still missing him bad if something so unrelated makes her cry," I said.

Doubt crossed Paul's face.

"What?" I asked.

"Here's the thing. I kind of got the impression she wasn't crying because she missed Dad."

I looked in my empty coffee mug. "I'm only one cup in. You lost me."

"I think she was more upset that she doesn't have that meatloaf recipe."

"Shut up," I said.

"I swear. She went on and on about how Dad always impressed people with his cooking and she couldn't do the same and now she needed to. It was weird."

I wondered who Mom was trying to impress. I wondered if he was short. And hairy. And could be found seasonally among the other lawn ornaments.

"Have you flat out asked her how she's doing?" I asked.

"Of course."

"And what does she say?"

"That she's 'fine'," Paul said. "It's always 'fine'."

"Maybe she is," I offered.

"Maybe. But then why doesn't she go to bingo, or see her friends, or do any of the stuff she did all the time before Dad died?"

I shook my head. "I don't know."

I didn't know how to tell Paul that Mom had made at least one new friend.

"Look," I said. "It's not like I'm leaving tomorrow. We'll figure it out with Mom."

Paul eyed me. "For sure?"

"Promise. Besides, I heard that clown college closed down."

"Sam?" Paul narrowed his eyes at me.

"Yeah?"

"What the hell is in your hair?"

Chapter Twenty-Two

Paul and I spent a couple hours catching up on our respective cases and Wanda Ames' shenanigans, then I dragged myself over to Gino's. Between working at the pizza shop and my nacho incident the previous night, I was in bad need of a shower.

I managed to unearth a fresh towel from one of the moving boxes and cleaned up in record time. I avoided thinking about soaping up in the same tiled box that Gino had by listing all the States alphabetically in my head. I lathered, rinsed, and repeated all before I got to Delaware.

I had just finished combing out my wet hair and was rummaging through empty cupboards in search of Mrs. Hubbard when Johnny called.

"What have you got going on today?" he asked.

"Unpacking," I said, pawing through my bag for anything I could call breakfast. "And I need to run down and get some pictures of an accident site for a fraud case."

"Can you fit in time with Roman?"

"Does he have something new?" I asked.

"He ran the plate info on Vanessa and said he'd give me an update, but he's leaving for Pittsburgh tonight and I'm swamped all day with one of my own jobs. He'll talk to you if you can fit his window."

"What's his window?"

"Noon. And he's gotta squeeze lunch in at the same time," he said.

I looked at the mangled half of a protein bar that I'd just unearthed from my bag.

"I'm in."

***

"Oh my god, that's so good." I licked relish off my thumb. "How can a hot dog be so good?"

"They deep fry them," Roman said.

I moaned a little as I took another bite.

"In lard," he said.

I put the dog down. Ah, hell. Who was I kidding? I picked it back up and added a spoonful of kraut.

"So, what's the scoop on this Vanessa girl?" I asked.

Roman popped his notebook out of his shirt pocket and flipped through several pages before finding what he wanted.

"White compact is registered to a Vanessa Goodacre. Twenty-three years old, address listed with the BMV is the same as the house you saw her go into. House is owned by a Roger Ownsby."

"Her dad?"

"Nope. Roger's address of record is down in Medina. He has rental property all over town, which may include the house you saw Vanessa go to. We did find a record of a Wanita Goodacre living at the same address. Age forty-one, 5'5", hair brown, eyes brown."

"Young mom," I remarked.

"Not unheard of, though." Roman flipped his notebook shut and wrapped a paw around his soda.

"Are you going to talk to Vanessa?" I asked.

"As soon as we find her," Roman said. I raised my eyebrows in surprise. "Another detective paid a visit to her house this morning, but only mom was there. Wanita gave us the name of the nail salon where Vanessa works day shifts before she goes to the restaurant, but the salon manager told our guys that she hadn't shown up for her shift."

"Did he say if that was unusual?" I asked.

"Sounded like it was more par for the course," Roman said around a bite of hot dog. "He was good and steamed. Told our guys if they saw her first, to tell her she's fired."

"Did Johnny tell you we saw her with Jerome last night?"

Roman nodded and wiped the corner of his mouth.

"Are you going to ask Jerome about her?" I asked.

"We already did. We had him down for another interview after you saw him at your nonni's bingo. He admitted that he'd had what he called a 'brief mistake' with Vanessa a couple months back and ended it right away, but Vanessa has been persistent. Her showing up at bingo was a total surprise to him."

"Must have been a nice surprise from what I could see in that nook," I said.

"We mentioned as much. He says he got caught up in the moment again and was just feeling lonely without his wife."

"Tracy's been gone for less than a week. How lonely could he be?"

"Didn't say it ain't bullshit. Just telling you the man's story."

I folded my napkin over the rest of my lard dog.

"It's so frustrating," I said. "There's something going on with him and I understand that you don't have proof, but it's hard to swallow the idea of him being cleared."

"I didn't say we cleared him. There's just nothing to tie him to it. The reality is we don't even know if there is an 'it'."

"How can you say that?" I asked. I started ticking off my fingers. "We know Tracy's gone and hasn't talked to anyone in her family. There was blood on her phone case in that car. A car which was abandoned. Has she used her ATM or credit cards?"

"Nothing on the cards."

I uncurled another finger.

"Tracy didn't tell her mom or sister she intended to leave," I added. "And she may not have many friends, but no one has come out of the woodwork saying they heard she had plans to leave. Not one," I said.

"So?" Roman asked.

"So, it doesn't make sense. Obviously something untoward happened to this woman."

"Untoward?"

I looked behind each of my shoulders.

"Why is my vocabulary being questioned lately?" I asked. "Hurt, taken, abducted, absconded, borrowed, whatever. This woman didn't just wander off on her own, hop into a stranger's car for kicks and giggles, then *get out*, and skip off onto some fantasy getaway vacation."

"I don't disagree," Roman said. "And I love that you're so passionate about this. The sad reality is that something bad has probably happened here. And if I could see one iota of a shred of a sliver of even a seed of new information to chase down, I would and I will. But we're at a standstill here."

"What about the fact that Jerome's last wife died? And that he's been playing grab ass with Vanessa?" I said.

"Sam, I'm not saying this guy isn't guilty. I just don't know of what."

"What about the blood on the cell phone case?" I pushed on.

Roman shook his head. "The lab tested the blood and it was Tracy's. It was a very small amount, though. For all we know, she nicked herself weeks ago."

"Any chance her sister is involved?" I asked.

Roman barked a little laugh and pressed back into his seat.

"I don't know whether you're a dog on a bone or just have a vivid imagination."

I pointed a French fry at him. "It's not completely out of the realm of possibility, though, right? Johnny and I met up with her and she definitely seemed to know more than she shared. She gave us a whole 'my sister and I aren't close' routine, but it seemed a bit too convenient."

"How so?"

"There seemed to be a tension underlying there. Like maybe there's a jealousy or something. From what I've heard so far, it sounds like their mom favored Tracy over Patty."

"Doesn't Patty work at the track?" Roman asked. "That would be enough to make me have some underlying tension. Serving gamblers all day?"

"What's wrong with that?" I asked.

"Have you seen some of these cats who sit there all day betting race after race?"

"You're eating lunch with one right now," I said.

"Well, I didn't say 'all'. I said 'some'. You are an extraordinary exception."

"Nice save," I grinned and snitched one of his fries. "So maybe it's not about their mom. Maybe Patty's jealous that Tracy got married first. Patty's older and based on the way she tried to lick the tan off Johnny, I'd suspect she's in the market for a man."

"That's not saying much," Roman said. "From what I've seen, Johnny gets that reaction a lot." His voice was neutral, but something in it made me look up from my pop. Roman pinned me with a look that was impossibly soft and intense at the same time.

"Is there a question there?" I asked.

"Not that it's my business, but are you and Johnny together?"

"No," I said.

"Do you want to be?"

I hesitated. "We have history."

"Ancient history or history that repeats itself?"

I shook my head, unsure of the words.

"You want to let me know when you figure it out?"

Chapter Twenty-Three

"I call bullshit."

"Can you take this before you dial?" Paul asked, shoving a box of cheese into my arms.

I passed the box to Vinnie, who in turn bent and spun it across the floor of the pizza shop. We'd made a human chain between the delivery truck and the back door of the restaurant.

"I'm serious," I said. "Jerome asking you to prove his missing wife was cheating on him while he's shnokking some other woman is ridiculous. Who does he think he's fooling?" Jerome had called Paul earlier to make sure he was still on the case, and I was officially grossed out.

Paul swung a sack of onions to me. "How does it look if he doesn't? If he's saying Vanessa was just a piece of side action, he still needs to look like he cares about finding his wife."

I launched the onions at Vinnie and turned back just in time to catch a bag of yeast. I took a ladylike squat and catapulted it to Vinnie.

"I'm just saying Tracy doesn't deserve this. She was a nice girl," I said. Paul stowed the last of the boxes and I reviewed the invoice.

"You knew her a long time ago, Sam," Paul said.

"What's that supposed to mean?" I scratched a hurried signature on the invoice, handed it to the driver, and followed Paul inside.

"Are you saying she deserved whatever happened?" I asked Paul.

He passed his box cutter to Vinnie and turned back to lounge against the prep table.

"Of course not. My point is you don't know what's going on in that relationship. Maybe she is cheating on him."

"So?" I asked.

"Maybe his affair or hers, if there even is one, has nothing to do with what happened to her."

I put the counter to my back and reclined next to Paul. "Okay, let's say that's true for a minute and look at what we know. For one, we've still got an unknown player in the Mercedes."

"A Mercedes with a stolen plate," Paul said.

"It's got to be someone Tracy knows, right? I mean, that woman went right into the house."

"Or it's someone Jerome knows."

"You think Jerome could be messing around with this woman?" I asked.

"Maybe. Is it impossible to think she went to the house to confront Tracy?"

"This is going to sound stupid, but that woman couldn't even stay on her own feet in those heels getting from car to door. If I'm gonna throw down with someone, I don't think I'd show up in silk and stilettos."

"I'd pay a thousand dollars to see you throw down in any shoes," Vinnie said as he maneuvered around me and Paul to stock the cold case.

"Hush," I said, kicking a tennis shoe-clad foot in his direction.

I looked back at Paul. "This mystery woman has to be tied in somehow, it's just too big a coincidence. But that doesn't mean Jerome is innocent. People kill their spouses for a lot of reasons."

"Money, most often," Paul said.

"Right. So, maybe Jerome paid the woman in the Mercedes."

Paul shook his head. "Roman said the life insurance on Tracy is only a hundred thousand. It's not exactly enough to run away with, especially if he planned to split it with this woman."

"Plus," Vinnie said, closing the cooler door. "Hard to cash in without a body."

"Jerome could have stashed Tracy someplace, thinking he could drop her body somewhere later. Make it harder on the police to solve, but eventually have a body for the insurance payout."

"Too risky," Paul said.

"Tracy's sister said her mom thought Tracy'd had some falling out with a co-worker. Maybe I need to talk to Maribeth again. When Angie and I talked to her before, she was pretty defensive of Tracy, but maybe she knows somebody who wasn't."

"Someone on Roman's squad already talked to Maribeth. Didn't sound like she knew much," Paul said.

"It's still worth a shot." I dug in. "I don't know how much Patty shared with the police, so who knows what they asked her."

"You think you can get Maribeth to tell you anything after what happened the other day?" Paul asked.

"No," I said. "But ten bucks says she'll tell Johnny anything he wants to hear."

"I've heard he has a knack," Paul said.

"It's more like he just shows up," I said.

***

"Turn into that strip mall, will you?"

Angie signaled and hung a right into a plaza that held the usual array of mom and pop stores. She parked in front of a shop selling needles and thread, and looked up at the plate glass window.

"How on earth do they make a living selling thread?" Angie

said with a shake of her head.

"Well, I'd say given the median age around here is eighty-five, this is probably a good market for some serious cross stitch."

Angie shuddered and turned to look at me solemnly in the eye. "Promise you'll shoot me before I become one of them."

I sketched an X over my heart, then held up two fingers. "Promise," I said.

Angie's mouth turned down. "What is that?" her eyes pointing to my fingers.

"My Girl Scout pledge."

"Sam, you weren't a Girl Scout."

"The hell I wasn't. I gave two full weeks to that troop."

Angie's eyes were not impressed.

"Hey," I said. "You sit at a table for two weeks and paste together paper shamrocks with half your name on each side, then tell me how long you would have lasted."

"There's those commitment issues."

"Cute," I said, gripping my camera bag and popping open the car door. "Come on, I need your help."

Angie and I crossed the parking lot to the sidewalk and walked down to the next corner. I dug my camera from my bag and handed the bag to Angie.

"Is this me helping? Holding your bag?" Angie held the bag in front of her like her toddler's used diaper.

"No. I need to get several shots from different angles here. You need to help me not get hit while I do it." I looked both ways, then ran into the intersection and snapped a dozen shots in both directions before racing back to the corner. Cars had eased up to the red light and I waited for the light to change again.

"Why can't you just stand here on the sidewalk and take them?" Angie asked.

"I'll get some from here, too, but I have to get the perspective the driver had in the accident." The light changed and I dodged back out behind the line of cars. I kneeled quickly in the street and snapped multiple shots before Angie shouted a warning at me. I jetted back over to the curb.

"I want it on the record that this is stupid," Angie called out as I took off at a trot across the side street that adjoined the intersection. I waited for a break in cars, sprinted to the middle lane, sat in the road, snapped a few shots, and hot-footed it back to the sidewalk.

By that time, Angie had crossed the side street and was standing to meet me, hands on curvy hips.

"What in God's name are you doing?" Angie asked.

"Getting a perspective of what the driver saw when he made impact."

"You scared the crap out of me. Why the hell did you sit down?"

I pointed to where I'd been sitting. "Because the driver who filed the claim said he saw a dog right at that spot and that's why he swerved into that ice cream store over there." I pointed behind us at a small shack that housed a seasonal ice cream stand with a walk-up window facing the street. The good news was the stand was closed at the time of the accident and no one was hurt. The bad news was twelve dozen gallons of ice cream and most of the equipment were destroyed. To top it all off, the owners had let their insurance policy lapse.

Angie walked the few feet over to look at the damaged side of the shack. I waited for another break in traffic, then shot into the intersection for one more pass. I got off several shots of the opposite side of the street, then spun on my heel to race back to the curb.

"Nooo!"

My eyes swung to Angie's face at the sound of her shriek. I should have been looking for what caused it.

Chapter Twenty-Four

The El Camino roared into the intersection. I skidded my feet to a stop, but my upper body kept going. I met the car's hood with a bear hug, my fingers finding purchase on a windshield wiper. The force of the blow bounced my legs up and across the hood. I lost my grip and flew off the other side of the car before landing in a seated position on the curb.

I was facing the street, wiper blade still clutched in hand, when the driver emerged from the car and ran over. He and Angie crouched in front of me, asking if I was okay. I felt my mouth open, but no words came out.

Angie was running her fingers lightly up and down my arms, as if asking my aura to tell her where I was hurt. I wish it could have answered for me. I heard sirens start up in the distance and was vaguely aware of the crowd gathering around the little cross legged girl and her wiper.

I blinked at Angie and tried to reach my hand out to her. She took my hand and cradled it.

"Help is coming, sweetie. I'm so sorry. I was looking at the stand. Sam, I'm so sorry."

I tried to draw her toward me and she leaned in close. "What is it, sweetie?" she asked.

I swallowed and opened my mouth again. "Good luck with the cross stitch."

Hours later, I opened my eyes and found eight staring back at me. Five brown and two gray. Vinnie, Mom, Angie, and Johnny hovered from both sides of the hospital bed.

"Honey?" Mom.

"Dude." Vinnie.

"I'm so sorry." Angie.

"Samantha." Johnny.

"Bunnies." Me.

"Oh, sweet Jesus." My mother's eyes welled and she wrapped her hand around the tips of my fingers, squeezing hard around the IV line taped to the back of my hand.

"It's okay, Mrs. Carter. That's probably just the pain medication." Johnny patted at my mom's shoulders and gently pried her fingers away from mine.

I blinked, shutting first one eye, then the other. I felt like grape jelly, but was vaguely aware of a burning sensation in my backside. I blinked again and swung my eyes around for a second look. No Paul.

"Did I get in a fight with a car wash?" I croaked.

Vinnie filled a small cup from a water pitcher, dunked in a straw, and held it in front of me.

"Sweetie, a car ran into you," Angie blubbered.

"Actually, from what I heard, you kind of ran into the car," Vinnie said.

I sipped some water and tried to shift onto my other cheek. A swell of pain rose up and the sweet yet sour taste of bile filled my throat. I waited for the taste to subside, then lifted the bed covers and peeked under. Beyond the hospital gown I saw two unshaven legs and a purple welt growing in the shape of a football, but nothing more serious.

"Is everything still there?" I asked.

"All accounted for and nothing broken," Johnny said,

smoothing back my hair. "But you're going to be sore for a few days."

"Can I go home then?" I asked, realizing as I said it that I wasn't sure where home was.

"The doctor said you have to stay here tonight," Angie answered. "Just in case. There doesn't look like any internal bleeding, but you smacked that car hard. And you went into shock," Angie said, a new wash of tears flowing down her cheeks.

"Crap," I said, memory flooding back. "My camera?"

"I've got them," Angie said.

I blew out a sigh. Wait.

"Them?" I echoed.

"Um, the pieces of it."

Unh.

"Where's Paul?" I asked.

"He's working, but I talked to him a few minutes ago," Johnny said. "He knows you're okay."

Gee-zuss, Paul really was pissed at me. Suddenly I felt a lot less like jelly and more like discarded crust. Maybe once everyone left I could call him. I looked at the side table wheeled across my bed where Vinnie had propped my water. No phone. No bag. I looked at Angie.

"Where's my phone?"

"With your clothes," Angie said, avoiding eye contact.

"Okay, I'll play," I sighed. "Where are my clothes?"

"Well, the thing is," Angie said. "You landed real funny and the paramedics had to tie you to a board because they didn't know if you'd hurt your back. Or how bad. And so they had to cut you out of—"

"Ange, honey, the drugs aren't that good. Can you give me the *Reader's Digest* version?"

"Your clothes are in the trash and your phone was in your back pocket. When you landed, you crushed it into pieces," she spit out. She turned her attention to the blanket tucked around my legs and began to softly pleat a small section back and forth.

Vinnie, Mom, and Johnny stood mesmerized by Angie's fingers. They all remained at the bed's edge, but I was no longer center of attention.

"It's just a phone, guys. I'm not gonna freak."

Angie cleared her throat. "There's more."

I looked around at the four of them. Not one eyeball so much as floated my way.

"Don't tell me they threw out my wiper."

Angie looked up from the accordion she'd made of the blanket, her gaze settling somewhere near my nose. "When you landed and, um, crushed your phone, one of the pieces. The force kind of, um…"

"The force kind of um, what?" I asked.

Angie looked sideways at Vinnie.

Vinnie leaned over and looked me dead in the eye. "Sam, you can take a selfie with your ass cheek."

Chapter Twenty-Five

I woke up the next morning and nearly wished I hadn't. I spent the better part of an hour willing my arms and legs to follow direction before. Visions of Humpty Dumpty swam through my head.

A male nurse, tall with skin that glowed like Celine Dion stage lighting, came in for the eighty-seventh round of vitals. A few minutes later, I was presented with a breakfast tray. I raised my bed, which incited the stabbing pain to flare up again. I managed a couple bites of toast and avoided the eggs. Calling them "yellow" was generous at best and my stomach was already raw from the pain meds.

I polished off the toast and rolled my shoulders back and forth until they felt reasonably loose. Angie had swung past Paul's office the previous night and brought me back a bag stuffed with laptop, *Fifty Shades of Gray*, and my current case files. God bless that woman, she'd also tucked in a baggie of Red Vines. I'd made it through the night and survived the excavation of the cell phone lens from my derriere, but was told I couldn't be released until the attending doctor made his rounds that afternoon. I figured I might as well get some work done.

I plucked out Wanda Ames's file, jammed a Red Vine in my mouth, and laid out my notes. I hadn't uploaded the pictures from the bowling alley and unless I could somehow retrieve them, I was starting from scratch. I'd seen Wanda's flexibility with my own eyes, but the lawyers and insurance companies would want documented proof.

Using the hospital phone, I called my cell phone carrier and explained that I broke my phone. I skipped the reason and very politely asked how long it might take for them to retrieve my photos and send them to me. When I hung up, I could still hear the laughter.

I dialed Tracy's sister, Patty. No answer on her home phone. I licked a finger and paged through my file to find her work number and called the race track bar. A guy with a grizzly voice smoothed only by boredom informed me that she wouldn't be on shift until three o'clock that afternoon.

The website for Tracy's realty agency provided me with a contact email for Maribeth, but no phone number. Somehow I didn't think she'd light up at the idea of talking with me again, and an email wasn't going to entice her to think otherwise. I scrolled through the website and perused each of the agent's profiles. If Patty was right about what her mom said about Tracy having a fight with another agent, I needed to find him or her.

I leaned my head back against the bed and closed my eyes. I'd lost two sets of pictures in as many days and now I was laid up for who knew how many more. Paul apparently wasn't speaking to me and now I was potentially costing him business. The police had all but put the file away on Tracy's disappearance and I had no new leads. The tears leaked out before I could stop them.

"Do you always cry when you eat licorice? Or, do you just eat licorice when you cry?"

My eyes popped open to find Roman standing in the doorway. I tossed the nub of licorice that was still perched between my lips onto the breakfast tray and swiped at my face.

"Hi," I mumbled. "Sorry, it must be the drugs." I didn't share the fact that the last dose I had was no stronger than aspirin.

Roman gripped a guest chair from under the window and placed it next to my bed. He leaned his large frame over the bed and rubbed a few renegade tears from my cheek before sitting down.

"How did you know I was here?" I asked.

"Johnny called."

"You didn't have to come. I'm okay."

Roman nodded and smiled. "He said you were. See, the thing of it is, I'm a cop. You can tell me something's one way, but that doesn't mean I don't have to see it for myself."

I smiled back. "I can relate to that."

Roman pointed to the files and laptop clustered on my bed tray. "Big paper due tomorrow?"

"I wish. Just trying to keep things moving on a couple cases."

"The Pentleys one of them?"

"Yeah. Any luck talking to Vanessa?"

"Nada. Our dear Vanessa seems to have rabbited."

"Like, with all her worldly possessions? Or on a broken-hearted weekend binge?"

Roman reached over and freed a Red Vine from the baggie on my tray. "To hear her mom tell it, she's just taking some time to 'get perspective' for a couple days."

"But?"

"But mom was wringing her hands like she was kneading dough for Sunday bread. That woman is worried."

"Worried because you're looking for her or because she doesn't really know where Vanessa is?"

"Door number two," he said.

"Are your guys looking for her?"

"I've got patrol who will do a drive-by now and then on her house and work. I'll buzz her mom again tonight to see if she's singing the same tune."

"Do you really think she's tied into this thing with Tracy?" I asked.

"Hard to say. I haven't gotten the sense that Vanessa is the brightest bulb in the box. The idea of Jerome killing Tracy to be with this young woman doesn't gel for me."

"Doesn't mean he couldn't have used her to help," I said. "From what I've seen, she seems very into him. Needy."

Roman chewed the last of his Red Vine. "Finding her would help."

A slice of pain cut across my bottom and I tried to shift my weight to the other side, but got twisted in my gown.

"Let me help." Roman stood. "Where you trying to go?"

"To the left."

"Where all can I touch you?"

"Excuse me?"

"I'm going to lift you straight up to shift you. Where can I touch you without it hurting too bad?"

"Oh, um, I guess just avoid my ribs and my bottom." I felt my cheeks flame.

Roman eased the covers back and skimmed one arm under my knees. "Put your arm around my neck."

I did as I was told and he wrapped his other arm around my back, then lifted me gently before resettling me back down on my opposite side. He replaced the bed covers across my waist and adjusted his chair.

"That was only slightly less embarrassing than a trip to the gynecologist," I said. "But thank you."

"Nothing to be embarrassed about and I should be thanking you. I usually don't get to first base until the actual first date."

I groaned.

"I know, I know," Roman said. "When do you get out of this joint?"

"Later today if the doc gives the all-clear."

"You need help getting home?"

"Thanks, but Vinnie's going to pick me up and get me back over to my mom's for a couple days."

"You going to take it easy or try to keep chasing this Pentley thing?" His voice was neutral, but I picked up a thread of caution.

"I want to talk to one of Tracy's agent friends. I heard you guys talked to her already and nothing came of it, but Tracy's sister mentioned there might be some bad blood at her work and I'm hoping this friend can shed some light."

"Maribeth Collins."

"Yeah," I said. "Did you talk to her?"

Roman shook his head. "My partner interviewed her and he debriefed me. Nothing major came out of it."

"What'd she say?"

"That she and Tracy were friendly enough, but didn't have much interaction outside of work. Didn't sound like there was all that much interaction at work either, really. They didn't share listings. Just saw each other in passing at the agency office."

"Did she mention any other co-workers that Tracy had a problem with? Or vice versa?"

"No. We didn't know what Tracy's sister said at the time about a fight with a co-worker, but my partner asked her general questions about whether she knew of anyone who had a beef with Tracy or would want to hurt her."

"And?" I asked.

"And she said she wouldn't know and repeated what she said about not having a lot of interaction with Tracy."

"How about the other agents?" I asked.

"We talked to all but two of the people who share the office, plus the manager and the title agent who works there part-time. No one cited having problems with Tracy or knowing of anyone who would want to harm her. We've got unreturned calls out to the other two, but they work very part-time and I'm not hopeful."

I chewed my lip for a minute. "The way Tracy's sister described what their mom said, Tracy went on at length about this falling out she'd had with a co-worker. Sounds like too big a deal to be with someone who's not around the office much."

"Any chance Patty's exaggerating the conversation? Or maybe Tracy's mom is?"

A knock on the door interrupted us and a female nurse rolled into the room behind a small cart.

"Time to change your bandage. Would you like your friend to stay or step out?"

Roman scanned me up and down. He'd seen my bare legs when he adjusted me and I could see the confusion bloom.

"Where's the bandage?" he asked.

Chapter Twenty-Six

Monday morning brought the first snow flurries of the season. The lawn in front of my mom's house was a mix of green, brown, and white. My butt and hips sported a merrier mix of purple and yellow.

Vinnie had picked me up from the hospital the prior night and I was settled back in my old room. Mom and I had passed the night and most of the morning without any mention of Wally and I wasn't anxious to press it. Mom fussed over me as usual, but hadn't made actual eye contact in twelve hours. She roasted up some breakfast and set me up in a kitchen chair with her old hemorrhoid cushion, then beat a path to the front door. She mumbled something about needing sausage for Sunday supper, which she'd moved to Monday in deference to my accident. Even a trip to the ER couldn't get me off the hook.

I hovered on my rubber donut and gnawed through a charred piece of toast, contemplating the logistics of a shower. I finished breakfast and searched through drawers and cabinets looking for any MacGuyver tools that would protect my wound. A wound which the mirror told me looked a lot like the great state of Texas, both in size and shape.

I cut open a gallon size baggie and strapped it to my hiney

with a few strips of athletic tape. It wouldn't win me a Doogie Howser of the Year award, but it did the job. I finagled myself in and out of the shower, dried off, and hauled on the loosest pants I could find. By the time I topped the pants off with a sweater and struggled into a pair of boots in honor of the snow, I was pooped. I propped my good cheek on the arm of the couch and deliberated.

My cell started buzzing in the kitchen and I hauled myself up to nab it.

"How's the patient this morning?" Johnny asked.

"Ready for a nap."

"Does she need help getting tucked in?"

I mentally smacked myself when I realized I was picturing the mechanics of that.

"Samantha?"

"Yes. And no on the tucking," I said. "But I could use a ride."

"Where to?"

"Gino's. Angie picked me up yesterday to take the accident pictures and now I'm stuck at my mom's without wheels."

"Where's your mom?"

"Either buying sausage or looking for one."

"What?"

"Never mind. Would you have time to run me over to Gino's to get my car?"

There was a pause. "You think maybe you should just take it easy today?"

"I don't want to get behind," I said. "I lost all my pictures for two different clients and have to start over."

"I'm sure the clients will understand a small delay."

"I promised Paul."

"Promised Paul what?"

"That I wouldn't get us behind," I said.

"Paul actually told you he wants you to keep working today?"

"He didn't say it outright, but I texted him last night saying I'd keep at it, and he didn't tell me not to."

"Sam—"

"You know, it's not a big deal. I can call Angie."

"Shit. Give me twenty minutes."

Twenty-two minutes later, I swung open the front door before Johnny could ring the bell.

"I'm so sorry," I said.

"No worries," Johnny said. "But whatever's going on with you and Paul, you gotta get it figured out."

"Nothing would please me more." I scooped up my keys and bag from the hallway table. Johnny took the bag from me while I locked up. We got to the truck and I thought maybe taking a day off wouldn't be such a bad idea. We stood together and stared at it.

"Does this thing come with a ladder?" I asked.

"I've got a chain in the back."

I wrinkled my nose.

"Or not," he said.

"To be fair," I sighed. "It's not the worst idea in the world."

"I got another one." Johnny opened the truck door and slung my bag across the bench seat, then moved to stand behind me.

"Okay, here's what we're gonna do," Johnny said. "Step up on the running board with your right foot, and then swing your left up over the seat so you can slide in on your left cheek. When you step up, I'll hold your waist so you don't have to put too much weight on that right side."

I lifted my leg to the running board and stopped short. "How did you know it was my right cheek?"

Silence behind me. I looked back at Johnny.

"Someone must have mentioned it the night you were admitted."

I turned completely around to face him. "Who? Who mentioned it?"

Johnny stilled. "I don't remember. Probably Angie. Come on, foot up."

"Johnny?"

He mumbled something and turned me back toward the open door.

"What did you just say?" I asked.

"I said I may have seen it."

I put a steadying hand on the side of the truck. "You saw it?"

"Mmm-hmm."

"How?"

"You asked me to look," he whispered into my shoulder.

"Liar."

"I swear," Johnny eased me around to face him again. "You were high as a kite and you asked Angie to tell you how bad it was. Angie was a train wreck. Couldn't stop crying. So you asked me to look."

"Why didn't you tell me no?" I shrieked.

"I did! Like six times. You kept begging me and then you smacked me and then you called me names."

"Now you're just putting me on, big fibber." I turned back around and put my foot on the running board again. Johnny hoisted me up as I swung my left leg in, then helped me slide the rest of the way. He stepped back to close the door, then paused and leaned back in.

"Hey, Sam?"

"Yeah?"

"Did I ever tell you about the time I went to Texas?"

Chapter Twenty-Seven

When we got to Gino's, Johnny helped me pack a bag of clothes to take back to Mom's. At some point, I'd need to start thinking of it as my house, but I couldn't bring myself to stay there for more than a few hours at a time, let alone think of it as my Tara.

After he got me packed, Johnny wedged me and my hemorrhoid cushion into my car. He took off and I dug out my notes from the hospital. I reviewed Maribeth's listings, and found an open house she was hosting that day.

I plugged the address into the GPS on my phone, hooked a U-turn, and headed off. I swung through United Dairy Farmers for a bacon and egg biscuit to chase down the burnt toast, and sidled to a stop at the curb just as Maribeth was placing an Open House sign on the sidewalk. She'd attached multi-colored balloons to it and was trying to untangle the strings as I humped myself out of the car and approached her.

"Hi," I said. "Need some help with that?"

Maribeth looked up with a toothy smile. "Good morning! I think I've just about got it. Are you here for the open—? Oh," she said, the smile fading from her eyes. "I know you, don't I?"

I tweaked my mouth in apology. "Yes. And I'm really sorry about the other day."

Maribeth gave up the fight with the balloons, letting one droop to the side. She straightened her shoulders and smoothed thick blond hair behind them. She would have been a tall woman even in stockinged feet, but her suede heels brought her close to six feet.

"I'm assuming you're not here to see the house," she said.

I dipped my head in apology. "And, my name's Samantha, not Debbie."

Maribeth's frown deepened. "What do you want?"

"I was hoping we could talk about Tracy."

Maribeth glanced down the sidewalk in both directions. Two houses down, a neighbor paused to let his Schnauzer do his business. It looked like the kind of business that takes a minute, and Maribeth's eyes relaxed a fraction as she planted them back on me.

"Why?" Maribeth asked.

"She's still missing and I'd like to find her."

"Aren't the police looking for her?"

"Yes, but Tracy's husband hired my brother to help look for her. My brother's a private investigator and I work for him."

Maribeth considered this some.

"Why would Jerome hire a private eye?" she asked. Her voice carried something more than curiosity. I took my turn considering her.

"The police don't have a ton of information to go on and they have a lot of other cases to work."

Maribeth's chilliness returned. "I've already talked to the police. I don't know what else I can offer."

"Please? Maribeth, I knew Tracy when we were kids. I'd hate to think I could have done more to help find her."

I caught the softening in Maribeth's face and went in for the close. "Just a few questions and I'll get out of your hair."

"Fine," she said, turning on a heel. "Come in the house, though. I have to finish getting ready."

I followed Maribeth up the paved walk and into the house.

140

One of the pavers was set slightly higher than the others. I would have taken a tumble had Maribeth not deftly side-stepped it, providing me warning.

The house was a craftsman cottage, its lawn manicured to the hilt, and equally composed on the inside. I trailed Maribeth to a sparkling kitchen at the back of the house and watched as she flipped the plastic tops off trays of fruit and cookies. She flitted from drawer to cupboard, trotting out serving trays, utensils, cheeseboard, and knife. The rooms we'd passed held minimal furniture, but Maribeth seemed at-home in the well-stocked kitchen.

"How long have you been a real estate agent?" I asked.

"Ten years." Maribeth pointed me to a bar stool, but I sidled up and braced my good side on the counter.

"How'd you get into it?"

Maribeth effortlessly hoisted a tall stack of ceramic plates off a shelf and arranged them next to the fruit. She dug napkins from a deep drawer and laid them out in an ornate fan pattern across the counter.

"I'd just broken up with someone I was living with. I had dropped out of college to help support them and by the time we broke up, I couldn't afford to go back. A realty license was cheap and I did okay with my lemonade stand when I was kid, so I'd thought I'd give sales a go." She tossed me a sardonic smile.

"You've been with the same agency the whole time?"

"Just the last four years." She cracked open a case of water and began lining the bottles up next to the cheeseboard.

"What about Tracy? She came to the agency after you, right?"

"Yes."

"I heard she'd tried her hand at a lot of jobs before this. Any idea how she got into it?"

Maribeth stiffened, but didn't look up from the bottles. "Why do you want to know?"

"Just curious. You never know what might be helpful."

She thought for a minute. "She worked in a clothing boutique for a while. And I know she did some admin work at the university because that's how she met Jerome. Beyond that, I don't know."

"Were she and Jerome having any problems?" I asked.

"I wouldn't know." She balled up the plastic packaging from the water bottle, then pivoted and shoved it hard into the under-sink trash can.

"Did she talk about her home life at all? Maybe she said something that didn't mean much at the time, but does in hindsight?"

"No, nothing." Annoyance pushed at the wrinkles forming around her nose. "I wouldn't be someone she'd tell even if something was going on."

"How about her relationship with the other agents?"

"What about them?" she asked.

"Was there anyone she didn't get along with?"

"Not that I know of."

"Anyone who was especially competitive with her?" I asked.

She shrugged in what I took to be a maybe.

"There could be some petty jealousy. Tracy's a fantastic sales woman," Maribeth said, her face brightening for the first time. "Clients love her. She's kind of shy when you first meet her—well, maybe 'reserved' is the better word. But with clients she's just so open right from the start."

"I assume she sells a lot of houses then?"

"She does well. She does better than some who have been doing this for years."

"Has she ever taken someone else's client away?"

Maribeth's face hardened. I threw my hands up in surrender.

"I'm not suggesting she did on purpose. I'm just wondering if maybe a client walked into the office and picked her over another agent," I said. "Maybe she got more than her share because people warmed to her so fast?"

"That's not how it works," Maribeth snapped. "Most people

don't just waltz into an agency. It's not like we're all sitting there waiting for clients, anyway."

"Okay. So, how does it work?"

Maribeth turned to the back counter and snatched a new dish towel from a drawer. "We network at different events, clients find us online, we get referrals. We're not usually competing directly for the same clients."

"What about the agency site? Did Tracy get more leads than the rest of you?"

"Maybe a few. But nobody was mad about it."

"What about personal beefs? Anybody in the office not like her for other reasons?"

Maribeth crossed back to my end of the counter and looked me hard in the eyes.

"No one had an issue with Tracy," she said. "I don't know how else to say this to you."

"I heard someone did," I said. "Quite a big issue, actually. 'Bad blood' may have been the description I heard."

"Where did you hear that?" Maribeth's annoyed look turned anxious.

"Is it true?"

She shook her head at me, but with less conviction. "I don't know anything."

"Could it be you?"

"I don't know what you're talking about."

"Yes, you do," I said, suddenly keenly aware that I was alone with this woman who had six inches on me and a cheese knife in hand. I straightened up from the counter. "Are you jealous of Tracy's success?"

Flashes of red burned Maribeth's cheeks. "You don't know what you're talking about."

"Then help me out here."

"I don't have any more information for you. And I have an open house to start." She walked around the counter and headed for the front door, leaving me no choice but to limp along after her.

Maribeth held the screen door as I passed through. I handed her one of Paul's agency business cards with my cell number on it and opened my mouth to tell her to call me if she thought of anything else. Before I could say anything, Maribeth pushed past me and waved enthusiastically to a couple climbing out of their SUV at the curb.

I followed Maribeth down the walkway and tripped over the paver that she once again side-stepped without missing a beat. Pain ripped through my bottom and I hobbled past the trio to get to my own car.

I fell into the driver seat, leaned my head against the backrest and closed my eyes to wait out the pain. I tried to replicate the deep breathing Angie's always trying to show me from her hippie meditation classes. The pained eased and I opened my eyes, noticing then what I hadn't when I first arrived. Directly across the street from the open house, sitting serenely at the curb, was a dark blue Mercedes.

Chapter Twenty-Eight

"How are you not excited about this?"

I tailed Roman around his desk and out into the hall of the police station. He dropped a folder off to an officer at the front counter, then looped back and stopped in front of a row of vending machines.

"Because it's not the evidence of the century." He jammed a dollar bill into a candy machine.

"Are you kidding me? She has a blue Mercedes exactly like the one I saw at the Pentleys'."

The machine spat the dollar bill out and Roman rammed it back in. The machine held it for a hope-filled second before rejecting it again.

"Yeah," he said. "But the Mercedes you saw at the Pentleys' had a stolen plate on it."

"So maybe she switched plates."

"Sam, come on. If she was going to go to the trouble, why not just use a different car altogether?" Roman traded his mangled dollar for another and tried again. The machine wasn't having it. I plucked the dollar from his hand and rubbed it flat against my thigh.

Roman watched with a mixture of doubt and desire.

"What about the open house? It's *her* house." It hit me on the way over to the station that there might be a reason for Maribeth's practiced ease in the kitchen and magical peripheral ability to avoid that broken paver. I'd asked Roman to look up the address and, sure enough, the house belonged to Maribeth.

"Again, so what?" Roman put his palm out for the dollar. I ignored him and went back to smoothing.

"Don't you think that would have come up? Why would she hide it from me?" I guided the dollar into the vending machine and the light strip turned green. Roman cut his eyes at me, but wasted no time punching three buttons.

"Maybe she just isn't the sharing type," he said. "You and Angie offend the hell out of her the first time you meet, then you show up asking her a thousand and one questions, including 'hey, you the jealous type'? Did you really expect her to share her life story with you?"

"I still think it's janky," I said, crossing my arms.

Roman pushed a ham hock through the vending window and fished out his snack.

"Janky as it may be, it doesn't prove anything."

"But don't you want to talk to her again?" I asked.

"To what end? She's told us and you the same story over and over. That she doesn't know anything. That she barely even knows Tracy."

I popped off the wall, sending a new spasm through my butt. "That's the other thing that bothers me. She keeps saying she doesn't talk to or work with Tracy much, but she used Jerome's name without having to think. If I don't know someone well, I'm gonna say 'her husband' before I'd say his name."

"That's your proof?"

"It's not just that," I said. "She even knew how Tracy and Jerome met. That's not something you share with a woman if you're not friends."

Roman looked doubtful.

"I know it's not a lot, but my gut is telling me this woman knows more than she's letting on."

"Can you say definitively that she's the woman you saw at the Pentleys'?"

I blew out a sigh of frustration. "So, that's one of two things bothering me. On paper, they could be the same person, but I don't think it was."

"Based on what?"

"Don't hit me, but it's a feeling."

"I'd never hit you, but a light swat after you're healed might be in the works." He started to pry open his snack package.

"Hear me out. The woman I saw was tall, blonde, dressed well. So's Maribeth. But there's something about the way they stood and walked that just felt...I don't know. Different."

"Number Two?"

"No, not even Number One. Just the overall way they carried themselves."

"No, you said there were two things bothering you."

"Oh, yeah. The whole time we were talking, Maribeth seemed either tense or annoyed. But when I asked her if any of their co-workers could have seen Tracy as competition, you should have seen her face. Roman, she lit up. She started raving about how Tracy relates right off the bat with her clients. When she described her, she was so specific about the words she used. If she really had a feud with Tracy, or had something to do with her disappearance, I just don't think she'd be so complimentary about her."

"Unless it was an act," Roman said.

"I don't know. It just doesn't add up."

"'Janky', I believe is the word."

I winked at him and for the first time noticed what he had unearthed from the vending machine. Red Vines. My face split in a grin.

"Welcome to the dark side." I held out a palm.

"Don't judge me," he said, and took off down the hall.

"Hey, sharing is caring," I called to his back.

***

I inspected my plate and felt a wash of regret. I should have raided the vending machine at the station while I had the chance. Note to self. Hit the Dairy Queen before Sunday Dinner. My sausage link looked like a water balloon with a slow leak as it lay defeated on a watery pile of bowtie pasta. If ever a sausage needed Prozac, it was this one.

"What's this?" Paul asked. He held up a small, green leaf pinched between his fingers.

"Basil," Mom said.

"I meant, since when do you use fresh herbs?" Paul asked.

"That's not fair," Vinnie said. "Didn't she use cilantro a couple weeks ago?"

"In banana pudding." Paul sniped.

I peeled another piece of what looked like plastic from my sausage link and added it to the pile on my napkin. I was ready to pass entirely on supper, but needed to make a food bed in my belly to support the painkiller I was planning on eating for dessert. By the time I left Roman, the events of the day had caught up to me. I was dreaming of a full-body hemorrhoid cushion and a Percocet.

"When does Erica get home?" I asked.

Paul's fiancé had been on the road for a couple weeks. She'd made a good gig out of freelance photography, but it took her out of town a lot and usually without much notice. She and I got on well during my visits home and I was missing the buffer. So far, she'd lucked out of the Sunday Supper club.

"Tuesday, maybe," Paul said.

"Where's she at?"

"D.C., I think."

"What's the assignment?" Vinnie asked.

"I'm not sure. Legislator profiles, something like that."

"You might want to tune in a bit more if you plan to be married long," Vinnie said.

"What would you know?" Paul snapped.

"Hey, Paul," I said. "Relax. He's joking."

Paul threw his fork on his plate, pushed back from the table, and took his dishes into the kitchen.

"What the hell?" Vinnie said to me.

"Mouth," Mom said.

Vinnie waved a hand in the air. "Sorry."

I picked up my own plate and followed Paul. By the time I got to the kitchen, he'd cracked a beer and had a hip braced against the jam of the back door. He was looking out at the backyard, but the stiffness in his shoulders told me he'd heard me come in.

I rinsed my plate and stacked it on top of Paul's. He'd already drained most of his bottle, so I popped the top on another one and placed it on the end of the counter next to him.

"Wanna talk about it?" I asked.

Paul stayed at the door, silent.

"Just tell me, is it Vinnie? 'Cause you know he's going to be upset for days if he thinks you're really ticked at him."

Paul shook his head but didn't turn around.

"Erica?" I asked.

"No, Sam. It's not anyone."

"Okay, okay. Sorry."

I limped over to the pantry shelf and snagged a Red Vine, then hunted up a Diet Coke from the fridge. I dumped ice in a glass, poured the pop, bit off each end of the licorice, and stuck it in the glass. I dosed myself a Percocet from the bottle on the counter, plunked it on my tongue, and sucked down some pop.

At some point in this charade, Paul had turned around. He was standing in the doorframe watching me, slack-jawed.

"What the fuck?" Paul asked.

"What?" I stopped mid-stride to the kitchen table.

"How old are you?"

"I'm hurting. What's the big deal?" I asked.

"You look like a fucking eight-year-old with that goddamn licorice in your glass."

"Are you kidding me right now? What the hell's wrong with you?" I asked.

Paul pushed off the door frame, tossed his bottle into the sink, slammed the back of an empty chair into the table, and stalked out of the kitchen. I heard my mom's questioning voice, then the front door slammed and it was silent.

I was still staring open-mouthed at the empty room when Vinnie poked his head through the door.

"What just happened?" he asked.

"I have absolutely no idea."

Chapter Twenty-Nine

I woke up Tuesday morning to a weak stream of sunlight warming my face. I eased my body over onto the other side and found I could move almost normally.

My alarm clock read 8:15 and I smiled at the realization that I woke up like a normal human being for a change. I divulged in twelve blissful seconds before the memory of the previous night flashed through and anxiety wormed its way back into my belly.

I rolled onto my back and gazed up at the ceiling. Our house had been built in the 1920s, remodeled in the 1960s, and "paint and powdered" in the late 1980s. Nowhere in any of those facelifts did it dawn on my parents or the previous owners to update the textured ceilings. There were circles upon circles in various sizes and shapes. Some were whole and others were broken, their ends not quite meeting. The overall effect looked like balls bouncing in ocean waves if you squeezed up one eye just right.

In high school, Paul smoked pot with his friends behind the little league field after school, then came home and watched his bedroom ceiling like it was a movie. I'd come in to nag him or borrow his tapes, and he'd ask me if I could see the elephants in the ceiling. I never could see those elephants, but one corner near the closet looked an awful lot like Richard Nixon.

I stared at my own ceiling now, reading it like tea leaves, trying to understand what was going on with Paul. He'd denied it, but I couldn't help thinking it was me. I took internalizing to the level of Olympic sport. When I was a kid, my dad took me to a Cleveland Browns game. I was whining about some girls at school who I thought were talking smack about me. My dad pointed to the huddled players on the field and asked me if I could see the guy with the number nine jersey. When I nodded that I did, he told me that was the quarterback, Bernie Kosar. Then he turned to me and said 'Do you think he's talking about you right now?'

Imagined or not, I felt like I had to step up my game to help Paul. It had been a full week since Tracy had disappeared. If I could just figure out what was going on, it would ease the burden. But there was also something to be said for low hanging fruit and I had two plums scraping the ground. Wanda Ames being the ripest.

I slogged through a few stretches, showered, re-bandaged my butt, slurped up a bowl of cereal and was still no closer to a grand idea for trapping Wanda. I threw in the towel and called Angie.

"What are you doing?" I asked when she answered. I heard squeals in the background but couldn't decipher whether they were playful or premeditative. "More importantly, what are those hoodlums doing?"

"They're playing jump rope."

"In the house?" Angie's house was a six pack of buns trying to wrap itself around eight hot dogs.

"Yes, in the house. And they're using my last nerve as the rope."

"Yikes, I'll catch you later."

"No!" Angie shouted. "Take me away from this. What's up?"

I gave her the rundown on Wanda Ames and my predicament.

"Why don't you just go back to the bowling alley?" Angie offered.

I cringed. "I can't bowl in the shape I'm in and besides, they only play once a week. That's four days away, If she doesn't show,

I can't afford to wait another week. I need to lock this one down for Paul."

"What's her home set-up like? Can you stake her out and try to catch her doing yardwork or something?"

"It's almost November. The leaves are already down. What's she going to be doing?"

"How about groceries? Maybe you can catch her throwing a bottle of Tide around while she's unloading her car."

"Negative, Ghost Rider," I said. "I could be waiting forever and for all we know, she uses those detergent pouch thingies that weigh nothing. I have to lure her out somehow."

"How lazy do you have to be to use those pouches, anyway?" Angie said. "And have you heard how little kids are eating them like candy and getting sick?"

"Ange, focus."

We were interrupted by the sort of shriek not normally witnessed outside asylums.

"Hang on," Angie said.

I picked at my nails while I waited. The shrieking rose to a feverish pitch, followed by dead silence. A few more seconds passed and Angie was back, sounding sweet as a fresh-picked peach. I pictured her kids sitting on the laundry room floor, a fresh pack of detergent pouches in hand.

"What if you call her and act like you're with the fire department and she has to evacuate immediately?" Angie offered.

"Mmmph. Even if I could get a good shot of her running out of the house, she could just say anybody would run if they were in that position."

"But what if she grabs a few of her favorite things? You know, so they don't burn."

"Unless one of her favorite things is her flat screen TV, I don't think a picture of her running with Grammy and Grampy's picture and a set of candlesticks is going to go very far in court."

"I give," Angie said. "Unless you can convince her you're Ed

McMahon and she's just won the lottery, I don't think you're gonna get a pic of her doing cartwheels or anything even remotely incriminating."

"Holy bells, Ange, that's it."

"Isn't Ed McMahon dead?"

"Not the lottery, but what about a prize?" I asked. "We know she's a greedy little thing. What if we make her think she's won something and the prize involves some type of physical activity?"

"In that case, let her win Johnny."

"Is this how it's gonna be?" I asked.

"Well, if you're not going to use him."

"I was thinking more like we give her a bowling pass or go-karts tickets at Fun 'n' Stuff."

"Pole dancing," Angie said.

"Come again?" I asked.

"You know, those 'exercise' classes they offer? You wear yoga tights and some cheap plastic heels, then swing around on a pole. They advertise it as a core workout, but I think it's just an excuse for women to act slutty until Halloween comes back around."

I hung up with Angie when the sounds of National Geographic Banshee Week started to climb back up through the phone. A quick internet search rewarded me with the name of a studio offering Pole Pilates that conveniently had a class scheduled in two days. I was still too sore to sit with equal weight on both cheeks, and my stripper skills were dive-bar level on my best day, but my book of stellar ideas was otherwise blank.

I popped three ibprofen, stepped into purple Vans, and took off for the office. I called the exercise studio on the way and convinced the woman who answered to let me sign up and pre-pay for three people. I told her one of the ladies I was treating had fallen on hard times, but was way too humble to accept any help, so could we make it look like a prize? She was so ecstatic at the idea of playing a role in the charade, it made me wonder how exciting her daily life was.

Paul's car was out front when I got to the office, but he was nowhere in sight. I rummaged through the guest room upstairs and came up with a digital camera to replace the one my bum had dined on. It wasn't as high-tech as the previous one, but beggars and choosers and all. I rifled through more drawers until I found an extra memory card and charger, then trucked my load downstairs. The camera had barely half a charge, so I rammed its cord into an outlet and went into the kitchen to make some coffee while I waited.

I used the percolating time to create an amateurish but passable award certificate for Wanda on my computer. I pasted in a couple pieces of clip art, centered her name, and sketched out a signature for the vice president of a bowling association. The association was real, but the VP's name was not. If Wanda was savvy enough to cross-check, she deserved the work comp money, in my opinion. When I was done with that, I logged back into Maribeth's realty site and scanned the profiles of the other agents. I jotted down names, along with phone numbers for those who had them, and looked for open houses for those who didn't. Of the half dozen agents aside from Maribeth and Tracy, three had phone numbers and two had open houses scheduled over the coming weekend. The sixth only had two listings and the listings were old enough that if I were the owner, I'd consider investing in a new agent.

By the time I finished my craft project and filled a to-go mug with coffee, Paul still hadn't appeared. I bagged up my equipment and stepped onto the front stoop. Paul's car was gone.

I loaded my wares into the car, then back-tracked to lock the office. I lumbered around the corner of the office and checked the parking lot of the adjacent building that hosted a dentist and a shrink. No Paul and no car. I smashed my renewed anxiety about our fight deep down in my donut-pit and took off.

Chapter Thirty

On my way to the accident site, I stopped at a dollar store and bought a frame for Wanda's certificate. We were in between rush and lunch hours, and traffic was light. I was able to get reasonably good shots of the intersection without incident. When I was done, I sat in my car and took a few minutes to upload the pictures to my laptop, then emailed them to myself. I wasn't taking any chances.

I stored the laptop, flipped through my notebook, and dialed the first agent on my list. Charlie Danzig's picture on the realty website was pure baby-face, but his voice made me think he was closer to death than to puberty.

I introduced myself and asked if he was okay as he hacked in my ear.

"Sure, sure. Hang on a sec." He was gone long enough for me to determine I badly needed a manicure. "Okay, who are you again?" he choked out.

"My name is Samantha Carter. I'm helping locate Tracy Pentley and was hoping you could help me out."

"Not sure how much help I can be, but I'll give it a shot, you know." Charlie's wheeze had petered out to a low rasp. Unless I'd caught him in the middle of moving a piano, he probably needed to get that checked.

"How long have you worked with Tracy?" I asked.

"Ever since she started."

"Do you know much about her?"

"I guess as much as you get to know anyone you work with. I mean, we don't spend all day together, you know. We tend to be all over the place with showings and whatnot."

"What about when you are together? Do you talk a lot?"

"We didn't like hang out," he said. "But we'd see each other in the office often enough. Share the old war stories, you know."

"What kind of war stories?" I asked.

"Oh, you know," Charlie wheezed. "Difficult clients, opposing agents trying to get the drop on you in a negotiation. That kind of stuff, you know."

"Any of those opposing agents have a recent issue with Tracy, or anyone else you know that had a problem with her?"

Charlie panted and thought about it. "Nah, you know, none that I can think of. Well, maybe one. Guy named Phil. Total weez."

"Weez?"

"Weasel," Charlie said. "He'll do anything to skim an extra buck, you know."

"What was his beef with Tracy?"

"He got a little testy with her over a deal maybe, uh, six months back?"

"You remember why?"

"Kinda. Tracy had pretty much sealed the deal on her end with her buyers and Weez—. Sorry, I mean Phil tried to talk her into getting them to go above asking price."

"Was the house worth it?"

"Nah, that's the thing. Tracy thought Phil wasn't doing it on the seller's behalf. He was just trying to up his cut, you know?"

"So, what'd she do?" I asked.

Charlie's wheeze turned into a full-blown hack. I covered my mouth without thinking and waited him out.

"Tracy told him in a nice way to stick it where the sun don't shine and threatened to spread it around what he was trying to do. The sellers accepted her buyer's offer and that was that, but Phil gave her shit about it for a while, you know."

"How so?"

"He came into the office once and made a jab at her about a listing that she'd lost to him."

"That's it? Doesn't sound that bad."

"Nah," Charlie said. He cranked out a chunky cough. I pictured a seriously abused tissue in his hand. "Tracy also said something about thinking Phil had been following her once, but I don't know."

"You didn't believe her?" I asked.

"It's not that, but I thought, why? I didn't see the point of him doing that, you know? Either way, she never mentioned it again."

"What about the other agents in your office?" I asked. "Everybody get along with Tracy?"

"We kind of have to. We're a pretty small group, you know?"

"Any competition?"

"I hear some ribbing time to time, but most everybody's got something else going, you know? It's not like the main bread and butter for most folks, except for two of them."

"Which two?"

"Troy Hoskins and Maribeth Collins."

"They do pretty well?"

"Yah, you know, I think so. Troy's driving a Saab. Got a primo condo on Lakeshore. It could all be financed to hell, but he looks to be doing okay on the face of it, you know?"

"And Maribeth?"

"She's not as vocal about her deals, so it's harder to know. But man, she's been doing this forever, you know? And she's been smart about investing her finds."

"Finds?"

"Property. She's got an eye for the flips. Buys 'em cheap,

cleans 'em up, sells them or rents them out."

"You know where?"

"There's one on Wagar Road," Charlie said. "And there's a condo down off Center Ridge somewhere. There's another single-family house that she rents out. Small, but real charming. Tin ceilings, the works. I think in Olmsted Falls, maybe?"

"She have any issues with Tracy?"

"She did, yah."

"What happened?" I asked.

"Well, hey, I'm not one to gossip, you know?"

Charlie had been two seconds away from telling me the stain color on Maribeth's hardwood floors.

"It's not gossip, Charlie. Just your opinion."

"Huh." He paused to take that in. "I like that, just my opinion. Okay, well, my opinion is that they seemed to get along pretty good up until this last year."

"What changed?"

Charlie was silent except for the hurricane-level breathing. I clonked my cell against my forehead and spoke slowly.

"Charlie, in your opinion, what changed?"

"Well, I'm not real sure. They were kind of buddy-buddy, you know? If they were in the office on the same day, they'd go to lunch. Sometimes I'd hint that I wanted to go with them, but they acted like they were in some secret sorority. Then out of nowhere, the lunches stopped. Tracy would ask me to go to lunch if Maribeth was there, or she would only come in the office late in the day. Maribeth usually came in only in the mornings."

"Did either of them say anything to you about it? Was there an argument that led up to them not talking anymore?" I asked.

"Nada. Whatever happened must have happened outside the office, you know? They weren't exactly mean to each other, but they just more like ignored each other, you know?"

"Has Tracy's relationship changed like that with anyone else?"

"Nah, not that I seen. Maribeth, neither."

"Thanks, Charlie. You've been really helpful."

Charlie's throat whistled in relief. "Good, good, glad to help, you know?"

"You definitely did. And Charlie?"

"Yeah?" he asked.

"Maybe you should see a doctor for that cough. You know?"

Chapter Thirty-One

After I wrapped up with Charlie, I called the other two agents with listed phone numbers. Neither answered, so I settled for leaving a brief message for each. I debated giving them the impression I was in the market for a house, in hopes they'd call right back, but figured they might not be so inclined to share with me when they realized I'd lied. Troy Hoskins was one of the two agents who didn't have a number listed, but he did have two open houses the coming weekend. What Charlie had described between Troy and Tracy didn't sound like the dispute of the century, but a lead is a lead and I wanted to track down Troy sooner rather than later.

I put Troy on my To Google list and called the racetrack again, looking for Patty. I was told she was heading out for her meal break, but her shift didn't end until 4:00. I packed away my laptop, puttered out of the lot, and headed for the ponies.

By the time Patty strolled back in from her break, I was lapping up the first drip of tuna from the bottom of my melt.

"Where's your little friend? Jimmy?" Patty perched sideways on the end of the booth seat opposite me, avoiding the commitment of sliding her legs all the way in.

"Johnny. And off somewhere with his boyfriend, I'd guess." I couldn't help myself.

"Hrmmph." Patty cocked an eye at me. "So why are you back here? I'd say it can't be for the tuna, but the way you're putting it down makes me second-guess that."

I daintily set down the sandwich half I was inhaling, and shot her a good-natured smile.

"I wanted to pick your brain some more about Tracy," I said from behind my napkin.

"What about her?"

"You mentioned a woman that Tracy hung out with at that baby shower. Could her name have been Maribeth?"

"Sure. Maybe." Patty tossed a non-committal hand in the air and shot a look toward the bar. She was technically back on shift, but the place was a ghost town aside from an old guy propped haphazardly on a bar stool. He was either dead or napping. Patty must have decided he didn't need another drink either way.

"Patty," I said, drawing her attention back. "I talked to a woman named Maribeth who works with Tracy. She didn't know of anyone who had a beef with your sister. Any other idea who it was that your mom thought Tracy was fighting with?"

Patty shook her head in annoyance and reached up to tuck away a rusted lock of hair that had escaped the giant bun on the top of her head.

"No," she said. "Like I said, I only half listened to my mom when she was telling me. Why don't you just go ask her yourself?"

I leaned back in the booth and watched her. She stared back sullenly.

"Patty, what gives?"

"Gives with what?"

"Your only sister is missing–for days, mind you–and you're sitting here treating me like a fly in your soup because I'm trying to figure out what happened to her."

"What's it to you?"

"I know that if it were my kid sister, I'd be a lot more worried than you seem to be."

"Well, let me go shine up a medal for you."

"What about your mom?" I tried. "Aren't you worried about what this is doing to her?"

"That's rich," Patty snorted. "The only thing my mother is worried about is protecting her precious little Tracy's secrets."

"And what secrets are those?"

Patty looked back toward the still empty bar. The annoyance dropped away from her face, replaced by a tired look. She looked back at me, but took a long time to answer.

"Nothing that'll help find my sister." Patty commandeered my straw wrapper off the tabletop and rolled it into a tight ball.

"Then why the comment?" I asked.

"Ma just doesn't want anyone to think badly of Tracy. Especially right now."

"Why not?" I asked.

"She thinks if the police know that Tracy has a history, they'll stop looking for her." Patty's tone told me she didn't agree.

"History of what?" I asked.

Patty looked down at her lap.

"Patty," I said. "I hate to be blunt about it, but the police have kind of stopped looking already."

"Seriously?" She drew her focus back to my face.

"You seem surprised," I said.

"Why did they stop?"

"There aren't any more leads to go on. They know something's off, but there's nothing else to run down at this point."

I saw the hesitance in her eyes and, for the first time, worry. "Patty, please."

Patty looked blankly at me, then shook her head like a pitcher shaking off a call.

"Tracy had an affair. It was early on in her relationship with Jerome, but it was bad."

"Bad how?" I asked.

"Jerome flipped. He hit Tracy when he found out."

"Why didn't she leave him?"

"I have no idea. We couldn't figure it out, Ma and me. It's like, Jerome explodes, hits her, kicks her out of the house, and won't even let her pack a bag of clothes. She lives on my sofa for two weeks and then one day he calls her and the next thing I know, she's moving back home with him."

"How did she explain it to you?" I asked.

"She didn't." Patty's voice hardened. "And when I pushed, she got shitty with me. Told me if I loved her like a real sister I should just shut up and support her."

I arched my eyebrows in question, but she didn't elaborate. "What do you mean, 'real' sister?"

Patty shot her straw ball into my empty water glass. "Tracy and I don't have the same dad."

"Tracy never told me that," I said, surprised.

"She wouldn't have. She was embarrassed about it for a long time. She only told a couple people, as far as I know."

"So, whose dad did I meet?"

"Mine," Patty said.

"He moved to California, right?"

"Yeah," Patty said with a snort. "Ma told everyone he went there to get into acting, but it was bullshit. He's still an accountant."

"Why the bullshit story?" I asked.

"Oh, see now. That's the fun part. Our dear mother didn't bother to tell my dad that Tracy wasn't his kid until Tracy was thirteen. Dad was pissed. He and Ma had a rough time for years. The main reason he had stayed was because Tracy was so young."

"Does Tracy know who her dad is?"

"I don't think so. She talked several years ago about trying to find him, but Ma refused to give her any info that would help. She's, uh, resistant to say the least."

"Any idea why she doesn't want Tracy to know?"

"She won't give either of us a reason, but my guess? Ma

probably doesn't even know who he is."

"How long ago did Tracy have her affair?" I asked.

"Mmm, three years or so. I don't know how long it went on, but that's when I found out."

"Is that why you hate her?"

Patty's startled eyes welled. "I don't hate her."

"You seem awfully angry."

"With my mother more than with Tracy. I don't care about Tracy's affair. I haven't always worn the shiniest halo myself. But it destroyed our relationship when we were just starting to finally have one. She and Ma have gone on like nothing happened, like they bonded over their cheating or something. That," Patty broke off, pointing a shaky finger at me. "That, I hate."

Chapter Thirty-Two

I left Patty and her anger at the bar, bet and lost two trifectas at Belmont, then wheeled back toward the office. I called Roman on the way and left him a condensed version of what Patty shared with me. Then I called Tracy's mom and got yet another voicemail box. I left a message letting her know I was checking in and would appreciate a call back. Light and breezy, no indication that I wanted to interrogate her about her cheating daughter.

When I got back to the west side, I cruised past the office twice, looking for Paul's car. On my third pass, my cell buzzed.

"Are you going to land the plane, or keep circling the runway?" Johnny asked.

"Where are you?" I asked.

"In the office, watching your indecision glide by."

"Punk," I said, but he'd already hung up.

I taxied my car into a slot in the neighboring strip plaza and walked back to the office. Johnny was parked at my desk, scrolling through his laptop with one hand and pillaging the Red Vine bucket with the other. I dumped my bag in the guest chair, circled the desk, and pinched the licorice strand out of his hand as he brought it to his mouth.

"I already licked that a little, fyi," Johnny said, reaching into the bucket for a fresh piece.

"Don't particularly care. Just need a little happy," I said, lowering myself into the guest chair.

"What's got you down, pumpkin? Tell Uncle Johnny."

"First of all, ewww." I gave him the rundown on my chat with Patty.

"Interesante," Johnny said.

"Muy. The affair was a long time ago, but who's to say Tracy hasn't just run off with another guy? Or, maybe Jerome caught her with some dude and didn't think a little slapping around was enough to send a message this time."

"You tell Roman?" Johnny asked.

"Mmm, left him a message."

"What was that?"

"What was what?" I asked.

"The smile."

"Come again?"

"You," Johnny said. "You smiled when I asked if you told Roman yet."

"So? I thought Uncle Johnny wanted his pumpkin to cheer up."

"Hunh." Johnny's eyes narrowed and my smile widened.

"So, what's next on your Nancy Drew to-do list?" Johnny went back to his laptop.

I dug into my bag for my own laptop. "YouTube. I need a few stripper videos."

Johnny's head popped back up. "If Paul's not paying you enough, I can lend you a couple bucks."

"It's not for cash, it's to lure our lovely Wanda out," I said.

"Smart. Prove she's a fraud by giving her a lap dance."

"Oh, Uncle Johnny, you're supportive *and* funny." I propped my laptop opposite his and clicked on the first video link I found. A woman in a leopard print leotard was straddling an oversized, stuffed leopard. When she reached off-camera and came back with a laser pointer and a rope, I closed the link.

"Holy shit." Johnny was leaning over me.

"I thought you were busy over there," I said.

"Never too busy to help a friend."

"I'm not giving you a lap dance."

"Role playing is a great training tool."

My phone buzzed in my pocket and I fished it out as I shooed Johnny back to his side of the desk.

"Feeling better today?" Roman asked.

"Mmm-hmmm," I said, smiling at Johnny. He glowered back at me.

"Sam, why do you sound like a 1-900 number?" Roman asked.

"Sorry, multi-tasking. I take it you got my message?" I asked.

"I did."

"Are you going to ask Jerome about the affair?" I asked.

"That, among other things. If we can find him."

"Don't tell me he pulled a Vanessa," I asked.

"It's sure looking like it. We decided to take one more run at him to see if we could use the info about his first wife to rattle his cage. When we showed up at his work, his boss told us Jerome came in yesterday morning and asked to take some vacation without any notice. The boss assumed Jerome needed to get his mind off Tracy and said yes."

"Where did he go?"

"Boss doesn't know. He didn't want to be nosy and Jerome had the time banked. We asked a couple of his co-workers, but no one knew he was planning to take off."

"Maybe he's just hiding out at home," I offered.

"We've had officers go there twice, but no answer so far. No house lights on during either patrol. Second time we were there, a neighbor told one of the officers that she'd seen Jerome getting into a cab day before yesterday, and hasn't seen him since. Doesn't mean he didn't come back home and hole up later, though. We're trying to get a warrant now to get into both the house and his work."

"How did you get the warrant? I thought there wasn't enough to go on?" I asked.

"We re-interviewed a few of Jerome's softball buddies and found out he pulled a disappearing act for a couple innings mid-game the night Tracy went missing. That should be enough to get the warrant on its own, but the info about Tracy's affair will help. Thanks for that."

"You're welcome," I said. "But why do you need a warrant for his office? Couldn't his boss just show you his desk or cube or whatever?"

"He's got a desk, a locker, and some kind of separate testing room he shares with a couple other researchers. The boss was nervous about letting us see the shared space so he told us to hold off on all of it. A lot of what they work on is proprietary and he wouldn't greenlight a search without their attorney's approval, and the attorney is stalling. We needed the warrant for the house anyway, so we just threw his office in while we were at it."

"How soon will you know if you'll get the warrant?" I asked.

"Hoping by end of the day or tomorrow morning at the latest."

"Can I come?"

"Not for this, Sam, I'm sorry. But I'll let you know what I can when I can."

"No worries. I've got a stripper thing in the morning any way."

"Do I want to know?"

"Probably not right now. I'll let you know what I can when I can."

"Touché," he said, and hung up.

Chapter Thirty-Three

I left Johnny alone to have some quality time with the strippers. I drove to my mom's house and found her in the kitchen, hacking a cantaloupe to death.

"Mom, gimme." I took the knife from her and tried to resuscitate the melon. She rooted around in the fridge, coming out with a tub of cottage cheese. She chose two bowls from the cabinet and started to scoop up the liquid goop. I took one of the bowls and put it back in the cupboard.

Mom frowned at me. "A half cup of this a day, Sam, and you could slip those extra ten pounds right off."

I looked down at my hips, then back at the lumpy mound of cheese and decided the adage about nothing tasting as good as skinny feels was a bunch of malarkey. A cheeseburger and fries got me closer to a cartwheel than occasionally spotting a hip bone. I dumped a handful of melon on top of Mom's cheese and she carried the bowl to the table.

"So, how do you want to do this?" I asked, perching on the chair across from her.

"Do what, sweetheart?" Mom unfolded her napkin and spread it across her lap.

"Are we going to talk about what happened the other night?"

"I think you should ask Paul. I tried, but he won't tell me why he was so upset."

"Mom, I'm not talking about Paul. I'm talking about Wally."

Mom chased her cottage cheese around with a wedge of melon, but didn't bring any to her lips.

"Mom."

"Samantha, I don't know what to tell you."

"How about we start with the basics? Where'd you guys meet?"

Mom spoke into her spoon. "At the market."

"When?"

"Not long ago."

"Okay," I said. I measured my breathing, hoping to relay an air of acceptance. It may have come off looking more like gas. "Is it serious between you two?"

"Of course not. We're just friends."

"Mom." I patted her non-spoon hand. "You brought this man home after ten at night. You can let go of the 'we're just friends' spiel."

"Samantha, a woman can have a gentleman friend without it being romantic."

Somewhere, Johnny was laughing his ass off.

"So, you're not dating him?"

"I told you, we're friends. Isn't that what you and the boys wanted? For me to pick up activities again?"

I tried to quell the visual of the "activities" Mom was engaged in.

"Well, yeah, we do. I'm just surprised you're keeping those activities a secret."

"I wasn't keeping Wally a secret," Mom snapped, scraping back her chair. She took her bowl of untouched cottage cheese to the sink and stood there, head bent over the porcelain. "Did you tell Paul and Vinnie?"

"No, but would you care if I did? Since it's not a secret?"

"Don't be a smart alec," Mom said, turning around to face me. "It's not a secret, but it's not your story to tell either."

I held my hands up in surrender. "I won't say anything, but you know at some point, you have to tell them."

Mom laced her arms around her torso and eyeballed her slipper-encased feet.

"Mom?" I asked.

Mom just squeezed her arms tighter and shook her head. I stood and eyed her until she turned around and ran water into her bowl.

I crossed the room and hugged her from behind. She nodded, but didn't turn around.

"Tell Wally I said hi," I said to her back.

***

I dropped Wanda's award certificate off with the front desk girl at the exercise studio. When I reminded her not to let on that I had nothing to do with the "prize" when we returned in the morning, she shot me a thumbs up and an attempt at a wink so mangled that it left my own eye watering in response. I looked heavenward and sent a prayer to whichever saint blesses good acting, and walked back out to my car.

I was still sitting in the parking lot, stewing about my mom and dreading my much delayed but inevitable first night at Gino's, when Tracy's mom returned my call. Carol said she had just come home from the market, but was free until early evening if I wanted to swing by. She'd picked up a coffee cake, if I was so inclined. I was.

When I arrived at Carol's house, her tears from my last visit were nowhere in sight. She was briskly unpacking the last of her groceries, a pot of coffee brewing on the countertop. She bounced between fridge and cupboards, arranging a tray of cups, forks, dessert plates, and napkins.

"How are you holding up?" I asked, taking the tray from her.

"I'm managing," Carol said lightly. She gestured at me to set the tray on the kitchen table and propelled me into a seat.

"Any word from the police?" I asked.

She pulled her mouth into a frown. "Not a one. I suspect they think she just drifted off."

Carol brought the coffee pot to the table and placed it on a hot-pad crocheted into the shape of a turkey. Its gaggle melted down into its breast plate, creating the illusion of a skin bib. If this is what retirement looked like, I needed to find a life passion. Fast.

I kept quiet while Carol cut us each a piece of cake and filled our cups. She seemed at ease, but entirely unmotivated to move the conversation along.

"Mrs. Simmons," I said.

"Carol." She corrected me as she dribbled cream into her coffee.

"Carol," I started again. "I talked to Patty today."

"Oh?" The creamer pitcher slipped in her hand.

"At the track."

Carol winced. "I wish she'd find someplace else to work. I don't understand how she can tolerate serving hoodlums and winos all day."

The racetrack wasn't exactly a 1930's brothel, but I chose not to point it out. I figured jumping in to defend Patty wouldn't win me any points and I had a feeling my odds of getting kicked out as soon as I asked about Tracy's affair were already even money.

"I take it that wasn't her first career choice?" I threw out as neutral a line as I could muster.

Carol emitted a sound somewhere between a snort and a hiccup.

"Patty's 'career choice' was to be an artist. She was smitten with the idea of improving the world through oil pastels."

"Did she pursue it?" I asked.

"Not on my dime. When she graduated high school, I gave her

the option to go to community college and live at home. I would foot the bill for everything. Otherwise, she was on her own."

"She turned you down."

"No. Worse. She accepted, smiled in my face, then signed up for a bunch of creative art courses. I found out and told her I wouldn't pay any more. She moved out, withdrew from all her classes, and got a waitressing job. She hasn't stuck with anything for longer than a couple years since."

"When we talked a few days ago, you mentioned that Tracy took a while to find work she liked, too," I said, choosing my next words carefully. "Did she, ah, struggle the same way Patty did?"

"Patty chose to struggle," Carol said with a ferocity that surprised me. "Tracy always had focus, she just took longer to find what she loved."

"Ironic, isn't it? Seems Patty found what she loved love early on," I said.

Carol turned cold eyes on me. "Love doesn't pay the bills, Samantha. Nor do husbands."

I nodded placatingly and changed course. "Patty said you mentioned that Tracy had a co-worker she didn't really get along with."

"That's right." Carol took a bite of cake, though out of hunger or avoidance, I couldn't tell.

"What did Tracy say was the problem?" I asked.

Carol shrugged and topped off her coffee cup. I palmed the top of my mug when she hovered the pot over it.

"I don't remember, really," Carol said. I can't imagine it was anything all that bothersome to Tracy. A meaningless tiff."

"Even though she told you about it?" I asked.

"Tracy tells me about a lot of things, Samantha. That's what mothers and daughters do. Not everything means something."

"I understand, but one of the agents in her office mentioned that Tracy and a woman named Maribeth seemed to have a noticeable falling out. Sounds to me like it was more than just a meaningless tiff if it led to them not talking to each other."

Carol's fork stopped mid-way to her mouth. "And what? You think this Maribeth has something to do with Tracy disappearing?"

I shrugged. "I don't know. I'm just trying to understand who may have had a problem with Tracy. Or a reason to hurt her."

"Over real estate?" Carol dismissed the idea with a flap of her hand. "It's not even good real estate."

My patience was wearing thinner than Karen Carpenter.

"Patty also told me that Tracy had an affair." I leaned back and put some distance between us. Not that I expected the woman to slap me, but I didn't want to encourage a motive.

No slap came. Nor any reaction at all. For a moment, I wondered if Carol had even heard me. Given we were sitting two feet apart with nothing but the still air to dim her hearing, I was sure she had, but all she did was carefully chew through another bite of cake.

"Carol, I—," I began.

"I heard you, Samantha."

She folded her napkin onto the table and laid her fork on top. She wet one fingertip and dipped it into the crumbs on her plate, running it around the rim, collecting the scraps like metal shavings to a magnet. I could tell the movement was meant to be casual, but the delicate china lifted off the placemat from the pressure.

I was torn between pressing her on the affair and showing her a better way to mix the sugar crumbs with the cake crumbs to get just the right flavor balance on the tongue. She saved me from a grueling choice.

"Things in life aren't always black and white, Sam," Carol said. I waited for her to go on, but she looked at me as if that should explain everything.

"In what way?" I pressed.

"In any way," she barked, then took a deep breath that appeared in no way to relax her. I felt my own chest tighten in response.

"Do you think the affair could be connected to Tracy's disappearance?" I asked.

"No, I do not."

"Do you know who she was cheating with? Could they have gotten together again?"

"She didn't *cheat*. It's not cheating when your husband has already quit you." Anger flashed in Carol's eyes and I wondered if we were still talking about Tracy.

"Did Tracy think Jerome quit her?" I asked.

"Tracy didn't say that outright, but I could see she must have felt that way. Jerome wasn't there for her the way a husband should be."

"How's that?"

Carol sat back in her chair and balled her fists in her lap. "Tracy wasn't perfect. A husband should accept his wife as she is and know that she can't be all things to him. Jerome wasn't willing to accept that. To accept her."

"What exactly didn't he want to accept?"

"Tracy wanted a life outside of her and Jerome. She wanted to have work and have friends. He wouldn't hear it. He wanted to wall her off, he didn't want other people in their lives."

"Isn't he in a softball league? Seems like a pretty social choice for a guy who wants to isolate himself," I said.

"That wasn't his choice. His company sponsors team. His involvement was mandatory."

"Carol, the man Tracy had the affair with. Do you know who he is?"

"No." I could smell the lie on her.

When we were kids, Vinnie broke my favorite glitter pen. You could have led a gay pride parade by the shine on his hands, but he denied it to the end. I still found him more credible than Carol.

"Do you know if he and Tracy were serious?" I asked.

Carol sliced the air with a flat palm. "No, I don't know who he is, but he's not in her life. If I thought he was, I would say."

"But if you don't know who he is, how can you know for sure? I know you must want to protect Tracy, but you could be making things worse by not talking about him."

"There is nothing to talk about. Patty is stirring a pot that she has no business stirring. As usual, she is just trying to make my Tracy look bad in order to make herself look better."

"Carol, I didn't get that feeling from her at all," I said.

"Then maybe you should find a different line of work, Samantha."

Chapter Thirty-Four

My chat with Carol left me exhausted, confused, and wishing I'd asked for a second piece of cake before I accused her daughter of being a trollop. I drove away without any destination in mind, and ended up cruising aimlessly through the Metroparks.

The leaves had escaped most of the trees and left gaping holes of sky between the branches. I glimpsed squirrels darting through the underbrush, foraging through the last of the winter stock-up sale. I was envious. I felt like that blind squirrel. If I could find just one nut.

I couldn't escape the nagging feeling that Maribeth knew more than she was saying. Even if she'd had a falling out with Tracy, they must have been decent friends at some point. It would explain why Maribeth knew so much about Tracy and why she was so complimentary of her relationships with her clients. But why hide the initial friendship even if they had a falling out?

An SUV came roaring up behind me, throwing the bird to the twenty-five mph speed limit. I eased to the shoulder to let it pass, then pulled off into the next observation point. I plugged my phone into the charger and dialed up Charlie. He answered on the fifth ring, out of breath.

"Hiya, Samantha. I was just talking about you," Charlie said.

His wheeze had petered out and he sounded like the twenty-something he likely was.

"Yeah, how so?" I asked.

"Gina Berlin, one of our part-time agents just came in a few minutes ago. I asked her if she knew anything about Tracy and Maribeth not getting along. To help you out, maybe, you know? She said you called her, but she hasn't had time to call back."

So much for my cryptically vague voicemail to throw off my scent. Jot that lesson down in my PI 101 handbook.

"Thanks, Charlie. What did she tell you?" I asked.

"She's still here. Why don't you get it from the horse's mouth, you know?" Charlie asked.

I heard a high muffled voice protesting in the background, then Charlie's voice in response. "No, that doesn't mean you look like a horse."

"Charlie?" I asked.

"Yeah, yeah. She's coming."

"Charlie, wait a sec. I wanted to ask you something."

"Sure, what's up?"

"Have you ever met Jerome Pentley?" I asked.

"Uh huh, once. Long time ago, maybe a few months after Tracy became an agent."

"At the office?"

"Nah. It was at a restaurant."

"Did he and Tracy seem to get along?" I asked.

"I guess so. He didn't talk much, but Tracy, Maribeth, and I were all talking about work so he kind of got drowned out, you know?"

"Hold up. The four of you went out together?"

"No, it was just them three. I was there on a date and ran into them," Charlie said.

"Do you know if Maribeth hung out with the Pentleys a lot?"

"I wouldn't say a lot, but sometimes when we were all in the office I'd hear them talk about where they went the night before, or making plans to go out. But like I said, that was a long time ago. Even when they were still chummy and going to lunch and stuff, I didn't hear 'em talking about going out at night anymore. Hey, Gina's waving at me that she has to go in a minute. You wanna talk to her or not?"

I said I did and waited through a lot of shuffling and mumbling in the background before the tiniest, highest voice I'd ever heard came on the line. I was talking to Mickie Mouse. Right after the castration.

"Hello?" Gina said.

"Hi, Gina. Thanks for stopping to talk for a minute."

"Okay, but I really do only have a minute."

"I promise I just have a few questions. Do you know that Tracy Pentley is missing?" I asked.

"Yes, Charlie told me the police were here."

"Did the police talk to you?"

"No," Gina stuttered. "No, they left me a message, same as you did. But I just haven't gotten around to calling back."

"Do you have any idea where Tracy might have gone or know anyone who'd want to hurt her?"

"No, how would I? I don't know. I thought..." Gina trailed off.

"Gina? You thought what?"

"I don't know what I thought. I hope she's okay." The squeak turned to a tremble.

"Gina, are you sure you don't know of anyone who'd want to hurt Tracy?"

"Positive."

"Was she fighting with anyone in the office?" I asked.

"Not that I ever saw. I'm not here a lot, though."

"How about in her personal life? Did she ever talk to you about problems she had outside of work?"

"No, never." The tremble ticked up a notch.

"It's okay, Gina. I'm sure we'll find her. If you think of anything, will you call me? Anything, big or small. You never know what might help," I said.

Gina hung up and I went back to studying the squirrels. I watched as one scampered partway up a tree trunk, only to be knocked back by a bigger squirrel sitting higher up on the trunk. The smaller squirrel righted himself and wandered off a few feet, then turned around. He sniffed the ground, ran back to the tree, caught his paw over a root and clonked his head into the trunk. He fell back, momentarily stunned.

Story of my life, bud.

While I waited to make sure the squirrel hadn't suffered a life-ending concussion, I juiced through what I'd learned. By the time the squirrel was taking a spritely run up a new tree, I hadn't been hit with any brilliant revelations.

I decided I'd put off my first night at Gino's long enough. I was a grown woman, for the love of Pete. Besides, maybe a good strip session with the kitchen wallpaper was just what the doctor ordered to clear my mind from the Pentley case for a bit. What is it they say about pieces falling into place when you're not thinking about the problem?

Throwing the car in reverse, I backed out of my spot and started making a mental list of tools I'd need from the Home Depot. I congratulated myself on my intestinal fortitude, popped the gear into drive, then promptly threw it back into park. I snatched up my phone.

"Ange?" I said when she answered. "How about I bring you and the boys some take-out tonight?"

Chapter Thirty-Five

"If I were a guy, I'd pay you *not* to sit on my lap," Angie said.

I stood in Angie's bedroom doorway, taking in her Angie Does Attica get-up. Ripped fishnets, black leather boy shorts, silver tank top, and stiletto boots. Her hair was kinked, teased, and sprayed into a gravity-defying nest. She was Debby Harry the morning after.

"Did you get that outfit from Urban Stripper Outfitters or Abercrombie and Whores?" Angie asked.

I looked down at my navy blue yoga tights, matching tank, and Pumas.

"It's an exercise class, for God's sake," I said. "We're not auditioning for the Crazy Horse."

"You're like a real PI now, Sam. You have to get into the spirit of the disguise," Angie cooed, grasping my hand and drawing me into her room. "Come, my child. Come see Angie's costume closet."

"Why do I have a feeling I'm about to learn a lot more about how you and Tony got those twelve kids of yours?" I said.

"Three. I have three."

"Anything over two is twelve to me."

We stepped into the closet. Angie's house was the size of a

thumb tack, but she'd convinced Tony to move an interior wall in their bedroom to shoe-horn in a walk-in closet. Angie had an outfit for any and every imaginable occasion, and for most unimaginable ones as well. Going to a donkey themed retirement party? Angie will open her closet door and ask you what color the donkey should be.

She rifled through two drawers and came up with what looked like a pair of socks and a scarf.

"Here," she said, shoving them into my hands. "Go put those on."

I was shaking my head before she finished the sentence. "Nuh-uh. No way, no how."

"Coward."

"Ange, I'll get arrested."

"You should be so lucky, maybe you'd meet a hot cop."

"I already met one. No arrest necessary," I said, pushing the clothing scraps back at her.

"Who?! When? And why am I just now hearing about him?"

I shushed her with my hand. "Calm down. His name is Roman and it's been all of three days since he even hinted at asking me out. And if you recall, I've been kind of busy getting hit by cars and hunting down a missing woman."

"Roman? Isn't that Johnny's cop friend?"

"Yeah." I unfolded the scarf, which turned out to be a tube top, and held it against my chest. With a stick of butter and a shoe horn, it might almost cover one boob.

"What does Johnny think of you going out with his friend?" Angie asked. She plucked the tube top out of my hands and went back to rummaging in her drawers.

"He doesn't know, but I doubt he'd care. I don't think they're like friend-friends," I said.

Angie turned around to face me. "Sweetie, you're a smart cookie. Don't act dumb."

"First I'm too conservative a whore. Now I'm a dumb

whore?"

"I just can't believe you don't think Johnny would have a problem with this. I know your thing with him was a long time ago, but it still happened, Sam. Nothing's resolved just because you've decided to ignore it. That boy has feelings for you."

"Maybe, but they're all beneath the button-fly feelings. Those don't count."

Angie shook her head. "Idiot."

"Can you save your accolades for my intelligence until after we get done on the pole?"

"On one condition."

"What?" I asked.

Angie held her clothes-filled hands out to me.

***

"Lift your butt higher."

I've imagined those words whispered in my ear in a dozen different scenarios, but this was not one of them. I shot the "dance" instructor an if-you-say-so look and shifted my weight forward. As I did, I felt more air on my hiney than I guessed was pleasant for my neighbors. I shimmied my left ankle higher on the pole to get more traction, and succeeded in tumbling straight to the floor.

"I think I see Dallas. Or is that Houston?" Angie asked from behind me. I flipped her the bird over my shoulder and heaved myself onto all fours to get the weight off my not quite healed tush. Somewhere the doctor who stitched me up was twitching.

I noodled my body around to face Angie and found her five feet off the floor. She sat in an I Dream of Genie pose, pole locked between her thighs, calm as a barbiturate.

"Seriously?" I asked.

Angie smiled serenely before kicking one leg straight out, flipping upside down, and slowly winding her way back down the pole. We were a wind-machine away from a Whitesnake video.

"If you weren't my best friend, I'd write some seriously nasty stuff about you in the bathroom stall." I said.

Angie popped back up and stood next to the pole, watching the instructor demonstrate the next move in her strip show sequence.

"You're just pissy 'cause Miss Wanda is a no-show."

Angie was right. I was out in broad daylight rubbing my klutzoid self against a metal pole, my bruised body stuffed into a sequined tank top and hot pants tight enough to make the children of the corn blink. I'd sacrificed my time, dignity, and possibly my fertility to catch a woman who hadn't even show up, let alone tripped her light fantastic in front of my waiting camera. Pissy didn't begin to cover it.

I waved my imaginary white flag at Angie and crawled to the wall where we'd rested our coats and bags. I rolled up my coat and wedged it under my butt, pitching forward to keep the weight off my right side. The angle pushed my boobs up over the lip of my tank top and I tried to mush them down with my palm, but they gushed right back out when I let go. I gave up when I felt my coat vibrating beneath me and dug out my phone. It was Johnny.

"Hey," I whispered, twisting my torso away from the class.

"Why are you whispering?" Johnny whispered.

"I'm in an exercise class. Why are you whispering?"

"I don't know," Johnny said.

"Then talk in a normal voice. I can't hear you," I whispered.

I peeked over my shoulder to find the dance instructor frowning at me. She pointed a French-tipped finger at the No Cell Phones sign on the wall.

"Can I call you back?" I asked.

"Actually, can you meet me at the office? I got a couple other calls I have to make, but I want to give you a quick update on Jerome. They got the warrant."

"Yes!" I felt a sharp poke on my shoulder, twisted around, and came face to face with a belly button ring in the shape of a smiley face. I looked up into the not as smiley face of the dance instructor.

"You. Out," she said. She pointed over her shoulder. "And take that one with you."

I peered around her and caught sight of Angie. She was bent at the waist, grasping the pole in both hands, and licking the air two inches in front it. Half the class was watching her in a mixture of awe and repulsion, while the other half stood hands-on-hips waiting for the class to start up again. A lone girl in the back pantomimed Angie's moves. She looked like a giraffe caught in a fence. Angie caught site of her, bounded over, and started showing the girl how to push her hips back for a better arch.

I gave the instructor a whaddaya gonna do smile and hung up with Johnny. I threw the high sign to Angie, who slinked over beaming. I shoved her coat into her hands, and hustled her out to the car.

"That was amazing," Angie said, as we buckled ourselves in. "I have to find out if they have monthly packages."

"Ange."

"Oh! Or, I wonder if they'd let me teach!"

"They'd have to charge people by the minute."

"Don't be such a prude, it wasn't that bad."

"Ange, it was like a halftime show at a gynecological convention."

"Where are you going?" Angie asked as I passed the freeway entrance that would take us to her house.

"I need to make a pit stop at the office. Johnny's got some scoop for me."

"About Tracy?"

"Yep. They got a search warrant for her house and Jerome's office."

"Did they find anything yet?" Angie asked as her cell rang. She answered and spent the next two minutes asking how much puke and what color was the phlegm. I made a U-turn and headed back toward the freeway even before she hung up.

"Curly, Larry, or Moe?" I asked when she ended the call.

"Moe," she said, referring to her youngest. "My mom's watching him for me. She said she's down for a little vomit, but not when it comes out on an arc. Sorry."

"No worries, Johnny will wait."

"Somehow I don't think he'll notice your tardiness once he gets a load of that outfit."

"Crap," I said, looking down at my boobs. I tried pushing them sideways in my bra, coercing them toward my armpits.

"Sam, that's a losing battle," Angie said.

"It's not that bad, is it?"

"I can see them and I'm looking out the window."

Chapter Thirty-Six

I dropped Angie off at the puke palace and wound my way through side streets to get to the office. I was close enough to Gino's house that I thought briefly about stopping to change, but didn't want to press my luck in case Johnny was itching to hit the road. My coat buttoned to the neck. That would have to be good enough.

Paul's car was parked next to Johnny's when I got to the office. I picked my way in Angie's heels up the front steps and clattered through the door. Paul was sitting on the front of his desk. Johnny relaxed in my chair, his back pressed to the wall and boots braced on the edge of the desk. Their conversation came to an abrupt halt as they both washed stunned eyeballs over me. I'd buttoned my coat all the way, but from mid-thigh down, I was naked leg and six-inch silver sparkle heel.

"I don't want to know," Paul said. He pushed off his desk and moved behind it.

"I—," Johnny began.

"And I don't want you to ask," Paul said, stiff-arming Johnny. He shut down his laptop and started stuffing things into his backpack. Johnny's attention wandered to my top button and stayed there.

I realized that sitting down would present a whole new set of challenges, so I jammed my hands in my pockets in hopes of adding an inch to my hem line and stood where I was.

"So, what's the story?" I asked.

"Story?" Johnny asked, eyes clicking down to my second button.

"Jerome? Warrant?" I asked. I looked over at Paul, who had zipped his bag and was walking toward me.

Paul stopped when his shoulder met mine. "Wanda?"

"I've almost got her," I said. "I had a plan this morning, but she didn't take the bait."

"Well, hook a new worm and get this thing wrapped up." Paul pushed past me without waiting for a response and strolled out the door.

"Aye, aye," I said under my breath.

"I take it you two haven't talked things out?" Johnny asked. He was finally looking me in the eyes. His pupils had retracted to a genuine level of concern.

"How am I supposed to? I don't even know what the 'things' are that we need to talk about and he won't stand in one place long enough for me to ask."

I clacked over to Paul's desk and commandeered his chair. I scooted in until my thighs disappeared underneath the wood surface of the desk and looked up in time to see Johnny squash a look of disappointment.

"Want me to talk to him?" Johnny asked.

"Nah, that would only make things worse. I'll figure it out."

"Offer's open," Johnny said. I smiled my thanks.

"Has he said anything to you?" I asked. "I don't want to put you in a bad spot, but he talks to you. Can I at least get a hint?"

Johnny pushed his chair off the wall. "Wish I had one for you. We talk about the cases that I'm helping him with and we trade ideas on the stuff I'm working on at the other agency, but that's about it."

"Nothing about me?" I asked.

"Not much. And it's always about how you're doing with your cases or what you and I are working on. Not anything personal."

I searched Johnny's face and couldn't find a lie. He popped the top of the Red Vine bucket and tossed a strand to me.

"Thanks," I said, catching it mid-air and surprising us both. "So tell me the news about the warrant. When do they start the search?"

"They already did. Roman said two units started on the house, car, and office at the same time. The house and car are done, but they're still working on the office."

"Wait, what car?" I asked.

"Jerome's."

"But it wasn't there the other day. And I thought his neighbor said he hopped in a cab?"

"Maybe he loaned it out. Or he came home with it and left again. Either way, he's still MIA."

"Huh," I said. "So what'd they find?"

"Bupkis."

"Really?"

I was surprised and couldn't figure out why. My belly had been telling me that Tracy's mysterious fight with one of her co-workers somehow tied into all this, and Maribeth's weirdness didn't ease that feeling any, but Jerome Pentley had felt wrong to me since the day he walked into Paul's office. To be fair, my gut wasn't always the most accurate barometer ever.

"Disappointed?" Johnny asked.

"Yeah, a little. Maybe I'm jaded because this thing with Jerome's first wife smells bad, but that guy is wound tighter than a two dollar watch."

Johnny cocked his head at me. "Two dollar watch?"

"Trust me, if you'd talked to him, you would have felt it," I said.

Johnny shook his head. "I'm amazed at your ability to eat like a twelve-year-old, dress like a twenty-five-year-old, and use the analogies of an eighty-year-old."

"Stick around," I said, chewing the last of my Vine. "I'm a fun ride."

My cell buzzed in my coat pocket before Johnny could respond and I fished it out. It was a text from Charlie saying he'd looked up Maribeth's rental properties and found that two of them had sold in the last few days. I pounded out his number.

"I thought that might pique your interest," Charlie said when he picked up.

"Charlie, look. I love that you want to help me out, but you have to put down the Blues Clues notebook, man."

"What? Hey, don't worry about me being above-board, if that's what has your goose in a noose. I'm only looking at stuff that's already available to me."

"Let's just leave this to the professionals, okay?" I asked.

"I hope you're referring to the police. Aren't you Annie Amateur at this investigating stuff?"

I pulled the phone away from my ear and wondered if I could reach far enough into it to wipe the smile out of his voice.

"Why do you say that?" I asked.

"It's called the power of Google," Charlie said. "I looked you up. You ain't been in town that long and, if I'm interpreting whitepages.com correctly, I'd say you're living with... your mom?"

"Let's stay focused here, Charlie. Lay off Maribeth and Gina and anybody else, okay? Last thing we need is to muck things up for the police or spread rumors."

"Oh-kay," Charlie sang. "But don't you even want to know one teeny little thing I noticed after I texted you?"

I counted to five, and looked both ways, but my better judgment failed to appear. "Fine," I said. "What?"

"Both of those rental houses sold for way under asking price."

"So? The market hasn't been smoking hot lately," I said.

"It's not just that. I took a look at the sale history on those properties. They're worth more than what Maribeth even listed them at, let alone what she accepted for them."

Johnny stood up, gave me the fork to mouth sign, and hooked his thumb at the door. I gave a thumbs up in return and watched with admiration as he walked out. Hey, you can take the girl out of the crush.

"You think she was trying for a quick sale?" I tried to re-focus on what Charlie was saying.

"I don't know," Charlie said. "I mean, she really rock-bottomed these joints. I don't know how much she put down at point of purchase, but she hasn't had either property for that long. I'd say odds are high she lost money in the deal."

"I thought you said she was pretty savvy with her investments?" I asked.

"She is. Or, at least she was. Maybe with her sales going down, whatever she's been making on the rentals hasn't been enough. You never know, though, right? Maybe she got a little taste for the ponies and found herself behind. Or, hey! I hear coke is back in."

"Alright, alright," I said. "Don't get crazy here. And back up a sec. Did Maribeth tell you that her sales have been down?"

"Not exactly, but since you and me first talked, I took a look at our records and Maribeth's sales have really tanked. Before Tracy joined on, Maribeth was kind of the cat's meow in this neck of the woods, you know?"

Not exactly how Maribeth had painted it to me.

"Do you think that's why those two stopped talking?" I asked.

"I'd be surprised if it was. It looks like Maribeth's sales had been sliding for months and I never heard her complain about how much Tracy was selling."

"Then let's assume it wasn't a problem. For all we know, Maribeth made a killing on these places, or she just wants to get out of the landlord business and doesn't mind losing a few sheckles to do it. Don't say anything to anyone about any of this right now, alright?"

Charlie's tone turned petulant. "I'm not stupid. But you just say the word and I might be able to accidentally pop the lock on the personnel files here, you know?"

"No!"

I hung up with Charlie only after he promised on a Boy Scout salute to put away his Hardy Boy badge. Johnny returned a few minutes later with two brown bags, one splattered happily in grease.

"For the twelve-year-old you," he said, dipping a hand into one of the bags and coming back out with a paper wrapped sandwich. I fingered back one corner and found a grilled triple cheese.

I tore off a piece of crust enrobed in cheddar and looked up at Johnny. "I might be in love."

"Again?"

I flung the crust at him.

"Too soon?"

Chapter Thirty-Seven

I'd plowed through most of my sandwich and was mid-prayer to whichever saint watched over elastic waistbands when Roman called Johnny with the news.

The search team hit the jackpot in Jerome's office. His desk proffered nothing more questionable than a Costco-sized bottle of vegetable oil, but in a mini-storage locker that acted as the base of Jerome's workspace in the research room, they found a red silk skirt and blouse matching the outfit Johnny and I had seen on the blonde woman the day Tracy disappeared. Stowed underneath the kick plate on the workspace table was a matching pair of size eight suede shoes. Upon close inspection, the skirt and top revealed a high-end label, but the shoes were a generic brand that was mass-produced for a dozen discount retailers across the country.

"Roman said their working theory is that Vanessa is our mystery blonde in the Mercedes and wherever she's run off to, they'll likely find Jerome. They should have warrant in hand for Vanessa's apartment within the hour."

"I'm guessing a blonde wig is high on the search list?" I asked.

Johnny shrugged a maybe. "Unless she dyed her hair. Length is about right, though. Why are you laughing?"

"You can't just dye dark brown hair to blonde and back again. Especially not in the span of one day. She was a brunette when I saw her at bingo. She had to be wearing a wig at Tracy's."

"Here I thought I was teaching you all the ways of the investigative world, and you trump me with the mere knowledge of women's hair."

"If you were a woman, you wouldn't have used the word 'mere'," I said. "And your supremely snide remark aside, what I don't get is why would Jerome keep the clothes and not the wig?"

"Assuming there is a wig in the first place. Or, maybe Jerome is playing the insurance game."

"How so?" I asked. I was starting to roast in my heavy coat. I snuck a finger inside my collar and pulled it out a fraction of an inch. The air on my neck felt delicious.

"Let's say Jerome and Vanessa wanted to play diddle-diddle for keeps and decided to remove Tracy from the picture," Johnny replied. "I think we can safely say Vanessa is way more into him than he is into her, or at least she's more demonstrative about it."

"Mmm, 'demonstrative'. I like it when you get collegiate on me," I said.

"And how about my diction?"

"Moving on," I said.

"Maybe Jerome's keeping the duds as a get out of jail card in case he breaks up with Vanessa or she gets nervous and threatens to go to the police. Her DNA's all over those clothes. He doesn't need both, so he tosses the wig."

"But how does that help him?" I asked. "The police found the clothes in *his* office. Hard for him to argue against collusion when he's got the clothes." I was now actively sweating at my hairline, but didn't dare open my coat.

"Yeah, but I'd bet Jerome didn't think he'd get caught. Based on how you described your first meeting with him, he sounds like a guy who's used to being in control."

"How long do you think it'll take to look through Vanessa's

195

place?" I asked.

"Depends on the warrant. But I'd say it'll happen fast, now that it looks more like Tracy was probably taken involuntarily."

"Any chance we can get into the Pentleys' house?"

"Doubt it. Why?"

The personal hot box I'd created under my coat was making it hard to think. "I don't know. Maybe it'll give us a clue as to where Jerome took her."

"What, you think he left a post-it behind? Stuck to a MapQuest print-out with directions to the ditch he dumped her in?" Johnny asked.

"No, I was thinking it might be stuck to a wig, smart ass."

"Let the wig go, Samantha. We need to focus on finding Jerome and Vanessa."

I leaned forward and back again, trying to kick up a breeze. "So, let's assume Jerome doesn't know the police know about Vanessa, in which case he probably thinks his vacation story is solid."

"Yeah?" Johnny asked.

"In his mind, he thinks he's got at least a head start."

"Which means he could be anywhere by this point," Johnny said. "Hopefully something helpful will turn up at Vanessa's place, but in the meantime, let's work the wonderful world wide web. I'll finish the property trace Paul started on Jerome, see if he's got any secret hidey holes they could be hibernating in. Did Paul's search turn up any family members out of state?"

I held up a hand. "Unless the reason he didn't take his car is because they took Vanessa's. Even in the dark, that thing looked like it was held together by rust and hope. If that's what they're driving, they couldn't get past the county line, let alone the state line."

Johnny grinned.

"What?" I asked.

"The grasshopper has watched and she has learned." Johnny

leaned back and rubbed a hand across his hard belly. "It's rewarding for the master to see."

"The grasshopper's going to punch the master with her tiny but powerful grasshopper fist if the master calls himself 'master' ever again. Can we please focus?" I swiped my hand up my forehead to chase the sweat off my face and into my hair.

"I think I've been demonstrating an insane amount of focus given what you're wearing."

"I'm wearing a wool coat up to my chin. How is that in any way distracting?" I asked.

"I can still see you from the ankles down."

"Of course. The stripper heels."

"It's not the heels, it's the woman in them." Johnny's smile was playful, but his eyes held an intensity that made my mouth go dry.

The trickle of sweat swimming down my spine ticked up to a small current.

"Samantha."

"Hmm?"

"Are you planning to avoid this conversation forever?" Johnny asked.

"I thought we cleared things up and were moving on."

"Exactly. It's the moving on part that we need to define."

"Can I get a rain check on that?" I asked.

"You've got five hours."

"Or what, I turn into a pumpkin?"

"Dinner. Your house. I'll cook."

"I haven't really had time to spruce up the place yet," I stalled. "Why don't you come over in a week or two, after things have died down here a bit?"

"Six o'clock."

"Okay. Six o'clock on two Tuesdays from now." I said. I began a thorough examination of the wood grain in front of me.

"Tonight, Sam."

My phone vibrated on the desk and I caught sight of Johnny's shaking head as I answered it.

"I don't care who it is," Johnny said. "No excuses. We're on for six o'clock." He stood and yanked his keys from his pocket, then strode toward the front door.

Vinnie's voice came careening at me through the phone when I answered.

"Hey, hey, hey." I said, cutting off his high-pitched ramble. "Bring it down, Lassie. What's going on?"

"You have to get over to Mom's right now," he said.

My stomach cramped. "Why? Is she okay?"

"Get over here!"

"Vinnie, what happened?"

"Sam, hangupandgetinyourgoddamncar!"

I slammed my chair backward into the wall and raced for the door, stumbling in the stupid heels. I kicked them off on the front lawn and stuffed myself into my car, ripping open the top three buttons of my coat with one hand as I stabbed my key into the ignition with the other.

I navigated the eight miles of side streets in seven minutes and called Vinnie back as many times, but got no response. When I skidded to a stop at the curb in front of Mom's house, everything was quiet. No sirens, no ambulance, and no Vinnie. I grappled with my seat belt and rolled out of the car at a dead run for the front door.

"Sam!" I heard my name shouted from behind. I pivoted halfway up the driveway and saw Vinnie parked across the street, several houses down, facing the wrong way. I looked back toward my mom's house and thought I saw movement behind the window curtain.

Taking off at a trot toward Vinnie's car, I became painfully aware of my bare feet on the near-frozen pavement.

"Get in," Vinnie hissed at me through the open passenger side window. He unlatched the door and pushed it out for me. I fell in and immediately turned his heater over to the a/c mode.

"What is it?" I ran my eyes the length of him. "Is Mom okay?"

Vinnie jabbed a finger at Mom's house. "Do you know what's going on in there?"

"Tell me."

Vinnie's head set off in a series of yanks and jerks. I put my hand on the back of his neck to stave off the worst of his self-induced whiplash.

"Vin, what is it?" When he still didn't respond, I reached for the door handle to go see for myself. Vinnie's hand shot out and gripped my elbow. I looked back at the house and it hit me. In the driveway, sitting behind Mom's car, was a tan Oldsmobile. Similar to the car I saw the night I ran from the house in my pajamas, racing for the refuge of Angie's house. I had a feeling that Vinnie had just discovered Mom had been visiting Wally World. Shit.

I turned back to Vinnie and put my hand on his. "Okay, Vin, listen to me."

"Sam, this can't happen." Vinnie's eyes had dilated to the size of salad plates.

"I know it seems like it right now," I said in what I hoped was a soothing voice. "But you have to remember that Mom needs to do what's best for her." Or whom, in this case.

"How can you say that? She's being a traitor to Dad."

"That's not fair, Vinnie, you know she loved Dad. But do you expect her to be alone forever?"

"What about you, me, and Paul?"

"We need to support her, Vin. No matter how we feel about it."

"But why wouldn't she tell us?"

"Maybe because she's afraid of this reaction, right here." I gestured at his face.

"I'm only reacting like this because she didn't tell us! We should be a part of this."

"I don't know, Vin. Maybe she needed to feel things out first, you know? See if she even liked the idea or not."

"Well, we should have been there with her."

"Um, not sure how that would have worked. I mean I was there for a tiny fraction of it, and I can promise you I did not want to see more."

Vinnie turned bulging eyes on me. "What do you mean, you were there? And you didn't call me to come over?"

"Seriously? Would you have called me? What would you have done, climbed into bed with them?"

"Not on my own. I would have asked you and Paul to be a part of it."

"Wait," I said. "What?"

Vinnie slid glazed eyes toward the house and I followed his gaze. Mom was standing in the doorway, waving to a chunky young woman dressed in an ill-fitting pants suit. The woman trotted down the driveway to her trunk, popped the lid, and pulled out a small, metal-framed sign. She fought with the contents of her trunk a bit more, then closed the lid and walked to the end of the driveway. She stood the sign on its end in the tree lawn and hammered it into the cold ground. After a moment, she stood back and appraised her work.

"Oh my god," I said.

"Still think we have to support her?"

The woman started back up the driveway, giving me a clear shot of the For Sale sign freshly staked in the ground.

Chapter Thirty-Eight

My mind was reeling and it was all I could do to talk Vinnie off the ledge. Two hours later, I had at least convinced him that it would be better to approach Mom when we were all together. For lack of a better plan, we decided to talk to her at Sunday Dinner. I called Paul, but he didn't answer. It was starting to piss me off. He could hate me all he wanted, but this was about the family. Enough was enough.

I called Vinnie's friend Bruce to come get him, with instructions to escort Vinnie immediately to a bar and babysit him through the night. Then I called our cousin Tina to see if she would work the closing shift at Dazio's. Tina said she'd heard Johnny was back in town and wanted me to set her up on a date with him in exchange for the favor. I told her I'd love too, but suggested we wait and see if the antibiotics worked first. She said she'd settle instead for a couple large pizzas to take home and I told her to throw some cheesecake into her bag while she was at it.

Bruce rolled up and I silently thanked him for being discreet enough not to mention my outfit, though he did something of a triple take when I climbed out of the car with my hands pressing my coat down between my legs.

We coaxed Vinnie into Bruce's car, I pushed three twenties

into his reluctant hands, and they sped off to the Island Grille. I waded through the detritus in my trunk and came up with an old pair of hot pink Converse. Holes were eating through the seams on each foot, but they would serve in a pinch if my car broke down. In Northeast Ohio, Murphy's Law dictated a flat tire would only happen in the winter, while you were wearing heels, and you were a half dozen miles from any kind of help.

Feet covered and arches grateful, I motored over to Ridge Rd and joined the drive-thru line at Dairy Queen. It was close to six o'clock. I rationalized the stop by telling myself I wasn't ruining my dinner. I was just replacing it. The perky girl at the window handed me my order and I pulled over and parked. I left the top on my ice cream long enough to leave a voicemail for Johnny, telling him not to come for dinner after all. I said there'd been a family crisis, nothing to worry about, but I didn't have the energy for a serious conversation. I promise-promised to call him tomorrow and hung up, then melted my frustration into my Peanut Buster Parfait.

As I sucked the vanilla ice cream and fudge syrup off each peanut one at a time, I dictated a state of the union to myself. I didn't know what was happening with Paul and me, or with Mom and absolutely anything, but I knew we needed to get our collective shit together. Paul's no-show act was no longer feeling like just a punishment to me, but a complete abandonment of Vinnie and Mom. I had to track him down. As soon as I tracked down Jerome, Vanessa, and Tracy. Oh, and fraud-loving Wanda. Geezuss, when had things turned into a life-size version of Where's Waldo? The only person I wasn't trying to find was Johnny. What a difference a dozen years makes.

I licked the last streak of fudge from the side of the plastic cup and put the lid on my pity party. I had to prioritize, and fast. Unfortunately, my mind was more committed than my body. Over the course of one day, I'd molested a metal pole, flashed a dozen people, kept my brother from committing either suicide or homicide, dodged both my past and future relationship issues, and failed yet again in my attempt to emulate Jessica Fletcher. In a word, this little kitty was beat.

It dawned on me as I pulled out of the Dairy Queen lot that I was finally coming face-to-face with my first night in Gino's house. I'd delayed it for so many days, it had become anticlimactic. That, or my exhaustion was so complete, the shine had simply worn off the rotting apple. I made a pit-stop at the Speedway gas station and stocked up on peanut butter crackers, coffee, and milk to get me through breakfast the next morning. The bright side of grocery shopping at Speedway is you don't get many second glances, regardless of what you're wearing. I was easily second best-dressed there, beaten out only by a woman in a sharply tailored white tuxedo covered with a light-up Cat in the Hat bib.

By the time I bumped over the ruts threatening to eat up Gino's concrete driveway, all I wanted was a shower, clothing that didn't bind as one with my skin, and a long, soft fall into any bed that would have me.

I hauled myself out of my car and tripped over the brick edging that lined the side of the house leading to the kitchen door. I cursed and made a mental note to replace the bulbs in the fixture hanging over the exterior door, then fished my keys from the bottom of my bag. Even back in flat shoes, I stumbled through the doorway, unfamiliar with the house in daylight, let alone in the complete dark. I skimmed my hand along the wall underneath the cabinets and made purchase with a switch.

"Let there be light," I mumbled. I flipped the switch and realized Gino wasn't packing more than forty watts. Add that to the home improvement list, I thought wearily.

I peeled off my coat and launched it vaguely in the direction of a kitchen chair. I lugged my gas station groceries up onto the counter, then passed through the dining room to the living room, picking my way in the dark as I headed for the stairs. I was already dreaming of the hot pulse of water that would soon shower down upon me when I tripped hard and hit the floor. I started to push up to my knees and felt something wrap around my chest and arms. The realization that I hadn't tripped on my own finally cut through my fatigue and thoughts of Paul's self-defense tips crashed against each other in my head. I tried to lift the restraint, but my attacker pulled it tight and my arms were locked to my sides. I kicked backward and clumsily connected my heel to a leg. I opened my mouth to scream, only to be smacked awkwardly in the side of the head. Stunned more than hurt, I registered the scent of perfume mixed with anxious sweat that wafted off the wrist that nicked me.

No need to hunt down Vanessa, I thought. I was pretty sure the hunter had just become the hunted.

I whipped my head backward, expecting to connect with the top of Vanessa's, but instead hit a chest. And part of a boob. Unless Vanessa had gone through a seriously delayed growth spurt in the last few days, I was dealing with something else altogether.

I was too close to the wall supporting the staircase to flip my attacker the way Paul had shown me. I reared my upper body backward, then flung it forward and buckled my knees, tucking my head. I felt weight on my back and heard a head connect with the wall. My attacker expelled a little whoosh of air. The force of the blow wasn't disabling, but she lost her balance. I lunged to the left to break her hold, but she took me with her as she fell to the floor, and I landed backward on top of her.

The restraint loosened in the fall, and I wrangled one arm out. The intruder garbled a couple words that I couldn't make out, but I wasn't in a chatty enough mood to stop to ask for clarification. I reached up and backward, grabbing at her face, hoping to jam my fingers into her eyes. I missed and came up with a handful of thick hair. I yanked as hard as I could, earning a grunt, before she flipped to her right and sent me tumbling off her.

"Wait," she panted from behind me.

Wait, my ass, I thought. I threw a fist backward and connected with either a cheek or forehead, sending the woman reeling back into the floor. It netted me another grunt, and I rolled into the dining room, trying to find the space and strength to get to my feet.

I managed to climb onto one knee before I felt hot breath on my ankle and a hand grab my hip. I shoved my adrenaline-filled, free leg backward, felt the woman's hold slip, and heard a sprinkle of sequins hitting the floor. I silently thanked Angie for dressing me like Tina Turner and shoved my leg back again. The contact was jarring and the woman fell silent. I risked a look backward as I crawled away. The kitchen light leaked through the room. I could finally see that it wasn't Vanessa's now still form attached to that handful of hair. It was Maribeth Collins'.

Chapter Thirty-Nine

A thousand fragmented thoughts thrashed around in my head. Maribeth and Jerome. Maribeth befriends Tracy, hooks up with Jerome, and then the women's friendship dies. Tracy disappears and now Maribeth is selling off her property. Jerome's already fled and Maribeth stays behind to play clean-up and close the shop. No wonder there was no wig to hide. Maribeth had the God-given goods.

I wondered fleetingly if Tracy realized what was happening between her husband and her friend. Or did she simply suspect it was a flirtation, and confront Jerome about it? Why wouldn't Tracy just leave Jerome, is what I couldn't understand, but maybe she thought the affair had stopped. Or maybe she saw the flirting and that's what broke up the friendship, but she didn't know Jerome and Maribeth had taken things further.

The one thing I did know for sure was that Maribeth was coming around on my living room floor. I willed my exhausted body back toward her and picked up the restraint that had come loose during the tussle and now lay strewn on the floor. In the light, I recognized it as the yoga strap Angie had lent to me. Maribeth must have pulled it from one of the moving boxes that still lined the living room wall.

Maribeth lay partly on her side, one arm tangled beneath her. I put my knee into her back while I dragged her other arm out. I tied her wrists, then her feet. It wasn't so much a hog tie as an interesting twister pose, but I just needed time to get to my phone to call for help. I pushed back to my feet and limped into the kitchen.

"Samantha, stop."

I grappled with my coat pockets, trying to feel for my phone.

"Please. I need your help." Maribeth's breath was ragged, her voice pleading from the other room.

I looked over at her as I finally freed my phone.

"Are you kidding me?" I asked. "You just attacked me."

"I wasn't trying to hurt you."

"You were trying to give me a nice massage?"

"Please, I need to talk to you."

"Why the hell didn't you just call me?" I asked.

"I didn't think you'd listen. I needed to see you face-to-face so you'd believe me."

"Believe what?" I had my finger on my phone, but the fear in Maribeth's eyes gave me pause.

Maribeth started to cry, a soundless wet affair. "Tracy's missing."

"No shit, Maribeth. Where did you and Jerome take her?"

"No. I—" she said, swallowing hard. "Jerome didn't take her. At least, not the first time."

"The first time?" Johnny's voice came from behind me. I wheeled around and found him standing in the side door, a bag of groceries in one hand and a bottle of wine in the other. He looked from me to Maribeth, taking in the bright purple yoga strap wrapped around Maribeth's limbs, her face mashed sideways into the floor, and the trail of snot that was now sliding down her cheek to mix with her tears. It was the urban sequel to *Blair Witch*, filming live in Uncle Gino's living room. Johnny stepped further into the kitchen and closed the door behind him.

"Ladies?" Johnny put the groceries on the table, flicked another quick glance at Maribeth's bound position on the floor, then turned me toward him.

"She was waiting in here for me."

He nodded as he rubbed his hands up and down my shaking arms, then framed my face in his palms. I blinked at him, which he must have taken as a sign my parts were still functioning because he kissed my forehead and moved past me into the living room. I followed him and switched on a table lamp.

Johnny leaned over to examine Maribeth's binding and then her face. "How bad are you hurt?"

"Nothing I didn't deserve," Maribeth said, raising her eyes toward me. I didn't argue.

Johnny picked her up and planted her on the sofa. He braced her partially against the arm to allow her to sit upright without untying her. He propelled me into an opposing armchair, where I perched on the edge, feet braced. He pressed his hand gently against my shoulder, easing me back into the seat. He gave me one last assessing look, but didn't sit.

"Why don't we try this again," Johnny said to Maribeth. "What do you mean 'not the first time'?

Maribeth looked back and forth between the two of us. This was not the woman I'd met twice before. Gone was the stiffness and irritation I'd seen at her showing. In front of me now was someone thoroughly broken. I recognized the mix of limpness and desperation in her eyes, but adrenaline was still seeping through my veins, rapidly turning to anger.

"You can lose the scared rabbit routine, Maribeth," I said. "You just broke into my house and clobbered me. Spit it out."

"I wasn't trying—."

"Stop," I snapped. "What does 'not the first time' mean? Did you or did you not take Tracy?"

Maribeth's head nodded up and down, then started to shake back and forth. She looked like she was drawing a Tic-Tac-Toe board on an Etch-a-Sketch with her forehead. "I didn't take her. I helped her get away."

"From Jerome?" Johnny asked.

More bobbing and weaving.

"Was he abusing her?"

"Not, not physically. Well, except for one time," she said quietly.

"How then?" I asked.

Tears dripped from Maribeth's eyes and pooled into the pockets of gray sunken beneath them. "He wouldn't let her spend much time away from him. He always had to know where she was and what she was doing. She said he, um, he called her some nasty names."

"Why didn't she just tell him she wanted a divorce?" I asked.

Maribeth shook her head violently. With her hands strapped behind her, the effort made the muscles in her neck strain taut. It looked painful and I felt momentarily bad, but not enough to untie her. The fresh friction burns on my arms were cutting into my empathy.

"She couldn't. She tried before and he threatened—," Maribeth cut herself off and squeezed her eyes shut. When she opened them, she addressed the coffee table. "Tracy has quite a bit of money. Jerome told her he'd make sure he got it if she divorced him."

If Tracy had money, she sure knew how to hide it from her family, I thought. But, why?

"How much are we talking?" I asked.

"Just north of a million and a half," Maribeth said.

"She made that selling houses?" I asked. I briefly debated whether to email Paul my resignation, or write it out on a nice piece of twenty-pound bond.

"Mercy, no." Maribeth said. "I mean, she's good, but she'd have to sell hundreds of homes to touch that kind of money in this part of town."

"So, where'd it come from?"

"Her dad."

"I thought she didn't know who her dad was?" I asked.

"She didn't. He reached out to her right before she got married."

"Is that when he gave her the money?" Johnny asked.

"No, he gave it to her as a wedding present. That's why she was worried Jerome could get at it if she divorced him. She didn't come into the marriage with it. Plus, she dumped a lot of the money into buying their house."

"So if Tracy ran away so Jerome couldn't get at her money, why make it look like a break-in?" I asked. "Why not just pack a bag and disappear?"

"We thought if we made it look like Tracy was kidnapped, Jerome wouldn't coming looking for her."

"You didn't think he would notice her tapping into her bank accounts? Or the police, for that matter?" Johnny asked.

"We weren't going to touch that money. I've been selling some property and we—." Maribeth stopped herself and flashed a hesitant look at Johnny and me.

"You and Tracy," I prompted.

"We planned to live off the proceeds for a while." Maribeth smiled as tears leaked from her lower lids. "Together."

Chapter Forty

Johnny and I locked on each other's face. The 'duh' in his eyes matched mine. We looked back at Maribeth, whose shoulders began to shake. Johnny crossed to her, where he untied the knot at her wrists. He started to untie her ankles, but I'd knotted the strap with adrenaline-driven strength, and he eventually gave up. He sat down on the other end of the sofa from Maribeth and nodded at me.

"How long have you and Tracy been together?" I asked.

Maribeth cleared her throat with effort and began worrying a thumb over a spot in her cashmere sweater.

"Close to a year maybe," she said. "It's hard to really put a date on it. We became close almost from the day she came to the agency, but I don't think either of us was ready to admit how strong the connection was for a long time."

"When were you planning to join her?" Johnny asked.

"We were going to wait another couple of weeks to let things cool down, then decide where to go next."

"You were running away without knowing where you'd go?" I asked.

"We had a couple places in mind, but we had to speed things up," Maribeth said, with what looked like regret pinching her face.

"Why?" Johnny asked.

"Tracy said Jerome was acting weird. Well, more so than usual. That really put her on edge, so she wanted to pull the trigger earlier than we planned."

"Weird, how?" Johnny asked.

Maribeth shook her head again and shrugged, rubbing her wrists in her lap. "She couldn't describe it, really. She just had this sense that something was off."

"Like he was going to hurt her?" Johnny asked.

"Maybe. I mean, she didn't say that, but she talked about hiring someone to keep an eye on him. Then right after that she said she just wanted to get out of there."

Johnny and I exchanged a glance, but didn't let on to Maribeth that Tracy had hired Johnny to be her eye.

"Where did you take her after you left her house Monday?" I asked.

Maribeth looked at me blankly. "I wasn't at the house. She threw some stuff around to make it look like someone took her and then she walked through the wooded lot behind her house, went down to the Speedway, and got on the bus to go to my condo."

"Wait, you weren't at her house on Monday?" I asked.

"No, I spent most of the day with clients. Then I met Tracy at the condo, and then I drove out to Sandusky."

"You bought that car and left Tracy's phone in it," I said.

Maribeth looked at me in surprise. "Yes."

"And no one else helped Tracy at the house?" Johnny asked.

"No, I told you. Why?" Maribeth asked. She turned a puzzled look at Johnny, but he was watching me. "Why?" she asked again, curiosity turning to urgency.

I raised my eyebrows at Johnny, unsure how much to share. Johnny shook his head a fraction, enough for me to keep my mouth shut.

"We're just trying to understand your story, Maribeth." Johnny said.

She craned her head toward him. "Story?"

Johnny held out a placating hand. "Look at it from our perspective. You broke into Sam's house, waited for her in the dark, and then attacked her."

"I came here for help. I swear," Maribeth pleaded. "I couldn't go to her office. I couldn't risk anyone seeing me and making a connection." Maribeth turned reddened eyes on me. "And I wasn't trying to hurt you. I wasn't thinking. I know I didn't go about it the right way, but I was upset and scared. I wasn't thinking straight...I'm not—"

"Why me?" I interrupted.

"I don't understand," Maribeth said.

"Why come to me and not the police?"

"I was afraid if I told the police, they would arrest me. That they would think I took Tracy and was making up a story to cover myself."

"And what's to stop me from thinking the same thing?" I asked.

"Back when you came and talked to me at my showing, it freaked me out." New tears trailed down Maribeth's cheeks, but her voice was calm. "I told Tracy and she said not to worry because you wouldn't let her get hurt and that I could trust you. She said you were her great protector in middle school. That you understood her, that she felt stifled and you got that about her. Oh, and something about you sticking up for her because of a lunch box? I didn't really understand, but it seemed important to her."

Johnny slid me a questioning look. I ignored it.

I rubbed a hand over my face. It felt marginally less gritty than my brain. "Okay, let's back up. Where did Tracy go when she left her house?" I asked.

"To my condo on Edgewater." Maribeth said.

"Why do you think she's missing? How do you know she didn't just go out for a while?"

Maribeth shook her head. "She wouldn't do that."

"Not for groceries? Does she smoke, drink?" Johnny asked. "Any addictions she'd risk stepping out to satisfy?"

"No." Maribeth gave Johnny an emphatic head shake. "Lakewood's not close to anyone we know, but it's not that far away either. She wouldn't risk letting anyone see her."

"Even if she was getting cabin fever?" I asked. "It's been almost a week. Maybe she took a quick walk down by the lake."

"It's freezing out there right now. And besides, she's had this chest cold for the last couple days. She wouldn't have had the stamina to walk down there," Maribeth said.

"How long has she been gone?" I asked.

"I'm not sure. I left the condo this morning around 7:00, maybe. I came back in around 2:30 and she was gone. Plus," she said and stopped herself.

"Plus, what?" I asked.

"The condo. The vase on my foyer table was smashed on the floor."

Chapter Forty-One

Maribeth sipped on a mug of warmed gas station milk and Johnny kept one eyeball on her while he called Roman from the living room. I dug out an extra blanket from one of the moving boxes for Maribeth and tried to not to keel over from fatigue.

Twenty minutes later, Roman filled my front door. He took me in with a hard set to his jaw and zero comment. My tank top was a hodgepodge of ripped fabric, glue strings, and dangling sequins. My micro shorts were split on one side, the rip stopped only by the elastic band securing the waist. Maribeth's snot was styling one section of my hair, and I had a sneaking suspicion that I had become one with the odor of Gino's house. Sadly, I realized, I'd looked worse.

"Where is she?" Roman asked.

"Kitchen," I said, opening the door wide.

Roman stepped inside and paused in front of me, placing one hand on my hip. He lowered his head to mine. "You okay?"

I willed the corners of my mouth into a semblance of a smile. I brushed my palm across Roman's bicep and caught sight of Johnny over his shoulder. Johnny looked at me blankly for a nanosecond, then dipped his head down and started scrolling through his phone.

Roman turned his head to follow my gaze and dropped his

hand from my waist. He strolled past Johnny with a casual nod. I followed and tried to make eye contact with Johnny as I passed, but he kept his head bent over his phone.

Roman stopped at the threshold of the kitchen and I watched as his eyes roamed over the ancient appliances and the floor that refused to release its stains even after three scrubbings. He tilted his head back and peered up at the brass fixture that was spitting a dim light down over the table. He pivoted his thick neck toward me.

"It's a family thing," I muttered.

Johnny came up and slipped between us to pass through to the table. He picked up Maribeth's mug, rinsed it in the sink, and settled his back against the counter. Roman took a seat across from Maribeth at the table. I hovered in the doorway.

"How you doing?" Roman asked Maribeth. He leaned forward, elbows on knees, and delivered her a wide, warm smile.

Maribeth squared her shoulders and looked him in the eye. "I'm sorry I didn't tell you before."

Roman showed her a palm and smiled again. "Let's worry about that later. Why don't we focus on finding Tracy first?"

Maribeth nodded and cupped her hands together as if the milk mug was still nestled between them. I glanced at the sink and debated giving it back to her, but the rigidity of Johnny's stance kept me rooted to my spot.

"Ms. Collins," Roman said. "I understand that you and Tracy had plans to, ah, start a new life together."

Maribeth nodded and pinched the inner corners of her eyes.

"Sometimes," Roman continued. "Sometimes, people in desperate situations make rash life decisions and then change their minds."

Maribeth was shaking her head even before Roman finished talking.

"Now, hear me out," Roman said, resting a palm flat on the tabletop. "It doesn't mean Tracy doesn't care about you. Or even want to go away with you. But you need to acknowledge the fact that she could have left the condo on her own terms."

"But the vase in my entryway was smashed," Maribeth whispered.

"Which conveniently, is kind of similar to how Tracy left her own house before she ran away the first time, isn't it?"

"No, no, that wasn't the first time, it was the only time. She wouldn't have left me. Jerome found her, I know it." Maribeth's head tipped back and forth, her lips mouthing words only she could hear.

Roman let her sit, watching her mouth, letting her work it out.

"Maribeth," I said softly. "If it helps us find her, isn't it worth considering that she left on her own?"

"No!" Maribeth's head roared back. "Listen to me. He's taken her. He knows about us. That has to be why he's been so weird to her lately."

"How would he know?" Roman asked. "If he was abusive, I could see him suspecting she might leave, but it's quite a leap to think you and she are in a relationship."

"Not as much as you think," Maribeth said and started to sob in big, wet gulps.

I moved to the table and sat next to her, patting her shoulder until the sobs subsided.

"What aren't you telling us?" I asked.

"I can't," she wailed. "Oh God, I can't."

"You have to. If Jerome has her, we may be running out of time." I said.

Johnny ripped a paper towel off the roll and passed it to Maribeth, She wiped the towel across her entire face, then pressed both hands against it, hiding behind the damp cloth. Her shoulders shook for several moments before she stilled again.

"Tracy," she began, lowering the towel. "Tracy had an affair a few years ago and Jerome's been holding it over her head ever since."

"We know about the affair," I said. "But why would—." The crack of the stupidity bat hit me right between the eyes. "Was that affair with a woman?"

Maribeth nodded. Roman pressed forward in his chair.

"And you're sure Jerome knows that?" Roman asked.

"Yes," Maribeth whimpered.

"That's what Jerome was threatening her with, wasn't it?" I asked. "This wasn't about him getting money in a divorce. It was about exposing her secret."

"Yes," Maribeth mouthed.

"Why was that so important to Tracy?" Johnny asked.

Maribeth's pupils flared in anger.

"Hold up," Johnny said, raising a conceding hand. "I understand she may not want everybody to know, but if she was in a horrible relationship, wouldn't it be worth revealing her secret to get out?"

"You can't understand," Maribeth said.

"I think I might, kind of," I said. "Tracy was a loner when we were young. I could see how she'd worry that people knowing would make her feel like an outsider again."

"It's more than that," Maribeth said. "Yes, she was insecure for a long time, but she'd mostly gotten over that. She didn't care much about what other people thought of her, but what scared her was the possibility of losing her relationship with her mom."

"Do you honestly think Carol would cut Tracy off if she knew she was gay?" I asked.

"It's not about Tracy, really. It's more about her dad. Carol is very bitter about him," Maribeth said. "When they had their affair, Carol thought she was in this long-term fairy tale, with the horse and the sunset and the whole bit. She really believed that he was going to take her and the girls and start a new family."

"But Tracy's dad wasn't as invested in the relationship," Johnny said.

"Not in the way you think. Tracy's dad was using Carol as a

cover. He worked real high up for some super conservative company and didn't want them knowing that he was gay."

"Tracy's dad is gay?" Roman asked.

"Holy crap," I said.

"Exactly," Maribeth said. "Tracy is worried her mom will think their sexuality is a bond Tracy and her dad share that Carol can't. Like Tracy betrayed her somehow."

"That's a whole other level of self-centered," I said.

"You see that and I see that, but Tracy doesn't. She loves her mom and she's not willing to take the chance of losing her." Maribeth drew in a steadying breath. "But it's not really an option now, is it?"

Chapter Forty-Two

I rolled over and repeatedly stabbed my finger onto the face of my cell phone in an attempt to shut off the alarm. I was on the brink of carpel tunnel when I realized a call was coming through. I focused one eye and tapped the accept button.

"Roman called. Jerome's car is gone," Johnny said.

"Um, good morning?" I said, rolling onto my back.

"That, too. I'm on my way to pick up Maribeth, then we'll swing by to get you."

"What for?" I drew my blanket higher up under my chin and snuggled down into the sheets.

"We're going to start hitting places Jerome could have taken Tracy."

"I thought we agreed last night that Roman's guys were doing that? He said it was off-limits to us right now."

"Yeah, well, that was before he picked up two separate stabbing cases overnight. He's okayed us to look around, but we have to call if we see anything off. No playing the cavalry."

"I need thirty minutes to paint my happy face on."

"You've got twenty," he said, and disconnected.

"Come home, they said. Help Mom, they said. It'll be fun, they said," I muttered to myself as I swung my legs to the floor.

Nineteen and one half minutes later, I stood showered and blow-dried on the curb. There'd been no time for make-up, so I swiped on some colored lip balm in honor of the impending snowstorm the morning news had touted, though it was probably an empty gesture. In the grand tradition of weather forecasters everywhere, Cleveland news stations heralded the possibility of stray showers as monsoons, and a light dusting of snow as the next nor'easter. Plus, it was still only the end of October, which meant we could either get a foot of the white stuff or need to break out the kiddie pool. Roll of the dice.

Five minutes into my curb warming, Johnny was still nowhere to be seen. A small, brown sedan rolled up in front of me. A hungover Vinnie rolled out, and with a toot of the horn, Bruce rolled away.

Vinnie was technically standing on his own two feet, but a tickle and a sneeze could have put him down hard. I linked my arm through one of his and we stood hip to hip on the curb.

"You alright?" I asked.

"Living the dream."

It was freezing, but I squelched the urge to bounce on my feet to get warm. I suspected Vinnie would be flat on the ground before the third bounce.

"You wanna talk about it?" I asked.

"Sure don't."

"That's cool," I said, looking off down the street. Still no Johnny. I looked back at Vinnie.

"Not to be rude, but why'd you have Bruce drop you off here if you didn't want to talk?" I asked.

Vinnie bobbed his shoulders up and down. "I thought I did, but, I don't know. Just feeling a little lost with this, is all."

"Grab an oar. You and me are kind of in the same boat." I smiled at him, but he didn't look amused.

Vinnie turned swollen eyes on me and I watched the cold air escape on his breath. "Sam, what if Mom plans to sell the restaurant, too?"

It hadn't even dawned on me that Mom might be picking up all of her roots. I squeezed Vinnie's arm and laid my head briefly on his shoulder.

"It'll be alright, Vin. Let's find out what's going on before we jump to any conclusions, okay?"

Doubt drenched Vinnie's face.

"Vin, I promise. We'll figure things out." I looked down the street again. "Listen, Johnny's coming to pick me up to work a case. You want to go inside and sleep it off for a while?"

"Nah," Vinnie said. "This still the case with that Tracy girl you're working?"

"Yeah. We kind of found her and then lost her again."

"Not for nothing, Sam, but maybe you should think about another line of work if you're going to stick around town for a while."

I swung my hip and gingerly bumped it into his.

"Hey now," Vinnie said, pulling away from me. "Just sayin'."

"It's a long story that I have a feeling is going to get even longer." I saw Johnny's truck cruising up the street out of the corner of my eye. "You want us to drop you off at your car?"

"Not if we have to ask him for permission." Vinnie dipped his head toward the truck. The day was overcast and Johnny's windshield sported a slew of dead bugs splattered across it, but that did nothing to disguise the chilly look on his face.

***

"Good luck to you," Vinnie said in my ear before he shakily stepped down from Johnny's cab. I scratched my nose with my middle finger and he smiled sickly back at me as I slammed the truck door shut. He waved as Johnny pulled away. I kept scratching.

"Thanks for dropping him," I said to Johnny.

"Sure thing." Those two words brought Johnny's total word count for the trip to four since Vinnie and I had climbed in.

I watched Johnny in the rearview mirror from the backseat. He hadn't exactly been cold when he left Gino's the previous night, but neither had he whispered sweet nothings in my ear on his way out the door. I suspected Roman's hand on my waist had effectively brought the flirtation period to an end. Maribeth's current presence in the front seat derailed any opportunity to talk to him about it, which didn't make me entirely unhappy.

"We're going to drive over and check out Maribeth's Edgewater condo, then we'll swing past her other two rentals," Johnny said. He glanced in the mirror at me.

"Maribeth, do you know of any other property that Jerome might own or rent?" I asked. "We didn't find anything in our records search, but did you ever hear Tracy talk about a vacation spot, a timeshare, anything like that?"

Maribeth shook her head. "No, never. Unless he's hiding it somewhere, I don't think he has any real money of his own for that kind of thing."

"How about his friends?" Johnny asked.

"I've never heard Tracy mention any. If he's not at work, he's usually home."

"And no family that we've been able to track down locally," Johnny said.

Johnny turned onto West 117th and headed toward the lake. West 117th is a major thoroughfare stretching from I-71 to Lake Erie. It changed from moneyed to eclectic to scary over the course of about a mile and a half. My all-time favorite West 117th sighting was of a guy strolling down the middle of the street in the middle of a sunny day, swinging his umbrella, and belting out 'Singing in the Rain' in between bites of his fried chicken leg. I looked for him as we cruised toward the lake, but the closest I could find was a woman in a fur vest walking her dog in an antique baby stroller.

Johnny neared Edgewater Drive, the last street you could turn on before plunging into the lake. We hooked a left toward a long bank of mid-rise buildings. Maribeth mutely pointed out one with her finger and Johnny turned in.

We piled out of the truck to stand in the cold and survey the tiny parking lot. Most resident parking on the street sat underground, beneath the condo buildings. The dozen visitor slots stationed outside were mostly occupied, but Jerome's car was not among them.

Johnny and I silently trailed Maribeth into an aging, but cared for lobby. Pots of cypress flanked either side of the entryway and tasteful floral prints adorned the walls. The effect was warm and disarming, broken only by the hard, rubberized black mats laid down in anticipation of the coming storm.

Maribeth's unit was a stark contrast to the lobby. Layers of decorator red were awash everywhere. Paint, pillows, and rugs spilled various shades of blood across an otherwise cream-colored backdrop. The broken vase still lay in pieces on the tiled entryway floor and crunched lightly under our feet as we trampled over them into the living room.

I bent to pick up a magazine and assorted knick-knacks that had fallen to the floor with the vase, but Johnny put a hand on my shoulder to stop me.

"Leave it for now. Let's let Maribeth look around first and see if there's anything else out of place," Johnny said. He stepped back into the small dining room that created an L with the living room, and peered down the adjoining hallway. I walked the length of the living room, taking in the tidy furnishings. I glanced behind me and realized Maribeth was still in the entryway. She stood staring forlornly at the broken vase, cheeks burned so red from the cold they nearly matched her furniture.

"Maribeth," I said, taking a step toward her.

"Don't," she said, gripping her coat around her.

"Maribeth, why don't you walk us through the rest of the place and see if anything looks out of sorts," Johnny said. He extended an arm to her from across the room as if asking her to dance. Her eyes followed it like a beacon as she passed me.

I took up the rear and we trekked from room to room. Maribeth paused at each doorway for a moment before shaking her head at Johnny. We circled back to the kitchen.

"Is this Tracy's purse or yours?" Johnny asked, pointing to a mahogany leather satchel slung across a kitchen chair.

"Hers."

"Have you looked through it?" Johnny asked. Maribeth shook her head and weakly gestured her permission.

Johnny rifled through the purse, then swept three fingers down into the outside pouch.

"Wallet and keys are here," Johnny said. He held the king ring out to Maribeth. "Can you tell if any are missing?"

Maribeth walked a finger through the ring and looked doubtful as she passed it back to him. "These are for her house. I don't know for sure, but she wouldn't have kept her condo key on the same ring. Jerome is…observant."

Johnny dumped the key ring back into Tracy's purse, unlatched the clasp to the wallet, and flipped through it. "ID, two credit cards, no cash."

"Do you have spare keys to the place?" I asked Maribeth.

Without answering, she turned and pulled out a drawer I would generously have labeled "junk". Whereas the rest of the condo was designed to magazine-spread level and we hadn't seen so much as a hair in either of the two bathroom sinks during our tour, this drawer rivaled any in Uncle Gino's house. Maribeth waded through the mess and came up with two matching keys attached to a Home Depot key ring, which she held out to me.

"You have any other spares stashed anywhere?" I asked.

"No, this is it." Maribeth said. She returned the keys and pushed the drawer back in. It snagged on a cardboard bar coaster, but Maribeth seemed not to notice.

"Any other way for Tracy to get back in without a key?"

Johnny asked.

"I don't think so," Maribeth said. "Unless she asked the staff down in the office. I had to register her as a guest, so they know she's been here. They could give her a key, I guess."

"And you're a hundred percent positive nothing is missing that she would have had to take if she did leave on her own? Medicine, glasses, anything like that?" I asked.

"No, nothing. I'm telling you, she didn't just leave me." Maribeth said.

"Alright," Johnny said. He crossed to Maribeth and touched his hand to the small of her back, propelling her out of the kitchen. "Let's go look at your rentals."

Chapter Forty-Three

We headed into Lakewood, sticking to the side streets. A rain and sleet mix had kicked up while we were scavenging in Maribeth's condo. The forecasters may have guessed right after all. Rain was already rushing through the gutters and by the time we covered the few miles to the first rental property, pea-sized hail pinged off Johnny's windshield.

Johnny pulled past the driveway of a small, tidy house painted out in cream and white. A tan Nissan Sentra sat in the driveway, but all the drapes were drawn and the house had an empty quality to it.

Johnny parked three houses down and let the truck idle. A charred, wet smell hit my nose through the vents, a sign that the first real bout of cold had homeowners breaking in their fireplaces.

Johnny and I both turned to look out the side window at the house. Maribeth stayed still in her seat, shoulders rounded in protective gesture.

"We'll find her," Johnny said, casting soft eyes on Maribeth. She leaned her head toward his voice without raising her eyes.

"You want me to go check it out?" I asked.

"No," Johnny said. "Stay with Maribeth." It wasn't a question, but he looked back at me with eyes seeking confirmation. I nodded to him and unbuckled my belt.

As soon as Johnny hopped out of the cab, I climbed over the seat and took his place next to Maribeth. Her eyes absently traced the pattern of the rain as it pattered sideways against the windshield. Pieces of larger hail flew into the glass intermittently, sending Maribeth's eyes darting, but her body remained slumped in her seat. I wondered absently if I would ever feel about a man the way Maribeth must have felt about Tracy. Tracy had been gone only a matter of hours and Maribeth was on the verge of checking out.

I reached over and gently squeezed her wrist. I adjusted the rearview mirror and watched Johnny. Through the rain pouring down the back window, I could barely make out his shape as he crossed the lawn and disappeared on the other side of the house, reappearing a minute later. He moved to the driveway and bent over the Nissan to peer in its windows, then straightened up and strolled down to the tree lawn. He started along the sidewalk in our direction, paused in front of the neighboring house, then picked up his pace as he returned to the truck.

I made like Gumby back over the driver's seat and was strapped in again when Johnny yanked open his door. He hiked himself up into the seat, threw his soaking hat onto the dashboard and popped the truck into gear.

"No dice," Johnny said as he pulled away from the curb. "Nobody's home, but I could see part of the kitchen and living room through the windows. I can't see how Tracy could hide there. Looks like a tiny house with a lot of kids. That sound like your tenants?" Johnny shot a quick glance at Maribeth, who gave a stunted shrug.

"I have a management company who handles the leasing, maintenance, all of that. I think a family's renting, but I don't know for sure," Maribeth said.

"How about the other place? Any idea who's renting there?" I asked.

"Two kids going to Baldwin Wallace, both boys, I think. I've met them. They started leasing two years ago, before I began using the management company."

We jogged up W 140th to Lorain Road before turning off on a side street full of single family homes and renovated duplexes. Judging by the number of Buicks and the stark absence of kids' toys, it looked to be a neighborhood of older residents. A "Smiles are Better Than Honey" windsock whipped against a porch railing, battered by the rain. Mailboxes up and down the street blasted out competing screeches as their metal doors flapped open on their hinges.

Johnny slowed as we passed the house and parked across the street. The driveway was empty, but as Johnny undid his belt, the front door opened and a young man came out. He was holding the hood of his red sweatshirt up over his head, the wind and rain knocking back the lip, giving the man a Red Riding Hood effect. He jogged down the sidewalk toward a bright yellow sports car pulling up to the curb, and hopped in. The driver hit the gas and the car's rear end fishtailed wildly on the hail pebbles before straightening out and rolling away.

I tapped Johnny on the shoulder.

"Let me do this one," I said.

"Sam, I don't think it's the best idea." His eyes met mine in the rearview mirror.

"I do," I said and popped open my door.

"Sam!" I heard Johnny call my name as I slammed the door shut behind me. I lifted the hood of my own sweatshirt up over my head and ran with one palm tamping it down against my skull. I navigated the slippery hail and coasted into the driveway, grabbing for the mailbox with my free hand to slow my approach. I missed by a foot and crashed into the box hedge bordering the lawn. I managed a reasonably soft landing, but left my right side soaking wet.

I skittered the rest of the way up to the porch, rang the bell, and shook like a freshly bathed puppy to get the top layer of wet off me. No answer. I rang again, turned to look back at the truck, and gave Johnny two thumbs up. The rain obscured my ability to see his face, but I was positive he was tracking me.

I turned back to the house and was about to press my face into the glass half-moon set into the door when it opened, revealing a doughy kid who looked like he must have skipped a couple grades if he was one of Maribeth's college renters.

"Hi," I chirped and smiled wide.

He grinned back, revealing a set of chompers large enough to make the Cookie Monster question his job security. It wasn't altogether unpleasant, but I struggled to keep my eyes on his. I wasn't the only one struggling, it seemed, seeing as how his were focused on my boobs.

"Hey, there," the kid said. He jutted his chin in and out approvingly. His eyes roved to my feet and back up again, stalling at the Ohio State Buckeye logo on my chest. Two molars the size of walnuts appeared as his smile widened.

"Ah, Buckeye fan?" I tried.

"Huh?" he said, finally meeting my gaze. This kid didn't skip lunch, let alone a grade.

I stuck out my hand. "I'm Debbie. Is Jack here?'

"There's no Jack here. Unless, you know, you're looking for Daniels." His chin jutted some more as he chuckled at his joke.

"Ohhh, that's too bad," I said, sticking out my lower lip. "We met at a party near campus last week and this was the address he gave me. Should have known it was too good to be true." I deepened the pout.

Walnuts gummed his teeth and looked slyly past me at the empty driveway. "How 'bout I be your Jack? Hey, it could be fun. I could call you Jill."

The banana I'd crammed in my mouth as I ran out of the house that morning launched a small revolt in my stomach. Man, I did not miss being nineteen.

"Come on," Walnuts said. "Mi casa es su casa, Jill." He opened the door wide and waved me in.

I caught an expanded glimpse of the house and knew in an instant Tracy would never have come here. The reek of beer-soaked carpet and stale cigarette smoke wafted out at me. The living room had been set up as a gamer's delight. I counted seven TVs and five consoles before I took a step backward to the end of the porch.

"Such a sweet offer, but maybe another time. Hey!" I said and pointed to the sky. "How about a rain check?"

Walnuts laughed and pantomimed tapping a drumstick on a cymbal. I turned, hopped over the two steps to the driveway and took off in a sliding jog. Johnny was halfway across the street when I hit the curb. I tucked my hand in his elbow and turned him back toward the truck.

"What the hell was that?" Johnny asked. "You took those porch steps like it was a slalom."

I gave him my best no-biggie smile and pushed past him to the truck. Maribeth turned her dispirited face toward me. I shook my head and she nodded her head, unsurprised.

"We're going to find her," I said. "And as soon as we do, we're taking you carpet shopping."

Chapter Forty-Four

Walnuts' pad was only a few miles from Carol's house, so we decided to swing past unannounced on the chance she'd be home. I was taken aback when Patty answered our knock. Given the strained picture she'd painted of her relationship with her mother, I'd have thought she'd be keeping her distance. Maybe the thought of losing one daughter was encouraging Carol to appreciate the other. Stranger things and all.

Patty's hennaed hair had been updated to a two-toned red-and-gold look that a flat iron had molded to her scalp. Her extra helping of boob was busy fighting to escape a thick, navy cable-knit sweater.

"I didn't expect to find you here," I said.

Patty lifted her chin and addressed the ivy clinging to the door frame. "My mother is having a hard time and called me this morning to come sit with her. I just got here."

While I hid my surprise, Patty didn't hide hers when she got a close-up look at Maribeth.

"We've met," Patty said to Maribeth in a flat voice. "Georgie's baby shower."

Maribeth blushed and unfurled a hand from the sleeve of her coat, extending it to Patty. "That's right. Hi, Patty."

The women shook and Patty called out to her mother, who appeared at the kitchen door. I could make out the gray pallor of Carol's skin from across the room. She'd donned a bright red, beaded tunic that did nothing to distract from her ashy, exhausted face.

At Gino's the previous night, we learned that Tracy had called Carol shortly after running away, to let her mom know she was okay. I understood now why Carol had gone from teary and Jerome-hating in our first meeting to flippant in our next. She knew Tracy was safe, and was trying to keep up the charade to throw off Jerome.

Roman's partner dropped in on Carol last night, to fill her in on the news that Tracy was missing. Again. She didn't look like she had taken it in stride.

Carol came to a halt at the sight of Maribeth. Her body stopped hard, and the beads on her hemline continued to swing, clacking loudly. Johnny and I reversed our descent onto the sofa. The five of us stood in an awkward circle. Carol opposite Maribeth and me. Patty and Johnny hanging on the fringe.

"Hi," Maribeth said to Carol. She seemed unsure about extending her hand, and settled for clasping both in front of her.

"Hello," Carol said, equally hesitant. She shot an expectant glance at Johnny, then turned rapidly filling eyes on me. "Have you heard something?"

"No, not yet," I said.

Carol exhaled and plunged her face into her hands, then quickly whisked them away, as if playing a peekaboo game with herself. Her shoulders sagged, but I saw her face relax a fraction.

"I thought," Carol started, flapping a hand at Maribeth, Johnny, and me. "I thought you'd all come to tell me..."

Ah, bells.

"I'm sorry, Carol, I wasn't thinking," I said. "We were out looking for Tracy this morning and were so close by, we just thought we'd stop and check in."

Carol nodded vigorously, short snaps of her neck. Her relief intensified, then faded away when she looked over at Patty, who rewarded her with a reassuring smile. An odd look flashed over Carol's face, and she pinned nervous eyes on me.

"Have you thought any more since last night about where Tracy may have gone?" I asked.

Carol darted her eyes back to Patty. "No, no."

I got the impression she wasn't saying no to my question as much as to the fact that I was asking it, but I pushed on.

"I'm sure you've thought it through up, down, and sideways," I said. "But are you absolutely sure she doesn't have any other friends she'd go to? Or relatives?"

"Why are you asking her that? We've been through this," Patty said.

"Patty, they're just trying to figure out where Jerome could have taken her," Carol said, turning pleading eyes back to me.

I looked over at Patty. She glared at her mother, her confusion blooming into suspicion.

"Ma?" Patty asked.

Carol's eyes clung to me like a politician to a lie. I inclined my head toward Patty.

"Tell her, Carol," I said.

"Tell me what?" Patty asked. She took two steps forward and lowered her face close to her mother's. Carol's eyes widened but refused to meet Patty's.

"Tell me what, Ma?" Patty persisted.

"Carol," Maribeth said. "Do you want me to tell—?"

"No! She's *my* daughter," Carol snapped.

Maribeth started, but quickly regained her composure and held up placating hands.

"Jesus, can someone for the love of Pete tell me what is going on?" Patty asked, flinging her arms to the side.

"Jerome didn't take your sister," Carol said.

"What? How do you know?" Patty asked.

"She ran away. She planned everything out…with her friend's help." Carol jabbed a beaded arm in Maribeth's direction. "They made it look like there was a break-in at the house to throw Jerome off."

"How do you know?" Patty repeated. The volume of her voice had risen while its temperature dropped.

"Tracy called me to tell me she was okay," Carol murmured.

"When?" Patty asked.

"A few days after she disappeared." Carol said.

"Why didn't you tell me?" Patty asked.

Maribeth opened her mouth, but Patty threw up a hand.

"You," Patty said, scowling at her mother. "I want to hear it from you."

Carol lifted her chin, defiance spreading in her eyes. "It had to be a secret. We couldn't risk Jerome finding out."

I rolled my eyes at the "we". My, how fast we move from victim to victimizer, I thought.

Patty's face was a kaleidoscope of emotions. Surprise, anger, and disbelief all competed for second place behind relief. Patty turned to the rest of us.

"Then Tracy's okay," Patty said. Hope and caution flitted across her face. No one answered.

Patty turned to Maribeth. "If you helped her, you must know where she's at."

Maribeth stole a glance at Carol, who had lowered her body into the loveseat, and her head into her hands.

"I don't know," Maribeth said slowly. "Tracy was hiding at my condo until we could find a better place to go. When I got home yesterday afternoon, she…she was gone."

Patty's eyes scoured Maribeth's face. "And you don't know where she went."

"No. We've been driving around to all the possible places she could have gone. We—. We don't know why she left. It's hard to know where she might have gone." Maribeth's voice cracked and the dam that had been building over the prior twelve hours finally broke.

The reality that Tracy may have walked away from not only the condo, but the relationship as well, seemed to finally take hold of Maribeth. Tears flooded her cheeks and cascaded in mini waterfalls from her chin.

Maribeth's crying rapidly turned to a racking sob loud enough to lull Carol into lifting her head. She eyed Maribeth apathetically for the briefest moment before propping one elbow on the armrest and lowering her head into it.

Patty sighed, stepped forward, and wrapped her arms around Maribeth. Patty held her silently for a long moment before pushing her back gently by her shoulders. Maribeth closed her eyes, bit her trembling lip, and breathed deeply through her nose.

"You're in love with my sister, aren't you?" Patty asked.

Maribeth's eyelids snapped back to reveal irises dilated with fear. Patty pasted on a surprisingly warm smile.

"I really do," Maribeth whispered, and buried her face back in her palms. Patty pulled her close again and peered over her shoulder at Carol.

Carol had cocked her head up, elbow still propped on the armrest, and now empty palm cradled upward. She looked like a pageant queen frozen mid-wave on the back of a parade convertible.

"You didn't want to tell me about this little detail either, Ma?"

Chapter Forty-Five

Carol's mouth gaped and her eyes bounced between the two women as if she was watching a ping-pong tournament.

Awareness washed over Patty's face. "Oh my god. You didn't know."

The 'O' of Carol's mouth lengthened into an oval and rounded back out again as she fought to form words. I moved to sit with her, but Johnny reached out and rested his hand on my wrist. He ran his hand down over mine and drew me to his side.

"Hang tight," he breathed into my ear. I squeezed in assent.

Carol levered herself up from the loveseat and slowly approached Maribeth. She stopped a foot away and planted her feet.

"I thought you were just helping Tracy. You're having an affair with her?" Carol asked. It was more dare than either question or statement.

"It's more than just an affair," Maribeth said.

Carol scraped out a laugh. Maribeth's resolve broke and she winced, but I couldn't tell if it was from the sound or the sentiment.

"I've heard that before," Carol said. "In fact, I've *said* that before."

"No, it really is more than that. For both of us," Patty said.

Carol rolled her eyes and began to turn her back, but Maribeth stopped her with a hand to her shoulder. Carol flinched, but lifted her chin and met Maribeth's gaze.

"Look, I know you're upset that Tracy didn't tell you she was planning to leave," Maribeth said. "But please, you have to know it's not because she didn't need your help. Or want it. She meant only to keep you safe."

"I wouldn't have said a word," Carol said, petulant.

"She knows that, but she didn't want to put you in the position to even have to make that choice. She was so afraid of what Jerome might do. There was no guarantee he wouldn't try to find her. Too many things could have gone wrong." Maribeth began to shake. "Things that probably already have."

Carol sank back down into the love seat. Patty followed and settled beside her mother. Her anger had dissipated some and she looked every bit the doting daughter. She slipped her arm through Carol's and lightly stroked the six inches of sleeve not choked with beads. Carol peered at her eldest daughter without appearing to see her.

"Kind of crazy, huh?" Patty said to Carol. "All this time we never knew. Sort of makes sense now why Tracy wouldn't listen to us when she went back to live with Jerome."

Carol sat stiff and unresponsive. Patty pushed on with a hopeful smile.

"Maybe that's why Tracy got so mad at me back then," Patty said. "Maybe she couldn't tell me why she really went back to Jerome because she would have had to tell me she was gay, so she was kind of trapped. Don't you think?" Patty stopped and searched Carol's face again. If she was seeking confirmation, she was shopping at the wrong store.

Carol laid distant, glassy eyes on Patty and began to laugh. Hard. Then she clapped. Loud.

Either I'd missed the joke or Carol had found a Mickie in the sofa cushions and slipped it to herself. Tears rolled down to her ears as she fell back into the cushions, laughing still as she wiped them away. Patty retrieved her arm from Carol's and pressed herself into the opposite corner of the love seat. The familiar bitterness crept back over her features.

Johnny mouthed 'what the hell' to me. I gave him my best hell-if-I-know shrug back. Growing up, we tended to fight crazy with crazy, but I wasn't so sure that was going to work here. I couldn't tell if Carol was crazy, or if the tilt-a-whirl of the last week had caused her to temporarily slide on her axis.

"Carol," I asked gently. "Can I get you some tea or something?"

"Tea?" Johnny echoed.

"You got Xanax in your back pocket?" I countered.

"Stop being ridiculous," Carol said. "I don't need tea or pills or anything else. My daughter just handed me the best gift ever."

Patty smiled tentatively in surprise and reached a hand out to cover her mother's, but Carol didn't so much as turn her way.

"And what gift would that be?" I asked.

"I never believed Tracy's dad was gay," Carol said. She spread her arms wide, a stage magician revealing her trick. "But if Tracy's gay, then it must be true."

Maribeth raised her hand as if we were in Science class. "I don't think it quite works that way."

"Why didn't you believe he was gay?" Johnny asked.

"I thought he was lying because he didn't have the guts to admit he didn't love me." Carol said. "That I was just a toy to him and when things got hard, he just...I don't know."

"All due respect, Mrs. Simmons," Johnny said. "I think it'd take more guts to tell someone you're gay than it would to tell them you just aren't that into them."

Carol cocked her head at Johnny and looked him up and down, as if seeing him for the first time.

"Excuse me if I don't pour myself at your feet with

understanding. Men defend men."

Patty saw her opening and scooted closer to Carol. "I think this is great, Ma. You're free from all that now. Just think, maybe things can be different between us. You know, between all three of us."

Carol looked at her daughter. "Why in the world would you want anything to be different?"

Chapter Forty-Six

By the time we escaped from Carol's house and sloshed through the wet snow back to the truck, I was ready to call my mom and tell her to feel free to shtup Wally all she wanted. Carol Simmons had delivered to me a whole new perspective on mothers.

Patty rolled out of the house right on our heels. She hadn't bothered to put on her coat, hurriedly scooping up her things in a sheer effort to escape. Her face was a blotchy mess and the heavy snow instantly melted into her hair, poofing up the flat-iron work like rice noodles in a hot pan. She crammed herself behind the wheel of a gold and primer Camaro, and ripped down the driveway.

Johnny blasted the truck heater and we buckled in as we watched Patty weave down the street. I sent a silent prayer to Saint Christopher that she'd get home in one piece. I belatedly realized she'd probably make it to a bar before she made it home, so I sent up a second prayer tagged with an open-ended destination.

I felt like we'd just gone four rounds in a cage match sponsored by Dr. Phil and Jerry Springer, but at least it seemed to have cracked the egg of Maribeth's near comatose state. She was still quiet, but I could see in the side mirror that she was thinking and more focused. Johnny's silent treatment largely continued, but his body language had defrosted.

"I wish I'd thought to ask Patty if she knows of anyone Tracy would hide out with," Maribeth said. "I don't have her cell number."

We all swung our heads and looked back up at Carol's house. My stomach and my right butt cheek clenched involuntarily.

"And something tells me Carol wouldn't be all that helpful right now," I said. "But what about Tracy's dad? If he gave her all that money, what's to say he wouldn't help hide her?"

"Good point," Johnny said, looking at Maribeth. "Do you know where he lives?"

"Chicago, somewhere," Maribeth said.

"What about an address book?" I asked. "Do you know if Tracy has one?"

Maribeth looked doubtful. "I haven't seen one in the condo and she only brought one small bag. I helped her unpack, even, so I don't think so."

"What about at her house?" Johnny asked.

"Maybe."

Johnny caught my eyes in the rearview mirror and I gave him a thumbs up.

"I'm game for a little B&E," I said.

Johnny laughed for the first time that day and I couldn't hide my pleasure.

"What?" I asked.

"Have you ever committed "a little B&E"?"

I opened my mouth and he cut me off.

"And Bingo and Entenmann's doesn't count."

"Ha ha. Do you remember Sabrina Tomasek?" I asked.

"Who doesn't? She was the blonde who was dumb enough to try to steal Angie's boyfriend in high school."

"Exactly. And you remember the story about how she showed up to school one day with all that gorgeous, long hair chopped off to her chin?"

Johnny turned around in his seat until he was facing me, hands gripping either side of the headrest. His voice lowered to the stuff of ghost stories.

"The rumor on the basketball team was that Angie snuck into Sabrina's house and cut her hair off while she was sleeping," Johnny said.

I winked.

"You did not," Johnny said. I swear I saw respect creeping into his eyes.

"Well, no," I said. "But I stood guard under her bedroom window."

"Then let me do the B&E and you stay on guard duty," Johnny said. I should have known the truth would hold me back.

"We'll see," I said.

"Sam, I'm serious about this."

"Come on, Jerome's long gone. How dangerous can it be?" I asked.

"Danger aside, it's illegal and I'd prefer not to destroy my pipeline with Roman."

The rain and hail had kicked up a notch to an even lovelier combination of ice and snow. The snow was pouring down in sheets. and I could feel the truck slip on the icy patches. By the time we hit the Pentleys' street, the truck ground to a crawl. Johnny navigated the turn by inches, but the back of the truck still fishtailed. We righted out and crept down the street. Johnny passed the Pentleys' house and slid in a wide donut to park on the Pentleys' side, two houses down.

"What the hell?" Johnny said, looking out the cab window.

"What?" Maribeth and I chimed together.

Johnny flipped the windshield wipers to high and pointed out the windshield. "Didn't Roman say Jerome's car had disappeared?"

We all peered out through the pie slices of glass cut by the windshield wipers. Jerome's Lexus sat sedately in the driveway, its shiny coat covered with the barest layer of snow.

"Well," I said. "Unless he came right home and threw on some skis for a quick trip to the Speedway for Funyuns, I'd say our boy is inside."

"What do you think the odds are that he'll just hand over the address book, no questions asked?" Johnny asked.

"About the same as the Browns making the Super Bowl," I said.

Johnny twisted his neck around to look at me.

"Maybe a little lower?" I whispered.

Maribeth turned to us and smiled.

"You two are cute together, you know that?" she asked.

I saw Johnny's mouth open to form a response, but the only sound I heard was the shattering of glass that used to call itself the Pentleys' bay window. We all pressed ourselves into the windshield, but I couldn't see anything more than the dark gaping hole into the Pentleys' front room.

"Stay here," Johnny growled. He cranked open the truck door and took off.

"Do you have your cell?" I asked Maribeth as I pushed open my own door.

"What? Yes, but where are you going?" she said, digging into her purse.

"Just stay here and call the police," I said. I jumped down into the snow, which was already ankle-deep. I turned and leaned back into the truck. "You'll have to keep an eye out and flag them down. It's a wall of white out here. And tell them to call Roman."

I slammed the door as Maribeth's fingers started dialing and trotted along the side of the truck to the sidewalk, running one hand along its cold side to keep upright. The good news was the snow flowed down fast enough to provide some traction over the ice.

I skated down the sidewalk, eyes peeled for Johnny. I spied his red shirt as he crouched behind the rear wheel of Jerome's car. I bent as low as I could and crab-walked, keeping out of sight from what was left of the Pentleys' window. As I got closer, I could see the snow shooting into the house as the wind pushed the storm sideways.

I made it to Johnny's side and put my hand on his shoulder as I kneeled next to him. The sound of the snow and wind had muffled my approach and I felt his back muscles bunch tight beneath my palm.

"Shit, Sam. What are you doing?" Johnny asked. He placed the palm of his hand on top of my head and peered up over the car.

"If they can't see you, they can't see me," I said, pulling his hand down. "Maribeth is calling the police."

"Please, please get back in the truck, Sam."

"Would you be saying that if Paul was crouching here?"

Johnny lowered his head and pressed it to mine, rolling until our foreheads met.

"You're killing me, you know that?"

"You have to trust me at some point."

"God, Samantha. It's not about trust."

"Then what's it about?"

A woman's scream peeled through the air, the sound dampened by the storm, but unmistakable. I felt the cold whoosh of air hit my naked forehead before I registered that Johnny had taken off toward the house. By the time I stood up, he had crossed the driveway to the lawn. I skirted Jerome's car and careened across the driveway behind Johnny, but he quickly realized what I had not. The grass had turned to a sheet of ice. Johnny came to a dead stop at the lawn's edge, but I couldn't halt my progress and slammed into his back.

We tumbled to the ground just as a bullet blasted through what remained of the glass in the bay window. A shower of glass mixed with hail poured down on our heads. Johnny rolled out from under me, snaked an arm around my waist, and rolled me underneath him. He looped my arms around his neck and yelled at me to wrap my legs around his waist. I lost no time in clinging to him like a baby monkey. He planted himself up into a plank and crawled into the line of bushes at the side of the house.

I thought I heard a low moan coming through the window, but it was hard to hear through the sound of hail hitting the metal shed that sat next to us.

"Stay right here," Johnny said.

"Stay here with me. Let the cops go in there."

I was over the GI Joe dream. A full load of bat shit crazy was in that house. And it had bullets.

"They'll never make it in time," Johnny said. "Whatever this is could go down in a very bad way, very quickly. Do not move."

Johnny pried my arms from around his neck and pushed back on his knees. My lower body dragged forward with his.

"Samantha."

I sighed and unwrapped my drenched legs from his waist.

Johnny got to his feet, ran low across the icy lawn, and stepped into the mulched flower bed. The flowers died along with summer, but the mulch provided decent traction, and Johnny raced along the bed to the front door.

I strained to hear over the wind and snow, but couldn't make out any other sounds. I levered myself up and traced Johnny's steps to the flower bed, where I paused, ear bent. Still nothing. Shit. Jerome was a tall guy, and Johnny had an easy thirty pounds on him, most of it muscle. But guns didn't distinguish between Doritos and protein powder, and I couldn't hear so much as a siren, let alone see a cavalry cruising down the street. I sent a prayer and hoped Saint Jude could hear me through the storm.

I stayed low and trotted to the walkway leading to the front door. The door was open several inches and I could see the base of a wide staircase and entryway directly beyond. Johnny was pressed up against the outside of the house. The slow shake of his head told me he knew I was behind him and wasn't happy about it.

Johnny edged his face around the doorframe. He pulled back a second later and glanced back at me, resignation on his face. He peered around the doorframe once more, then stepped up into the foyer. I dashed up the walkway and stepped in behind him, and came face to profile with Jerome Pentley. He was sitting in a straight-backed chair, rigid as ever with knees pressed together, on the far side of the living room. He was staring at a spot on the floor, some five feet in front of him. He clasped his hands tight in his lap, just as he had when Paul and I first met him, but the rest of his appearance was starkly different. Gone were the sharply pleated trousers, replaced by cheap, rumpled khaki pants streaked with dark stains. His face hadn't seen a razor in days, nor his hair a comb. My nose was assaulted with a combination of sweat, urine, and vapor rub.

From where he sat, Jerome's peripheral vision didn't pick up Johnny or me in the foyer. Johnny and I inched forward another foot, stopping when we saw a pair of women's shoes splayed on the hardwood floor, Tracy's feet stuffed into them.

Chapter Forty-Seven

Tracy was a mess. She was bound at both ankles and wrists, but even without restraints, I doubt she'd have gotten far if given the chance to escape. Her skin and eyes were the color of wet cement, a plane of gray broken only by her illness-reddened nose. Skin peeled around the edges of her nostrils where tissues had wiped away both mucus and a layer of her face. Her body and spirit looked equally limp, but I couldn't tell how much of that was a result of her chest cold or the hopeless position Jerome had put her in. Adding insult to injury, he had stuffed some type of pink fabric into her mouth. Most of Tracy's energy poured into the effort of simply getting breath in and out.

Tracy's position on the floor gave her a better view of the doorway, and her eyes caught on Johnny and me, dragging Jerome's with them. He took us in without comment, but Tracy closed her eyes tight and moaned around her gag. Johnny lifted both palms flat out in front of him and kept focused on Jerome, but Jerome kept his hands in his lap and made no move to rise, let alone attack.

I pried my eyes from Tracy's and looked again at Jerome, noticing now that despite the otherwise military posture, his shoulders were rounded in. Belatedly, I realized it was because his hands weren't clasped, but rather tied with a tan rope. The rope wound around his waist and through the slats at either side of the chair-back. His knees were locked together by the tension of the rope connecting his waist to his ankles. The rope trailed out from under the chair and was tied taut around an old-fashioned cast iron radiator set against the wall. It hissed with its steam heat, trying to battle the cold of the storm forcing its way in through the broken window farther down the wall. Spreading his legs even a few inches would guarantee Jerome a burn to last a lifetime.

I felt Johnny eyes land on me and I shook my head minutely. I was just as confused. I looked back at Tracy, whose eyes had grown more frantic during our inspection of Jerome. Oddly, she never laid eyes on him, only widened them at us as she struggled to push words past her gag. Nor did I see a gun, but I knew it wasn't a spit ball that had shattered that window.

"Sam," Johnny said, and pressed an urgent hand on my forearm.

What my conscious couldn't calculate, my subconscious finally spewed into my frontal lobe. Jerome was bound and Tracy was afraid, but not of him. Her moaning had been a warning. And most pressing, I realized the hissing sound coming from the radiator on my left was now louder on my right. I slowly twisted my head and blinked at what I saw. Hunched in the alcove underneath the staircase, hate glowing in her eyes, Vanessa stared out.

Vanessa's hair was dry and tangled about her face, strands caught in her cracked lips. Two high spots of color on her cheeks dotted an otherwise pale face. The effect would have been almost clownish if not for the feral look in her eyes. They say when a dog goes rabid, he can become so irritable and aggressive, he'll chew his own leg off. I involuntarily cast my eyes down to Vanessa's denim-clad legs.

I held my hands up and away from my body as I cautiously sank to my knees. Johnny slipped a hand under my armpit to stop me, but I patted the air with a calming hand.

Vanessa's fevered eyes tracked my movements, scratching her gun arm faster and faster as I drew closer to her eye level. I saw the lines of scabs running the length of each of her forearms and decided I'd come close enough. I placed my palms loosely on top of my knees and sat back on my heels. I fought to ignore the gun and clung my eyes to Vanessa's.

"Get out," Vanessa growled. The scratching picked up speed. "You can't have him."

"Who?" I asked.

"He's mine." Vanessa flicked bright eyes at Jerome, but I didn't turn around to catch his reaction.

"That's cool," I said. "I'm not here for him, okay? We're just here to pick up Tracy."

"She can't have him either." Blood sprouted from one of the scabs and I swallowed hard, willing myself to maintain eye contact. Vanessa worked her chapped, bleeding lips around in a frenzy, then spit in Tracy's direction. It was an arid smattering, more show than substance, but Tracy still flinched.

"That's okay." I tried a soothing voice. "Tracy doesn't want him either."

"Lying bitch!" Vanessa spat dry air at me.

Tracy shook her head rapidly from her prone position on the floor.

"I'm not lying, I swear," I said.

"Then why did she come back here?" Vanessa hissed.

Valid question, I thought. Maybe this chick wasn't quite as nuts as I thought. She started shaking her head violently, the ends of her ratted hair spiking out from her head. Or, maybe she was.

"Vanessa, I don't know why Tracy came back, but I'm positive it wasn't to see Jerome."

I looked back at Tracy briefly. She was mumbling again behind her gag, but any reason she could utter for coming home would have fallen on deaf ears. Deaf, nuttier than a hoot owl ears.

"No, no, no." Vanessa vibrated the words between her lips. A small crust of spit formed at one corner of her mouth.

"Vanessa, listen to me. Tracy is in love with someone else," I said.

A flash of uncertainty streaked across Vanessa's face before her eyes hardened over again.

"Stop it!" Vanessa shrieked. "Stop trying to trick me!"

"It's true. She's in love with me." I wheeled my head toward the sound of Maribeth's voice. She stood at the bottom of the staircase. She took a step further into the room and I heard Johnny swear behind me.

"No! You're trying to trick me, too!" Vanessa screamed at Maribeth. She shifted and jabbed her gun arm in Jerome's direction.

"He said we'd be together," Vanessa wailed. "But I got here and he was packing a bag." The disbelief of the earlier moment shone fresh in her eyes. She pivoted toward Tracy, using her gun arm like a laser pointer in a boardroom presentation.

"Then this whore shows up saying she's only here to get some ring she left behind," Vanessa sneered.

I caught movement peripherally and saw Maribeth massaging the empty ring finger of her left hand. Ugh. So, Tracy did leave the condo on her own. The one time they shouldn't have gone to Jared.

"But I'm not stupid. And you," Vanessa keened as she swung the gun back toward Jerome. "You *promised* me."

I risked turning my head to peek at Jerome. He was watching Vanessa. I watched as the disgust edged in and overtook the fear in his eyes.

Bad move.

I felt the air shift more than I actually saw Vanessa spring from her place under the stairs. She had only a millisecond lead, but in my wet, heavy clothes, I couldn't beat her to a standing position. She lunged forward, her trajectory propelling toward both Jerome and Tracy, and I had to make a choice. It was a no-brainer.

I pushed off my heels and flung my upper body in front of Vanessa to land on top of Tracy. Johnny rushed forward at the same time and blanketed me in a facedown bear hug. Vanessa tried to hurdle our human pancake stack and caught her foot on my rib cage. She floundered, then twisted back on one leg and used the other to kick the side of Johnny's face. She lost her footing again, but quickly rebounded.

As Vanessa straightened up and raised her gun arm, Maribeth howled. She put her head down and ran at Vanessa, ramming her in the side. Maribeth outweighed Vanessa both vertically and horizontally, and Vanessa crumpled, her gun firing on impact. Maribeth dropped on top of Vanessa as she fell to the floor. Vanessa stilled and Maribeth peeled the gun from her hand roughly enough to make me bury my head. When no more shots rang out, I twisted my head to the side and peeked at them through one eye.

Johnny's cheek brushed against mine.

"You okay?" Johnny breathed.

"Yeah, you?"

"Yeah."

"I don't mean to sound ungrateful," I said. "But it's kind of hard to breathe."

Tracy moaned beneath me. I wedged my hand back into our body pile and fished the gag from her mouth.

"How do you think I feel? I'm on the bottom," Tracy rasped.

Johnny pushed against the floor and lifted his weight off me. He pulled me backwards off Tracy, and I rolled to a seated position on the hard wood floor. He moved to help Tracy up, but she shook her head.

"No strength," Tracy said. Johnny set to work untying her hands instead.

Maribeth flipped Vanessa onto her stomach and sat on her back. Overkill, given the woman was out cold, but who was I to tell Maribeth her business. Her hands were shaking, the adrenaline ebbing, and shock was taking its place. It was then I noticed the blood spattered on the floor near Vanessa's head. I pointed at it.

"Did she shoot herself?" I asked.

"No," Jerome's voice came thinly from across the room. Four pairs of eyes swiveled around to follow it. "She shot me."

Chapter Forty-Eight

Jerome Pentley survived a bullet to the gut. An able-handed surgeon and months of rehab would eventually morph his injuries into memories, but only time would tell whether the healing would unfold at home or in prison.

Vanessa was also rushed to the hospital, the kind boasting beds with straps and padded walls. No release date was in sight and likely wouldn't be before her trial.

The Pentleys' house was lit up like a Griswold Christmas through much of the night. Those of us who weren't shot or bleeding were separated into different rooms and floors, injuries triaged in between questioning by the police.

Vanessa's punch to the head knocked some of the crazy out and made room for denial to return to roost. By the time doctors treated her scalp wound and set her up in her own private cuckoo's nest, she was reconvinced that Jerome loved her and wasn't leaving her after all. Jerome had loaded three suitcases with clothing, bank books, passport, and all the contents of the Pentleys' home safe. When a detective pointed this out to Vanessa, she said she knew full well Jerome was leaving and she was going with him to start a new life. When the detective countered by telling her they'd found evidence that she'd tied Jerome up for days against his will in Dolly Parton *Nine to Five* style, she just smiled serenely. When pressed further, Vanessa began rocking back and forth, humming "Rock-a-bye Baby". She hasn't uttered a word since.

Tracy Pentley was also escorted to the hospital, out of an abundance of caution. Her chest cold, combined with being left in a prone position for as long as she was, was too much for her respiratory system. She spent the night benefiting from breathing treatments, and earned a couple stitches in her leg, too. Turns out Tracy was both the perpetrator and victim of the broken vase in Maribeth's condo. She'd knocked it over in her rush to get to her old house, and earned a respectably deep gash for her efforts.

Roman finished relaying all of this to us in Paul's office the next morning. He'd shown up a half hour earlier, a bag of warm bagels nestled under his arm. I knew he couldn't have logged more than ninety minutes of sleep, but his starched shirt and freshly shaven face suggested a jolliness that pounded at my fully matured headache.

Johnny, Paul, Roman, and I huddled around the conference table. While Roman hungrily tucked into a bagel, the rest of us lazily picked at ours. Johnny's bashed eye had blossomed into a smoky black mess. Between my left rib and right butt cheek, a dull pain chased me relentlessly. Paul hunched at the end of the table, fatigue dripping from his shoulders, his face resigned. The anger I'd felt coming from him during our recent encounters was gone, a distracted weariness left in its wake.

We let Roman work through the first half of his bagel in silence.

Paul rubbed his face tiredly. "Am I awful for disliking my client so much that I can't stand him for being right about his wife cheating on him?"

"He was cheating on her, too," I pointed out.

Roman chased errant crumbs from chest to plate and shook his head. "I don't think Jerome knew Tracy was cheating."

Paul, Johnny, and I looked at each other. Maybe I was more

tired than I thought, but Paul looked confused too. And he hadn't spent most of the night with Cuckoo the Cocoa Puffs girl.

"But that's why the guy hired me in the first place," Paul said.

"Maybe not," Roman said. "One of our officers rode along with the bus that carried Jerome to the hospital. Jerome started rambling when our officer asked him what happened. A bunch of disjointed shit that my guy couldn't make any sense of. He was babbling about irony and bad luck, saying 'I thought she hated her' over and over."

"Jerome thought who hated who?" Johnny asked.

"My guy assumed Jerome was talking about Vanessa and Tracy, but he was only on-scene for a few minutes and he doesn't know anything about the case. He wrote Jerome's rant down nearly word for word, and relayed it to me. I'm thinking Jerome was referring to Maribeth, not Vanessa. When I interviewed Tracy, she said she had no idea Vanessa existed until she came back home two days ago, so Jerome couldn't have meant Tracy and Vanessa."

Roman paused and brought his coffee cup to his lips before continuing.

"So I asked her if Jerome knew Maribeth, or had any reason to think Maribeth hated Tracy. Tracy started crying and said she'd been telling Jerome at every turn how much she hates working with Maribeth. She was paranoid that he would find out about their affair and thought she was boosting her cover by setting up this mutual hatred story."

"So what?" Paul asked. "Jerome may not have known the affair was with Maribeth, but he obviously sniffed out that Tracy was cheating with *someone*."

"It's not about the affair at all," Johnny said, his good eye narrowing at Roman. "You think Jerome was planning to do something to Tracy and hiring Paul was just a decoy."

"Bingo," Roman said.

"And he tried to set Maribeth up to take the fall," Paul said. "The alleged arch enemy."

"Yup," Roman swallowed a bite from his second bagel. "Even if he couldn't pin anything on Maribeth, he could create a lot of doubt. His DNA would be all over that house anyway, so he could use her to muddy the waters in case any neighbors were out and about the afternoon Tracy went missing. So, I'm guessing he dressed up like Maribeth, drove to his house in a Mercedes that looks an awful lot like Maribeth's, then went in and found out someone had beaten him to the punch."

"Which would explain the fake plates," I said. "But, if Jerome was trying to frame Maribeth, why wouldn't he tell the police about the fights she and Tracy had?"

"Why risk it?" Johnny said. "Pushing the police toward Maribeth would make them dig, and his set-up was only superficial. He got the Mercedes color right, but used the bogus plate. He couldn't bank on Maribeth having an alibi, but the presence of a stranger would be enough to cause confusion. He knew later that he couldn't be tied to the disappearance because he didn't have anything to do with it, so there was nothing for him to hide by pointing out his original ruse."

Roman's cell rang while Johnny was talking, and he held up a hand to excuse himself. When he returned a few minutes later, he tracked in both snow and a satisfied smile.

"Detective Schmidt up in Michigan. Looks like someone took a shovel to Abby Pentley's grave site. Got at least a few feet deep, but hard to tell for sure. There's been rain the last couple days up there, and the caretaker hasn't been through that section of the cemetery since Tuesday, so it must have happened over the weekend.

"They think it was Jerome?" I said.

"What are the odds it's not? Guy disappeared for days before coming home and getting the Kathy Bates treatment." Roman said. "Local PD recovered a stolen car abandoned four miles from the cemetery. The car's owner says nothing is missing, but she knows she didn't leave behind the mud we found tracked across her driver side floorboard. Or the shovel in the trunk."

"Jesus," Johnny said.

"They'll process it for prints and Schmidt's team will let us know."

"It doesn't prove he planned to hurt Tracy," I said.

"No," Roman said. "But if we tie Jerome to the car, Schmidt thinks it'll go a long way in getting the family to green light an exhumation of Abby's body. If an autopsy shows what he thinks it will, it may help them get Abby's case into court. And it helps us with Tracy's case. Her mil and half is all the motive we need, and if the testing on the clothes we found in Jerome's office show he's the one who wore them, we may have enough."

"If nothing else, maybe there'll be some justice for Abby," Johnny said.

I nodded, but my heart wasn't in it. I'd hit my limit of twisted relationships and the awfulness of what people were willing to do for money. My phone vibrated on the table and I nudged it toward me with one finger until I could see the read out.

"Hi Mom, what's up?" I answered.

"Samantha, I have a problem."

"What kind of problem?"

Sniffling.

"Mom?"

"It's a boy problem."

Chapter Forty-Nine

Mom's boy problem turned out to be more of a flatulence problem. She and Wally were taking in a matinee at Ridge Park Square when Mom fell victim to her weakness for malted milk balls. She loves the malt, but the malt does not love her. By the time the climactic ending arrived, she and the onscreen cannon were both blasting. I convinced her that if Wally broke up with her over a little caboose music, he wasn't the man for her.

I also convinced her that I couldn't carry the burden of her secret any longer. Time was up for her to tell Vinnie and Paul about her new beau. Mom relented and suggested a nice family dinner would be the perfect time to tell them. She also told me she thought it would be 'lovely to bring your and Paul's little friend Johnny along'. Or as I liked to call him, The New Buffer.

"What is this?" I whispered to Paul. I leaned over and stuck my fork into the slop on his plate. I withdrew my hand and the fork stayed put.

"I'm pretty sure it's eggplant," Paul whispered in response, yanking the fork out and sticking it into my own pile.

"But it's pink," I said.

"And it is delicious." I looked up at the sound of Johnny's voice, and caught the toothy smile he sent my mother at the opposite end of the table. My mom gave him a tight, but appreciative smile and returned to monitoring the tension on either side of her. Mom eyed Vinnie, Vinnie eyed Wally, and Wally eyed the slice of muted television he could see across the hall in the living room. The Browns were dragging down ratings on Thursday Night Football, and Wally looked like he'd prefer to get tackled on that field more than taking a beating in our dining room.

Vinnie ran Wally through a rousing game of twenty questions, Mom agitating in her seat the entire time. Paul made appropriate noises, but seemed wholly unfazed by it all. By the grace of God, Mom managed to knock the sharpest edge off Vinnie's fears when she announced that she'd changed her mind about selling the house. She'd put it on the market on a whim, thinking she should move into a condo village with her other widowed friends, but the level of anxiety she'd incurred during FartGate made her realize she probably needed to tackle one life change at a time.

When dinner was over, which was signaled by half full plates and a general air of defeat, everyone scattered. Vinnie begrudgingly invited Wally into the living room to watch the Patriots finish off their massacre of the Browns. Mom voiced her intentions to 'whip up some real, homemade cream' for the torte she brought home from Colozza's. Johnny offered to help her and after much poo-pooing and declaration that she could do it herself, she surreptitiously waved him into the kitchen ahead of her. I slipped past all of them and joined Paul, where he'd retreated to the back porch.

"Company?" I asked as I stepped out onto the cold planks.

Paul inclined his head toward the empty spot beside him on the ancient porch swing. I sat and burrowed deep into my coat. We stared mutely out into the yard. The previous day's storm filled deep divots in the grass, creating tiny ponds with shards of ice floating on top.

"You can't keep telling me nothing's wrong," I said quietly. "If you're mad at me, you have to tell me. And if you're not, please tell me what really is going on."

Paul's gaze lengthened across the top of the neighbor's fence.

"Paul, I'm sorry," I plowed on. "I really, really am. I shouldn't have left again so fast after Dad's funeral. I couldn't—. Shit." Tears rose before I could stop them.

Paul leaned forward and rested his elbows on his knees. He craned his head toward me. "I get it."

"You do? Then can you clue me in?"

A weak smile flitted across Paul's face. "Listen, maybe I was kind of mad. Not because I had to manage things after Dad died. But, I don't know, it would have been nice to have somebody on my side while I was doing it. Moral support, maybe."

"I'm not making excuses here, but I thought Erica was your moral support?" I asked.

Paul's face clouded over, and the anger I'd seen the past week reappeared. It left as quickly as it came and fatigue set back in.

"Erica and I haven't been a support to each other for a long time. She's barely even been in town these last six months." Paul rubbed his face and looked down at his shoes as he scuffed his heels back and forth on the porch slats.

"What's going on?" I asked.

"She wants us to move to Washington. Thinks it'll be a better hub for her work."

"You don't want to go?" I asked.

"I don't think so. At least not right now."

"And that's a deal breaker for her?"

"She moved out last week."

"Oh." I took it in for a moment. "Are you okay?"

"I will be."

Paul picked up his heels and we swung for a bit.

"Why didn't you tell me?" I asked.

"I wasn't sure you'd understand."

"Why not?" I asked.

"Because you got out of here to go chase your dream and

that's what Erica's doing," Paul sad.

"And you didn't think I could see your side of it?" I asked. "That's why you've been so pissy with me?"

Paul didn't answer. He stuck his heels in a wooden slat, bringing the swing to a stop.

"Look," I said. "I haven't exactly been lighting the world on fire out there. It's more like I've been running around with a wet match. And besides, you never had to leave town to chase your dream. I thought your agency was your dream."

"It is."

"Then hang onto it," I said. "You'll find the right person, whether that's Erica or not."

Paul looked thoughtful, but not convinced.

"Give it some time," I said.

Paul nodded and we rocked.

"Can I get a mulligan for being a dick to you?" Paul asked after a while.

"One per year. You just cashed."

"Thanks."

"So, is this why you're not upset about Mom and Wally being an item?" I asked.

"Who am I to tell her what's right? I'm not exactly the relationship whisperer at this point."

"You do realize Mom's getting more nooky than any of us, right?"

Paul laughed, deeper than I'd heard in days. Candy to my ears.

"In a desperate effort to get that image out of mind, can we talk about you for a minute?" Paul asked.

"No nooky here."

"Holy crap, stop."

"Couldn't resist."

"I meant, what are you going to do now? It doesn't look like Mom needs the big assist that we thought. You're not tied down here anymore."

I took in a slow, deep breath and exhaled through my mouth, watching my breath puff in the cold air.

"It doesn't seem as claustrophobic as it did growing up," I admitted.

"Stay."

I looked at Paul and smiled.

"I'm serious. Why not? You're starting over whether you stay or go, so why not try it?" Paul paused. "If you want to work at the agency full-time, the job is yours."

"Are you sure you want that? I wasn't even able to bag Wanda Ames, and she was all but handed to me on a silver platter."

"Crap, in all the mess of last night, I forgot to tell you," Paul fished his cell out of his coat pocket. He tapped the screen a few times and handed me the phone. The video was wobbly, but clear enough to discern the agile if not attractive moves of Wanda Ames. Hot pink short-shorts, matching belly shirt, and body glitter were on full display as she writhed upside down on a stripper pole. When she spiraled around, the teddy bear tattoo came clearly into view. I sent a thank you to whichever saint watches over benevolent insurers.

"Where did you get this?" I said, eyes still glued to the video. It was mesmerizing, not the quality of the show as much as the unquestionable confidence that splashed out of Wanda's glitter-lined eyes.

"It was sent to Wanda's employer from a generic email account. They traced the account back to a woman named Jeannie, whose boyfriend she alleges Wanda stole. Jeannie works at the nail salon next to that stripper school you found. Turns out Wanda did show up after all. She begged and boo-hooed the front desk girl into redeeming her award for a later class and Jeannie followed her. She doesn't admit to it, but we think Jeannie wanted to confront Wanda face-to-face, then decided the video would be even better."

"A lifetime memento," I said.

"And not just for Jeannie." Paul grinned. "She's plastered it all over the internet."

"Amazing."

"Wouldn't have happened without you coming up with the prize idea," Paul said.

"To be fair, Angie kind of sparked that idea."

"But you parlayed it."

"But it would have been a bust without Jeannie."

"You're killing me here. I'm trying to tell you that you can do this job," Paul said.

I flashed back to all the reasons I'd left town, and all that I'd left behind.

"Come on," Paul said. "What do you say?"

Chapter Fifty

When Paul and I walked back into the house, Johnny was standing behind the open fridge door, watching my mother stare down at her dress. Whipping cream coated her dress, the floor, and counters. It was everywhere but in the mixing bowl. Paul walked right on past her and out the door to the dining room. Mom gave us a helpless look and followed Paul, nattering on about changing her dress.

I wiped the budding grin from my face and pulled a handful of rags out of a cabinet. Johnny closed the fridge door, snatched a rag from my hand, and mopped up the counters while I tackled the cabinets.

"So what's the verdict?" Johnny asked.

"On?"

"You sticking around for a while."

"That seems to be the question of the night."

"What's the answer?" Johnny asked. He stopped mopping and faced me.

I tossed my rag in the sink and shoved my hands in my pockets.

"I told Paul I'd give it a shot."

"Samantha." Johnny gave me a soft smile. The smile grew wider as we contemplated each other.

"Johnny."

"Does that mean we get to give our friendship another go?"

"Depends on what kind of friendship you want."

"Depends on what kind you have with Roman."

"I don't have anything with Roman," I said.

"Didn't look like it the other night."

"Looks are deceiving. Besides, Roman's not my concern. Paul is."

"Like in a Greg and Marcia off-camera kind of way?"

"In a professional way. I don't want to do anything that might hurt Paul or the agency," I said.

"Neither do I. But things are easing up with Paul's caseload, and I don't think he'll need my help after a couple more weeks."

I hesitated. "It's not just that."

"Sam, if I could do things over again, I would have told you good-bye myself. I never meant to hurt you. You must know that."

"I do." And I did.

"We can go slow," Johnny said, wrapping one arm around my waist.

"I'm good with slow."

"How slow?" Johnny tilted his mouth toward mine just as Mom pushed through the kitchen door. I heard her squeak as Johnny straightened and dropped his arm. I twisted my head in time to see her retreating form. Paul's head poked through on the return swing.

"You know, I was thinking," Paul said to Johnny. "We should think about working together full-time. Make the agency a partnership."

Johnny opened his mouth and Paul shushed him with a palm.

"Just juice it around. I think it could be good for both of us." Paul flicked a finger between Johnny and me. "You two think you can keep working together?"

"Absolutely," Johnny said.

"Sure thing," I mumbled.

Paul's head disappeared and I looked up at Johnny's spreading grin.

Gee-zuss.

ACKNOWLEDGMENTS

I'm blessed to have a ridiculously supportive circle of family, friends, and peers. These generous folks have collectively nurtured this journey from seed to tree, and I simply don't have enough ways to say thank you.

To Mamow, who gave me her artist's blood, which started it all.

To Tania, who said yes to the first seismic shift.

To Beth, who not only threw me an unexpected shovel, but who introduced me as a writer before I was willing to do so myself.

To Ben, for his righteous pursuit of perfection and always asking 'what's next?'. And for driving the U-Haul the whole way.

To Jay, for always listening without judging.

To Brian, both the Boy Who Saved the Blurb and Sam's first champion.

For every opinion, idea, yea-say, nay-say, stroke of inspiration, gesture of encouragement, line edit, and gift of humor along the way, I shout my endless thanks to Dee Dee Collura, Cheryl Magat, Junior, Tom Seger, Heather Lewis, Neal Drell, Mel Guest-Smith, Dog Eared Pages Books, Desert Sleuths, Book Passages, and the collective independent bookstore family in Cleveland, Ohio.

Above all, to the city of Cleveland and its many characters, both real and imagined. For those who choose to dig beyond the jokes, stereotypes, and stories of a burning lake…and happen upon the heart, humor, weirdness, and warmth of a truly terrific community of folk. You are lucky souls. As am I.

ABOUT THE AUTHOR

Deborah "Nelle" Lewis is a Human Resources professional and fiction writer who splits her time between Phoenix, Arizona and Cleveland, Ohio. She has roamed all over the country, hopping lily pads coast-to-coast. Her eighteen-year stop in Ohio cemented the state forever in her heart as home.

She can be found online at dlwrites.com.

Made in the USA
San Bernardino, CA
24 November 2017